I0549291

Watch for More
Novels by J. Busskohl

from Indigo Sea Press

indigoseapress.com

The Deputy's Widow

By

J. Busskohl

Stiletto Books
Published by Indigo Sea Press
Winston-Salem

Dagger Books
Indigo Sea Press
302 Ricks Drive
Winston-Salem, NC 27103

Copyright 2015 by J. Busskohl

First Stiletto Books edition published
January, 2016
Stiletto Books, Moon Sailor and all production design are trademarks of Indigo Sea Press, used under license.

For information regarding bulk purchases of this book, digital purchase and special discounts, please contact the publisher at indigoseapress.com

Cover design by Pan Morelli

Manufactured in the United States of America
ISBN 978-1-63066-313-1

For Chris . . . now and always.

Chapter 1

Crane Haven, New York
November 1948

Detective Baker climbed from the Packard. The smell of snow hung heavily in the air, and he searched the sky for signs of the storm to come. There were none. There was only a quarter moon, but it was bright enough to cast shadows on the day-old layer of white crust spread over the ground. He spied the Big Dipper too, almost laughing at the ridiculous surge of pride that swept over him whenever he was in a group and was the first to see it. There was no sign of snow. But it would come. Sixteen inches of snow so far this month and more on the way. Already, fingers of cold slithered into his coat, pawing at him; and he lifted his collar against the feeling.

A man in heavy boots climbed from the back seat, and two more climbed from the front. They too shivered as they stepped into the wind, looking for the snow that had yet to arrive. "Over there," one of them said, jerking his head toward the ravine. The second front-seater was looking into the sky. "There's the Big Dipper," he said. And Baker resisted the urge to shout that he'd seen it first.

The man with the heavy boots leaned against the car and rolled a cigarette. Baker hated the gangster, but he had to admire the way the man could roll a smoke in this wind. The thug caught Baker looking and winked once before jerking his head again in the direction of the ravine.

Baker pulled his coat tighter and moved off toward two large rocks overlooking what used to be the Goosely River. Three decades ago, the river dried up and residents took to throwing their garbage over the cliff. The bottom of the ravine was littered with rusted Fords and Chevys, old tires, bottles and cans and scrap metal from every imaginable source. And, what with this being so close to the city and all, the occasional stiff turned up as well. Baker knew he hadn't been brought here to view the sorry remains of an old car. Gangsters didn't like to show off their garbage...unless it served a purpose. And the only garbage that served a gangster's purpose was a corpse.

Baker moved closer to the ravine, circling around the larger of the two rocks overlooking the dried riverbed below. Frigid wind surged up from the gulch, carrying stinging sand that scraped his cheeks. He made his way around the rocks and paused as his toe touched the body.

He recognized the scarf first. Red plaid. He had one just like it in blue. Their mother loved to buy them the same gifts in different colors, and three years ago the scarves had been Christmas gifts.

"Stewie." He whispered his brother's name, as if saying it aloud might wake the too-still form lying at his feet beside the boulder. Stewie lay on his side, his outstretched hand clutching a fistful of snow. Entranced, Baker knelt beside him and touched the cold flesh. In this weather time of death was impossible to estimate, and determining how long ago a stiff was zotzed became guesswork at best. Baker looked over his shoulders, past the boulder, to the three stooges standing by the Packard. He figured an hour for them to come and get him and another for them to drag him out here to the ravine. That meant Stewie had been dead for two hours at least, probably more.

Baker had seen his share of stiffs in the war. He drove the ambulance. Meat wagon, they called it. And he'd taken more friends than he cared to remember for their last ride. Occasionally he was able to put a soldier back together before making the trip to the field hospital…where the guy could die in a bed. But mostly he just picked up whatever was left, put it on a stretcher, loaded it in the back and drove away. There was no meat wagon waiting here at the top of the ravine for Stewie. There was just Baker and the three thugs hungry for another corpse.

The sound of heavy boots on frozen ground grated on Baker's already taut nerves. He looked up into the face of Leadfoot Barone, who had just finished that smoke he'd been rolling. "Funny thing about dead men," Barone said, "they can't pay their debts."

Baker's jaw tightened, but he said nothing. He smoothed the collar on Stewie's jacket and let his numb finger trace the hole left by the bullet as it drilled through the left temple. The medic in Baker took over, and he forgot about Barone standing behind him and about the sand grating against his cheeks. He assessed the body as if he were back in the field, preparing to give a report should it be asked for later. There was a single bullet wound to the head at the left temple. Judging by the powder burns, Stewie had been shot at close range. But not before putting up a fight.

The hands were bloody, the knuckles bruised. There was a gash across the left cheek, and the left eye was swollen shut. The left hand was clenched, tightly gripping its tiny pile of snow. Baker gently pried the fist open, not giving a shit if he destroyed evidence. There was nothing there, just frozen snow in a dead man's hand.

Barone's heavy breathing competed with the wind for Baker's attention. Baker felt his muscles tense as he listened to the wind howl through the ravine below and to the breath finding its way down Barone's fat neck into a fatter chest. Baker wanted revenge for Stewie. And he would get it. It might take a while, but he would make Barone pay.

Baker tossed a look over his shoulder in the direction of the Packard that had carried him here. The two toughs Barone brought along leaned against the hood of the car. Baker suspected that, if he checked, he'd find they had hands that looked just like Stewie's. Stewie always mixed with bad people; but, when push came to shove, he gave as good as he got. *Until the bullet*, Baker thought, letting his eyes slide to the blackened hole in his brother's head.

He shivered. The temperature was dropping, and Baker would rather be anywhere but here. He *had* been somewhere, he thought bitterly. He'd been with a woman named Celia.

Or Sarah.

He blinked with the effort of trying to recall her name, wondering why it suddenly seemed so important. When she'd sat across from him in the bar, she said her name was…Celia. No. Sarah. Damn. It didn't matter, he supposed. Everything about her said she was willing to give him what he needed. Plus, she had red hair and Baker hadn't been with a redhead since his divorce from Ginger. Red hair was what it would take to put his wife behind him and move forward.

As Celia-Sarah leaned forward so he could light her cigarette, her dress opened in front just enough to let him see the gentle swell of her breasts. And it occurred to him that it was going on eighteen months since he'd had a woman. Eighteen months of celibate agony.

Celia-Sarah bought him a drink, and he still couldn't get over the shock of it—a woman buying a man a drink. He figured it could be a

3

headline in the local paper. But if she were as bold in bed as she was in the martini bar, he was willing to let her wear one of his suits if she asked. She did unusual things to the edge of her glass with her tongue, and Baker lost himself in imagining that tongue on him. A band was playing, but Baker didn't hear them. He was busy watching Celia-Sarah with the red hair...and the wicked tongue.

He bought the next round of drinks, as well as the round after that. And he finally worked up the courage to ask her back to his office, wondering as they walked the block and a half in the cold, clear air that smelled of snow if she would put that tongue to work for him if he asked.

He wondered how to ask about something like that.

The office was cold and dark and sterile. Celia-Sarah burrowed a little deeper into her fur coat as Baker switched on the overhead lights. He took one look at her, thought about it a minute, then turned the lights off and let the glow of the street lamp outside be their guide.

She relaxed a little then, letting her coat slide to the floor. Baker picked it up and laid it over a chair. He offered her a drink, thinking of the dusty bottle of scotch he vowed never to touch again lying in the top drawer of the filing cabinet, but she shook her head. She stood, staring at him with enormous eyes. Baker tried to stare back, but he wasn't sure he should. Maybe she would be offended. He looked away, but she touched his arm and his eyes were drawn back to her face.

Christ, he didn't know if he could do this. What did women want? Was he supposed to say something charming? Was he supposed to keep quiet? Her red hair was gathered behind her neck; and he carefully reached around and loosened it, expecting it to fall down her back in a cascade of red fire. But after he removed the clip, the hair didn't move. He remembered that after a trip to the beauty parlor, his ex-wife's hair was the same way: too stiff to blow, bend or break.

But Celia-Sarah didn't seem embarrassed. She smiled, looking up at him from under heavy lids in a way that made her seem almost shy. Baker didn't know what to do with his hands, so he rested them on her shoulders and leaned forward. His kiss was gentle and he felt the woman smile as his lips touched hers.

Celia-Sarah wrapped her arms around his neck, letting her fingers tangle in the back of his hair. And she kissed him deeply. Baker felt that mouth of hers go to work on his like he'd seen it go to work on the martini glass in the bar. He thought he would explode. Somehow, she loosened his tie. Or maybe he did it. Things got hazy after the kiss. He lowered her to the floor, wishing he'd had the foresight to unfold the cot he slept on before he'd gone out tonight.

But Celia-Sarah didn't seem to mind. He unzipped her dress and slid his hands inside, savoring the moans she blew into his ear as he touched her breasts. He groaned too when she ripped his shirt open, sending buttons scattering all over the office floor. While her tongue went to work on his chest, her hands busied themselves with unzipping his pants. Baker lost himself then. This was it. Eighteen months of monk-like existence was going to end here and now.

He pulled away from her long enough to retrieve the fur coat and spread it beneath them. Celia-Sarah smiled and said, "Nifty." Then she put that mouth to good use again, letting it slide over his chest and belly and to points lower. When Baker had enough, he flipped her onto her back and settled between her legs. They were just getting down to business when Barone's goons beat down the door and dragged him out. Celia-Sarah swore a little at first and then pursed her lips, sighing with regret as she straightened her stockings, zipped her dress and pulled the coat on. She followed as the thugs dragged Baker into the cold night and stuffed him in the back of the sparkling white Packard. Baker looked out the back window as the car pulled away from the curb. Celia-Sarah stood on the sidewalk with her coat wrapped tightly around her, that stiff red hair blowing like a tavern sign in the icy wind.

As she faded from sight, Baker nearly laughed at his situation. He found himself with two problems. First, he was sitting next to Leadfoot Barone. Second, he had a raging hard-on and nowhere to stick it.

Some days it just didn't pay to get out of bed.

He knew why they'd come for him. Stewie was in trouble.

Stewie was always in trouble.

But Baker never figured his impulsive younger brother would be dumb enough to get involved with the likes of Larry "Leadfoot" Barone. Leadfoot Barone, who took two goons wherever he went.

Two goons who would watch while Barone beat the shit out of Baker. Two goons who would finish the job when Barone got tired.

Baker was going to have to break some kneecaps tonight. And he didn't want to. What he really wanted to do was get drunk and finish what he started with Celia-Sarah. That dame had a laugh that could curl his toes. But the only sound here was the wind blowing through dried grass half buried in snow. Baker's pants were wet from kneeling on the ground by the body, and he began to shiver—as much from the cold as from the thought of what he would tell his mother about her youngest son.

It was two years ago when Baker saw Stewie for the last time. And they'd fought. About Stewie's gambling.

"You're an asshole, Stu. A goddamned asshole." Baker ran a thick hand through his hair in frustration. *"They'll kill you. You know that, don't you?"*

Stewie just smiled. "They gotta catch me first."

"Shit. I can't bail you out forever."

"I never asked you to. Keep my car. I don't need it. I've got faster legs than you. Always have. Always will."

Not fast enough, Baker thought now.

Barone stood behind him, lifted one of the heavy boots that made him famous and kicked Baker in the ribs. The two goons behind chuckled to themselves as Baker sprawled in a heap on top of his dead brother. When he could breathe again, he pushed himself up.

"That was just to get your attention, Detective," Barone said.

Baker held his ribs and looked over his shoulder at the fat man, his eyes cold, his mind on the revenge he'd get one way or another. "I'm all ears, Barone," Baker said through clenched teeth. "Why did you bring me here?"

"To tell you I didn't kill your brother."

Baker made a noise that sounded something like a snort.

Barone lifted a boot and Baker tensed, bracing himself for the impact. But Barone set it back down, and Baker watched it sink back into its deep imprint in the snow. "I'm only going to repeat myself just the one time, Baker," Barone said. "I didn't kill your brother. I don't know who did. But the fact remains: he owed me money. And seeing as how you're next of kin...."

"Go fuck yourself," Baker said.

This time Barone kicked him in the face. There was the rending of flesh, the feel of frozen air as it touched exposed muscle and the splatter of crimson blood on white snow.

Baker's cheek hung in a mangled flap over his lower jaw. Frigid wind assaulted his teeth and his tongue. For a moment he sat in the snow watching Barone come closer, surprised to see the gangster shaking his head. "I told you I didn't kill him," Barone said again. "I'm getting tired of repeating myself." He scratched his chin. "In fact, I said I was only going to repeat myself the one time." Now he shook his head. "I must be getting soft."

Baker knew the roughing up would come now. It was Barone's favorite thing: beating people up. He enjoyed it.

Hell, he fucking loved it.

And now the thug was lifting that infamous five-pound boot to finish the job on Baker. "Not tonight," Baker said, watching the world pass in slow motion. "I have a headache." He caught Barone's ankle as it rose, cradling it in his hand for an instant before tossing the gangster backward. Barone landed on his back, staring up at the quarter moon, his coat falling open, exposing the Colt revolver he carried on his hip, his fat neck causing his breathing to rasp and whistle.

The two goons launched themselves forward, but Baker was quicker. He grabbed Barone's Colt, gave it a half-spin in his palm so the butt faced outward and smashed goon number one's kneecap. The man crumpled in a heap, howling in agony.

Goon number two pulled a gun, but again Baker was faster. He shoulder rolled in the snow as he righted the Colt, thumbed the hammer, came to a crouch and fired. The bullet ripped through number two's knee, and he dropped next to goon number one.

Baker turned his attention to Barone, now struggling to sit up. Baker's smile through the torn cheek was gruesome as he tossed the gun away, sprang to Barone's side, dropped and straddled the fat man, pinning his arms in the snow.

Baker pulled the small dagger he carried from the sheath on his lower leg. "Here's a little something for you, Barone," he said, letting moonlight flash on the blade.

Barone squealed like a schoolgirl as Baker gouged a hole similar to his own in the man's cheek. When he was satisfied, he put his nose to the thug's. "Stewie's debts were his own. If you wanted your money so bad, you shouldn't have killed him."

"I didn't kill him," Barone said as he struggled weakly, held in the snow by Baker and his own heavy boots. Baker punched him once and the fat man stilled, watching Baker with cold eyes.

"I'm supposed to believe this isn't your work?" Baker asked.

Barone continued to stare, those hard eyes unwavering, so Baker punched him again. "If you bother me about this again, Barone, I will tear your nuts off, light them on fire and cram them down your fat neck."

He didn't wait for an answer. He climbed off Barone and moved past the goons that lay, moaning and bleeding, in the snow. Cradling his cheek, he made his way back to Barone's shiny white Packard and headed back to town.

Baker let himself into the front room of his office, turning on a lamp on the desk of his secretary, Edwards. The door to his own office stood open, the light off. And it smelled faintly of Celia-Sarah's perfume. Despite the hole in his face, his body responded to the smell of her. She was gone. Long gone. And his body still wanted her.

He pulled the dusty bottle of scotch from the drawer of the filing cabinet and poured a healthy shot over his cheek. It burned like a son of a bitch.

Next he shuffled into the dim bathroom and pulled the hand towel from the rack, running it under cold water before putting it to his face. After soaking a needle and scissors in a glass of the old scotch, he found a spool of nylon thread and set to work closing the wound.

Barone's boot had sliced him good. Baker knew his parotid gland was ruined and wished he'd had the good fortune to have it cut out before he got the mumps as a boy. His mother made the diagnosis by feeding him a dill pickle. It was a week before he forgave her.

Tonight he counted the gland as a lost cause and prepared himself for a future of dry mouth. He closed the inside flap first, working through tears that ran from his eyes, pouring scotch alternately down his throat and over the wound.

When he finished the inside, he approximated the muscle as best he could, then closed the outer layer of skin. He was dizzy and nauseated from the scotch by then, but the wound was closed.

He leaned over the sink and was sick.

Stewie was dead. And Baker wondered about the body, still lying by the ravine outside of town. *Dead men can't catch cold,* he told himself, and wondered why he didn't find comfort in that. If Barone hadn't killed Stewie, who had? What was the kid involved in this time? Baker hadn't seen him for two years, and he wasn't sure he wanted to know what Stewie had been up to. He put his hands over his face. His kid brother was lying by a rock outside of town. There was a bullet hole in his head. And their mother would have to be told. *Jesus Christ,* Baker thought.

He pulled the cot from the corner under the window. He'd put it there after Ginger left because, by then, there was really no point in going home at night. He told himself it was easier this way. In case he needed to work late. For times when he was on a big case. No sense in going back to that empty apartment.

That's what he told himself.

Now he wheeled the bed away from the wall and carefully unfolded it. He was going to succeed this time without pinching his—

There was a loud pounding at the outer door....

—fingers. "Damn," he muttered, striding to the adjoining bathroom and running his hands under cold water. "Come in," he yelled, his voice muffled by the swelling in his face.

The door in Edwards' office creaked open. Baker stood by his desk, drying his hands as Sheriff Doug Ferrebee maneuvered his bulk through the narrow doorway and into the room. Baker regarded the man with hooded eyes.

Ferrebee stood as tall as the doorway and was just as wide. His red hands hung limply at his side; but Baker knew the sheriff would start working them soon, rubbing them together like dry leaves, littering the floor with dead skin.

"Evening, Detective," the sheriff said, his own eyes guarded. "Not out photographing cheating husbands tonight?" His gaze swept over Baker, starting with shoes and pants still wet from kneeling in the snow, to the blood-soaked shirt and ending on the ugly Frankenstein patch job on his cheek.

9

Baker didn't say anything. He tossed the towel on the desk and began spreading blankets on the stiff mattress.

Ferrebee nodded. "I see." He hitched his belt up and crossed his arms over his chest. "Found a coupla thugs outside of town with their kneecaps busted. You know anything about that?"

Baker shook his head. "Nope. Don't know a thing," he said in a voice muffled by the swelling in his face. He finished with the blankets and took his seat behind the desk, propping his feet up. He knew his eyes were glazed with booze and pain, and he forced himself to focus on the sheriff's red face.

Ferrebee leaned against the door, keeping his arms crossed; but his palms pointed down, so he could reach for his gun if necessary. Baker tried not to smile. After a minute, Ferrebee cleared his throat. "A guy named Barone is over at the doc's getting his face put back together. Don't suppose you know anything about that neither."

"Not a damned thing."

Ferrebee's face swam in and out of focus, and Baker knew he was blinking too much. He looked away, dropped his feet and began to remove his shoes.

Ferrebee uncrossed his arms and began to rub those sausage fingers together. *Rasp, rasp, rasp.* Baker watched the flakes of skin fall to the floor like snow. "We found your brother's body, Detective."

Baker sat up and looked at the sheriff from across the desk. "My brother mixed with bad people, Ferrebee. I don't. I refuse to." His eyes hardened. "And if they don't take no for an answer, I tend to get very angry."

Ferrebee nodded, his hands still working. "I get you, Baker. Enough said. Come down and make an ID on the body when you get a chance." He looked Baker over. "And get the doc to look after that cheek."

Baker nodded, thinking about Stewie in the morgue.

Ferrebee turned to leave and then paused. "You wouldn't know anything about that white Packard parked in front of your office with the keys still in it, would you?"

Baker shook his head. "But it's in my spot. I'm going to have it towed."

"I'll take care of it," Ferrebee said.

Baker nodded and closed his eyes, but Ferrebee didn't move to leave. When Baker opened his eyes again, the sheriff smiled and his face reddened a bit. He crossed and uncrossed his arms, his huge bulk swaying with the effort. "Effie and I never heard from you about Chet's wedding. The invitations went out over a month ago. You'll be there, won't you?"

Baker allowed himself a small smile, then winced with pain. "I'll be there, Sheriff. I appreciate the invitation."

Ferrebee grinned and ducked out, his vast weight lumbering through the darkness of Edwards' office with ease. Baker waited until the outer door closed. Then he stood, passed through Edwards' office himself and locked the outer door. He locked the door to his own office too. Normally security was not a concern of Baker's. But Barone was probably a little angry about his cheek.

Baker knew two locked doors wouldn't stop the gangster, but he figured he'd hear the locks being picked...or the windows being shattered as Barone tried to break in. The noise would give him a head start on loading his gun.

At last Baker settled down on the cot wearing his trousers and a t-shirt. He tucked the Colt under his pillow and picked up his book. He'd been wading through the works of Edgar Allen Poe for the last month. He turned to the place he'd left off and lost himself in the story.

But as brick after red brick was laid so as to entomb Fortunato in *The Cask of Amontillado*, Baker couldn't help but think of the box that would soon swallow his brother.

11

Chapter 2

Baker felt worse than before he'd closed his eyes. The sutures pulled at the bruised skin in his cheek, and the wound pulsed angrily. His mouth was dry, a combination of too much scotch and a ruined salivary gland. His eyes burned as if sand had been sprinkled under the lids, and he squeezed them shut against the artificial brightness of the gray light oozing through the blinds.

And Stewie was still dead. The realization sank in slowly, teasing him at first with the possibility of unreality as he eyed the empty scotch bottle. But the hazy feeling changed to certainty as he fingered the ugly mass of patched flesh on his cheek.

He sat on the edge of the cot and cradled his head in his hands while he groaned, feeling older than his thirty-four years and wondering how he would get through the day. He willed his feet to move, to take him across the room to the closet. It was after eight o'clock, and Edwards would be in shortly. The suit from last night, covered in blood, was ruined. Baker had stuffed it under a chair, but Edwards would find it. And a lecture would follow.

However, he thought, *it was possible to appease Edwards by being resplendently dressed by the time he arrived.* Baker just needed to figure out what looked best. He eyed the closet door with dread. Walter Edwards was a British snob. Furthermore, the Brit had procured Baker's endless supply of suits, ties, shoes, shirts and hats by what Baker suspected were less than legal means. Textile trucks on their way to regional department stores were repeatedly hijacked in this part of New York State. Rumor had it the gang of hijackers was employed by Pockets O'Hurley.

Occasionally Pockets sent out a posse of hoods to look for trucks that had, in turn, been hijacked from him. It seemed to Baker that whenever new suits appeared in his closet, word hit the streets that Pockets' supply trucks had been hit. Baker tried not to think too much about it. He stood and padded across the cold floor to the big black door and pushed it open. There was a slight hiss as air escaped, and he imagined he knew how the banker felt opening the vault first thing in the morning.

Were Baker to dig deep into Edwards' past, he was sure he

would find a police record miles long, detailing an endless trail of robberies, bootlegging and possibly murder. Needless to say, Baker had no desire to dig where Edwards was concerned. Edwards was a friend, possibly the only one Baker had.

He sighed. Friend or not, Edwards was still a British snob, determined to see Baker in suitable attire at all times. "Bloody good for the agency's image," he said. Baker took a step into the closet, fearful of going in too deep. He fished around for a suit and selected one he thought would meet with Edwards' approval. He thought he did fairly well, although he had some trouble when it came to the necktie. He was hopeless with ties. Dames should choose ties.

Dames and Edwards.

After some careful rummaging, he selected a brown and yellow spotted number that would have to do.

He started the coffee, then moved to the windows and opened the blinds. Sunlight elbowed its way through heavy clouds that, even now, were pregnant with snow. It would storm soon; but for the moment, light and dark had called a fragile truce, and they shared the sky with cautious amity. He left his post for a moment to pour a cup of coffee and returned to the window, allowing what little sun there was to warm his face as he looked out onto Main Street.

Shades in darkened store windows were lifted, one at a time, signaling that the small town of Crane Haven was officially up and at 'em.

Phil Farmer and his mother rounded the corner on their way to the bank. Baker raised his coffee mug in silent salute to them. They couldn't see him through the glare on the window. Not that the superior third and fourth generation bankers would deign to acknowledge the shamus who occupied the office across the street. But he toasted them just the same. Phil held his mother's elbow, guiding her around patches of ice not yet melted beneath the pellets of salt the city workers spread before dawn.

An image of Stewie flashed in his mind: Stewie with a buckeye he'd picked up from under the tree in the backyard. He was laughing as he tossed the small nut in the air, caught it, then tossed it to Baker. They were shooting sparrows with a slingshot. Baker had better aim. Stewie had faster legs.

The image faded and Baker laid a hand to his cheek, then closed the shades. He looked at the bloody suit stuffed under the chair. It was hopeless, he knew. The front was covered with a mixture of Barone's blood and his own. And even if the suit were salvageable, Baker didn't know how to begin to explain how all the buttons had been ripped off the front.

He was smoking his second cigarette and fingering the bandage he'd put on his cheek when the outer door opened, and he heard the unmistakable tread of Edwards' giant feet in the next office. "That you, Edwards?" he called, trying to sound normal.

The office door swung open, stopping with a thump when it struck the filing cabinet. Edwards, all six feet five inches of him, loomed in the doorway, shoulders as wide as a refrigerator, fists like Virginia hams.

"I understand you ruined a suit last night," he said, looking Baker over head to toe with that withering British glare.

Baker blew out a cloud of smoke and tried not to think about his brother. "Word travels fast."

Edwards took a step into the room and shrugged. "There's talk at the diner about broken kneecaps and severed heads."

"No one's head was severed." Baker pushed the thought of the blackened hole in Stewie's temple from his mind.

Edwards eyed Baker's swollen cheek. "Forgive me, sir. *Nearly* severed heads." He across from Baker and studied his employer without emotion. "Do you wish to tell me what happened? All I know is that you injured some men outside of town. At least that's what the rumors indicate. And there's talk of a dead body. But beyond that, I know nothing."

Baker shrugged, thinking the Brit already knew plenty, and crushed the cigarette in the ashtray on his desk. He wasn't ready to talk about Stewie yet. Not to Edwards. Not to anyone. "I'll fill you in later," he said. "Right now I have to go."

"You aren't going anywhere dressed like that, sir. That tie is a monstrosity."

Baker looked down and assessed the necktie. "It was with the others."

"It has its place, sir; but with that suit, it is a monstrosity."

"You haven't commented on my face."

Edwards was in the closet rummaging. "Under the

circumstances," he called, "I felt it best to pretend not to notice."

"Don't you want to know who did it?" Baker asked.

Edwards returned from the closet and held three ties up, one at a time, looking from them to Baker in turn. "Not particularly." He held up a black and purple job. "I think this will do nicely. It matches your head."

"Funny." Baker touched the bandage on his cheek. "Guy named Barone worked me over," he said, watching Edwards for a reaction.

And there it was. There was a flicker, a twitch of something in Edwards' eyes at the mention of Barone's name; but it was gone as quickly as it appeared, and Baker decided to let it be. For now.

Baker stood still as Edwards pulled off the tie Baker had chosen and went to work assembling the new choice. Baker didn't like standing beside Edwards. The Brit's height and bulk dwarfed Baker's own six-foot frame and made him feel small. And then there was the way Edwards cinched the knot on the tie, as if trying to crush his larynx. Baker didn't appreciate that either. "There," Edwards said, standing back to assess his handiwork. "Much better." He offered a small smile, but Baker sensed something beneath the look. Something dangerous.

And, as usual, he wasn't sure what Edwards was thinking. He opted not to loosen the tie.

"I'll be back later," Baker said, his thoughts returning to his brother. And the morgue.

Ollie Tate ran the city morgue, performing autopsies on the rare occasions they were needed. He also ran Tate's Funeral Parlor. Mainly he performed the embalming and dressing of the dead. His wife, Linda, saw to the bereaved. Ollie's manners were a little too coarse for polite society.

"Baker," he growled when the weary detective pushed his way into the cold gray room. "Looks like they tried to off you as well." He eyed the bandage, already wet again with fresh blood and pursed his lips. When Baker didn't say anything, the fat mortician said, "Sorry about your brother. Didn't know he lived around here."

"He didn't." Baker walked to the steel table that held Stewie and stood with his legs pressed against it. A sheet had been pulled up to cover Stewie's face; and Baker lifted it carefully now, peering at the form beneath.

"You can see where they shot him over here," Ollie said, coming around the table now and pointing to the wound Baker had seen last night. Baker kept his face impassive as he noted the wound had been washed and probed. "And over here," Ollie continued, rolling the body to its left side, "we have a stab wound. Those Chicago boys like to play with knives, don't they now?"

Baker's jaw worked. He couldn't remember if Barone had a knife. "Chicago boys?"

Ollie shrugged and stepped back, picking up a cigarette he'd left smoldering in an ashtray on a nearby counter. "Face is pretty busted up. He's got a broken knuckle. Third one on the right hand. I'm guessing the other guy don't look so good neither." When Baker didn't say anything, Ollie grunted. "If that don't say Chicago, then I don't know what does."

Baker wasn't thinking Chicago. Baker was thinking Barone. If Chicago was in on this, then all hell was about to break loose. He cleared his throat. "Sheriff said you needed an ID before you could finish up here."

Ollie put the cigarette back in the ashtray and wiped his hands on his stained white scrubs. "True enough, son. True enough." He moved over to a clipboard with an official-looking piece of pink paper attached to it. "He had his wallet on him—empty of course—and his identification, but we like to have a family member make a positive whenever possible." He looked down and scribbled something on the pink paper. "I'm citing the cause of death as head trauma secondary to a bullet wound."

Baker nodded, pulling the sheet over Stewie's head again. "I want him cremated and sent home."

"Home?"

Baker nodded. "To Iowa. Cedar Rapids. Our mother is there. She'll handle the burial."

Ollie cleared his throat. "We don't get much call for cremations around here, son. I'm not sure…"

"Cremate the body, Tate. Mom couldn't handle seeing him like this."

The look in his eyes must have been intense because Ollie only nodded. "Fine, son. I'll take care of it. We'll use the furnace over at the school. They still burn coal there, and I'm sure we could get a blaze hot enough to do what you're asking."

16

"Send me the bill," Baker said, pushing his way out of the dingy room and into the cold morning air.

And that was it. He'd handled it. His brother was dead. Soon to be burned and sent home to Iowa to be scattered somewhere on the family farm. And Baker felt nothing but hollowness inside. There was no grief, no sadness, no anger. Just...space.

Edwards was polite when Baker returned, and it was clear he'd heard about the hit on Stewie. There was a fresh pot of coffee brewing, and he'd set out a clean ashtray and a fresh pack of Lucky Strikes on the corner of the desk. This was as far as Edwards' proper demeanor allowed him to go with regard to condolences. And even this gesture pushed the bounds of convention.

Baker frowned as he removed his necktie and sat behind the desk. He swiveled his chair and was staring out the window as Edwards brought in the mail and a cup of coffee.

"Letter from Mr. Hedron, sir."

"Barone shot my brother, Edwards," Baker said, ignoring the mail as he turned to face his friend. Again, he watched Edwards closely for a reaction.

Edwards' broad forehead wrinkled and his eyes narrowed. "Impossible," he said.

Baker took a drink of the coffee. "Why?"

"Because a bullet through the head isn't Barone's style."

Baker scoffed. "Funny. I thought a bullet through the head was exactly his style."

"Your brother owed him money, correct?"

Baker nodded.

"Then Barone didn't kill him." Edwards tossed an envelope on the desk in a way that let Baker know the conversation was over. "Letter from Mr. Hedron."

Baker didn't appreciate the change of subject, but he was too tired and angry to argue with Edwards just now. He picked up the envelope from Mr. Hedron, the office landlord. He slit it open and read the letter inside with a frown before dropping it onto the desk in disgust. "We're to be evicted in two weeks if I don't pay the rent on the office."

Edwards said nothing, but he looked uncharacteristically glum.

Baker lit a cigarette and gestured to a chair opposite him.

Edwards had always been uncomfortable with familiarity; and he took the chair with reluctance, keeping his enormous bulk perched precariously on the edge of the seat. "Maybe it's just as well, Edwards," Baker said, absently fingering the bandage on his cheek. "This cold weather is bad for business. No one cheats on his wife in this kind of weather. It's too cold to take his pants off. No cheating means no dough." He pointed with the two fingers holding the cigarette. "I may have to fire you if this keeps up."

"So you've said." Edwards plucked at imaginary lint on his jacket.

Baker leaned back and took a drag on his cigarette. His face was drawn, heavy. "When was the last time I paid you, Edwards?"

"I couldn't say, sir." But it didn't really matter and they both knew it. Baker didn't know the extent of Edwards' moonlighting, but he suspected the Brit's income far exceeded his own. The secretarial work Edwards performed for The Baker Agency was for amusement only. His real source of income lay outside the legal arena.

Baker was quiet for a moment until he noticed Edwards fidgeting. Then he looked at his friend and said, "I'm not going tonight," and exhaled a cloud of smoke that settled over the desk between them.

"Truly, sir? But you were so looking forward to a night out. If it is about your face, I'm sure…"

"It isn't about my face, Edwards." Baker closed his eyes. A memory of Ginger, her red hair and pale skin, surfaced suddenly and without warning. The freckles dusting her cheeks were the same golden color as her eyes, and in the glow of early morning she looked like an angel. When he remembered her, it was always of her in the morning when she lit the room more brightly than the sun.

Baker closed his eyes as his body fused to the chair, and the world stopped spinning. He was standing in the bedroom of their apartment. She was there, kneeling on the bed with the sheet wrapped around her. Her hair filled the room with fire. She smiled at him and beneath the smile was desire. His heart lurched with need and the agony of knowing she was no longer his. She raised her pale arms, and Baker resisted the urge to reach for her. She wasn't real. *She wasn't real.*

Ginger smiled, letting her arms drop to her sides and the sheet fall away. Baker shook his head and remembered that this was why he'd stopped drinking. This... hazy space between what's real and what's fantasy...was a place where he'd indulged too often and for too long. No more. No more.

In the vision he shook his head and watched the softness of desire in her eyes transform into cold rage. Slowly she began to fade.

Baker willed her to fall, to sink to that place beneath conscious thought where she usually lived. There, she was barely palpable, like a fading bruise, something to be caressed on occasion to make sure it was healing. Ginger resisted, her amber eyes cold and angry. But fade she did. And he was the worse for it.

Baker sighed and opened his eyes. The room was there, cold and gray and sad, as always. And Edwards was still perched on the edge of his chair, looking concerned and uncomfortable. Baker cleared his throat and leaned forward, resting his head in his hands.

Ginger.

Would she care that Stewie was dead? Would she care that Baker was alone? Again?

After a moment, he felt his breathing ease. The sounds of the traffic outside his window grew more frantic as businesses opened. The wind blew dust against the glass. And Edwards continued to stare.

Baker held up a hand and took a drink of coffee. After he swallowed, he cleared his throat again. "Sorry, Edwards. I'm fine, really. I don't feel up to a wedding, that's all. Even if it is the sheriff's kid who's getting hitched."

The large man nodded. His face was stern, but his eyes belied the worry Baker had come to recognize over the past months. "Shall I phone the young lady and make your apologies, sir?"

Baker fingered the fresh bandage on his cheek and nodded. "Tell her it's because we've got a big case we're working on. It's just about to break wide open."

"I'll take care of it, sir."

Edwards left, closing the door softly. Baker gave into the ache in his cheek and leaned forward, resting his head on the desk. Maybe he'd go see the doc today. Just to get something for the pain.

His mind drifted and he floated with it, letting images rise and fall with his breathing. Stewie in the barn. Stewie on the football field.

And then Ginger was there, reaching for him again and Baker was too weak to send her away. He whispered her name, "Ginger."

Had it really been a year?

The phone rang. At the same time a gust of November wind pitched pebbled debris against the window. Baker jumped, tipping back in his chair, catching himself before he fell over. His cheek screamed with pain; and he thought about the bottle of scotch from last night, wishing he hadn't emptied it.

Edwards' knock was tentative.

"Yeah?" Baker said. But it was more of a moan.

The Brit opened the door, quivering with excitement. "Sir, there is a woman on the phone in need of your services."

Baker lit a cigarette and searched through his drawer for a bottle of aspirin. "So make her an appointment." There were rubber bands, paper clips. Where the hell was the aspirin? "The sooner the better."

"I tried, sir, but she declined."

Baker looked at his friend. "Declined?"

"Yes, sir. She said the matter is one requiring a certain amount of *discretion,* and she does not wish to be seen."

Baker's stomach growled. So far this morning he'd had coffee and cigarettes but no food. How could he get food with no money? "Have you forgotten our clients usually pay at the first meeting?"

Edwards' frown deepened. "I did mention that to her, sir."

"And?"

"When I told her of our policy, she indicated I should check our mail slot. I took the liberty of doing so, and this retainer's fee was among your other mail." He pulled a sealed envelope from his breast pocket and handed it to Baker.

The envelope was small, the address written in a woman's hand. Baker slit it open. Five crisp twenty-dollar bills were tucked inside. "Well, I'll be," he said, leaning back in his chair.

"Do you wish to speak with her?" Edwards' brows were arched, his blue eyes blazing with eagerness.

"Hell, yes, I wish to speak with her." Baker thought a moment. "Only don't rush. I don't want her to think we're just sitting around in here wondering what to wear."

"Very good, sir."

Baker hurriedly pulled a pad and pencil from his desk and picked up the phone when Edwards put the call through. He cleared his throat. "Detective Baker speaking." His voice was smooth as silk, a practiced quality not unappreciated by the fairer sex.

"Detective Baker. Thank you for agreeing to speak with me." Her voice was deep and smooth. Like a spoonful of honey drizzled over Lauren Bacall.

Baker sat up straighter, letting thoughts of Stewie and memories of Ginger evaporate.

The woman took a deep breath. "I find myself in need of the services you offer in your newspaper advertisement."

Baker leaned back. "How may I be of service?"

"Please call me Diana. My name is Diana Kramer."

"That your real name?"

There was silence on the line. Then, "Of course it is my real name, Detective. Why would I lie?"

"I have no idea. Why would you give me your real name and refuse to meet me in person?"

She had a throaty laugh, the kind that implied long legs and a slim waist.

Baker swallowed hard and imagined what she was wearing.

"Oh, Detective, I do like you," she said with a smile in her voice. "I do not wish to be seen in the vicinity of Crane Haven. I assure you, once you hear my request, you will understand my reasons for remaining hidden."

"I'm listening."

"The man I love is to be married to another woman this afternoon."

Baker's neck tingled, and he wondered for a minute if there were any other wedding besides the one for Ferrebee's kid.

"I see. Does this man have a name?"

"Chester Ferrebee."

Well, hell. "The deputy?" Baker was going to have to change his mind about attending the wedding. Again.

"Yes. He is to wed Marian Drake, a mousy little thing, whom some declare a beauty, although I never really saw anything overly spectacular about her. Do you know her?"

"I'm afraid I don't."

"Well, she's not much. And she's marrying my man."

21

"You're involved with the sheriff's son?" Baker leaned back, drumming his pencil on the pad of paper. "I'm not sure about this, Miss Kramer."

"Diana."

"I'm not sure about this, Diana." He dropped the pencil and picked up his cigarettes, lighting one and inhaling deeply, ignoring the growling in his stomach. He eyed the envelope of money, thinking it would get Stewie back to Iowa with no worries; and he could buy a helluva lot of roast beef on rye with whatever was left.

"I take it you know Chet, Detective?"

Baker blew out a cloud of smoke and pulled his eyes away from the cash. "What? Oh, yeah. Everyone knows Chet."

"I see. Chet is in possession of some letters I've written him over the last several months."

"And you want me to find the letters."

"Yes. I want you to find the letters. For sentimental reasons, of course."

Baker placed the cigarette in his ashtray and stood. "Of course," he echoed, feeling the familiar hollowness. Were all women master manipulators? Or just the ones he had the misfortune to encounter? Holding the phone with one hand, he turned to look out the window and sat on the corner of the desk. "Why are you unable to ask Mr. Ferrebee for these letters yourself?"

There was silence on the line again. Baker watched pedestrians struggle to stay upright as the wind propelled them across the narrow street, lifting skirts and snatching hats as it picked up steam. The clouds were winning the battle for possession of the sky. When Diana Kramer spoke, Baker shivered.

"I am not currently welcome in his circles, Detective, and won't be for some time. Although I fully anticipate my relationship with Chet to resume once this ceremony is out of the way, I am concerned that an accidental discovery of the letters by his new bride may hinder our reunion. Have I made myself clear enough?"

Baker shook his head, not at all sympathetic with the "other woman" who had just secured his services. "Perfectly," he said, his voice clipped.

"You will take the job?"

He thought about Edwards and the need to offer some sort of

paycheck. He thought about dinner. A hot dinner with mashed potatoes and gravy and real beef. He thought about Ginger and alimony. He thought about his landlord and eviction. And he thought about Stewie. And funeral expenses. And his grieving mother in Iowa.

"I'll take the job," he said with more conviction than he felt. "But I still think it would be easier for you to ask Chet for the letters yourself."

She laughed again and Baker grimaced at the sound. "That would be impossible for reasons too numerous to count at this time. I need your help, Detective. And I am asking for your discretion."

Baker shrugged and kicked his chair out of the way. "This isn't always a discreet business, Miss Kramer."

"I understand. Do what you can. I will, of course, pay the remainder of your fee upon completion of the case." She hung up.

Baker stared at the dead phone in his hand. "Edwards," he said softly, knowing the Brit was, as always, listening just outside.

Edwards opened the door, clutching the familiar drinking glass he used for eavesdropping. "Yes, sir?" he said.

"It appears I will be going to the wedding after all," he announced.

"Shall I call the young lady again?"

"Don't be ridiculous, Edwards."

Edwards appeared relieved.

"It will be much easier to corner the groom if I'm not saddled with some dame."

Edwards looked stricken. "Please tell me you don't intend to make a scene."

Baker shook his head. "I'll pull the groom aside and ask him about the letters. If he has them, fine. If not, fine."

"And if he kills you, sir?"

"Kills me?"

Edwards was exasperated. "Yes. For asking about his lover during the wedding in which he is marrying another woman."

Baker shrugged and looked at his friend. "You'll be there to make sure he doesn't."

"And if I choose to let him, sir?"

"Then at least follow along to see where he dumps my body.

Now I'll need my tuxedo."

"I didn't pick it up from Deirdre's."

Baker scowled.

"You said you weren't going," Edwards reminded him.

"Well, call her. Or something. I need that suit."

Edwards sighed. "Fine."

"Can you get a date?"

"Me, sir? Of course I can, but—"

"Good. I'll want you there."

"Really, sir. This case involves simple love letters. I hardly think I'll be needed."

But Baker wasn't listening. He was in the bathroom. Shaving.

Deirdre floated into the office at 5 p.m. in a gown the color of heaven. She was a hat-maker. And a dress maker. And Baker's friend. She ran the shop next door and lived in the apartment above. She took care of his dry cleaning, made him soup when he was sick and knew every single secret he had. They were pals. Chums. Buddies.

So why was there a lump in his throat when he saw her tonight? He scowled to cover his surprise.

She frowned at his expression. "Stop that," she said. "Don't look at me; look at this." She held up the tuxedo for his inspection. "Your attire for the evening," she said with a slight bow as she laid it on the desk in front of him.

Baker looked it over with his eyebrows raised, and Deirdre laughed. "It won't bite you, Detective. It's just a tuxedo."

But Baker hadn't worn the tuxedo since his wedding. He and Ginger hadn't made it to the bed in the small flat in the city before her dress was off and in the corner, with that tuxedo crumpled on top of it. They'd picked it all up from the floor the next morning, giggling, and hung everything in the back of the closet, vowing to treasure every wrinkle in their wedding clothes. Forever.

Baker took his suit to Deirdre last week for cleaning. And now the wrinkles were gone. Just like Ginger.

He touched the suit, tamping the memories down, swallowing with the effort.

"Is something wrong?" Deirdre asked.

Baker shook his head and nodded at her evening gown. "What's all this?" he asked, trying on a smile to see how it felt. It felt terrible.

Deirdre didn't notice. She tossed her head, allowing a curtain of chestnut hair to spill over her shoulder. "Do you like it?"

Baker nodded. "Very nice. Will you allow me to escort you?"

Her face froze, the smile trembling slightly as her eyes filled with something. Pity, maybe?

"Oh, I didn't...I'm going...I have a date," she said, her voice no more than a husky whisper.

Baker felt his face flush and stepped back even as Deirdre took a step forward. Her lips were parted like she wanted to say something; and Baker held his breath, wondering what it would be. But Edwards knocked and charged in, oblivious to the thick tension in the air; and the moment was gone.

"I have a date," he announced. "It was short notice, but the young lady seems rather excited about it."

Deirdre smiled and stepped away from Baker as she turned to Edwards. "Of course she's excited. You're very charming."

The tall man shifted uncomfortably, his cheeks tinged pink. "You are too kind, Miss Deirdre. Once again, you've stilled my heart."

She smiled, avoiding Baker's eyes. "It was nothing." She stood and walked to the door. "Well, I have to go, men. Philip is picking me up next door."

Baker started. "Philip? As in Philip Farmer? The banker?"

Deirdre turned to look at him, her hand on the doorknob. "Yes," she said.

Baker snorted.

Deirdre frowned. "What's wrong with Philip?"

"Nothing, if you like men with weak chins."

Her eyes flashed. "He asked," she said, opening the door. "That's something anyway." The door slammed behind her, leaving a silence that was somehow louder.

Baker kicked his chair. Edwards cleared his throat and stood awkwardly in the middle of the room.

Baker turned and glared at him. "You have something to say, Edwards?"

Edwards cleared his throat. "No, sir."

"Good. I'll meet you at the club after the wedding."

Chapter 3

Wet, heavy snow was falling as Baker stepped out of the Crane Haven United Methodist Church. The wedding had been the usual affair: mothers crying, bridesmaids making eyes at the groomsmen, the groomsmen pretending not to notice.

Cock and bull as far as he was concerned. Every last bit of it.

His 1932 Chevy Cabriolet was parked under a streetlight over a puddle. The puddle, thankfully, was frozen. He stood for a moment, smoking the cigarette he'd lit as soon as he'd escaped the church, and wondered about Chet Ferrebee. He didn't know Chet well, but the man had seemed happy enough during the ceremony. He exchanged chaste looks with his bride, Marian Drake. She smiled brilliantly, her eyes glazed by the hallucinogenic ideal of true love. The true love part was bullshit as far as Baker was concerned. Nevertheless, Chet and Marian didn't look like a couple with troubles. Baker thought about Diana Kramer and wondered what she had done to lure Chet from fidelity. Baker figured she must be some dame, because Marian Drake was a heart stopper.

Marian Drake had black hair and dark eyes. Baker couldn't be sure of the eye color from where he sat in the church, but it didn't matter. She was lovely. Diana Kramer described her as *mousy*. Baker would have said *modest*. Reserved. Perhaps even shy. But *mousy* Marian Drake was not. She was beautiful. Flawless. Like a doll made of porcelain. And it was very clear that she was in love with Chet Ferrebee. And Chet was keeping time with Diana Kramer.

Baker tossed the cigarette. What a fucking mess.

Now he had to climb in his car, drive to the country club and ask for the damned letters. If there were a scene, it wasn't his fault. If Marian Drake got her heart broken, that wasn't his fault either. He lit another cigarette and hated himself just a little. Marian seemed like a sweet kid, her innocent eyes blind with trust and love. She was probably a virgin with big dreams about her wedding night and a future filled with kids and Christmas trees and Little League. Baker was about to destroy all of that.

Then he thought of Ginger. And how he'd trusted her. He hadn't suspected a thing during the last six months of their marriage when she'd taken up sleeping with Tucker Lewis. And, oh, how he wished someone had told him about it—had saved him the humiliation of discovering them on his own. Well, Marian Drake was a first-class chump if she believed Chet Ferrebee was going to be faithful.

And with that thought, any reluctance Baker had about approaching Chet regarding illicit love letters during the wedding reception vanished.

Baker dropped the cigarette, crushing it into the snow with his heel. All around him, wedding guests climbed into cars and drove away through the snow toward the reception.

"Come on, Baby," he said, climbing inside the Chevy. "I know it's cold. Just a short trip to the country club." When the temperamental car belonged to Stewie, he spoke to it, coaxed it and even talked dirty to it when necessary. Baker had kept up the sweet-talking ritual after the car became his. Now he smiled to himself, enjoying a rare fond memory of his brother, and rolled down the window. "It's not because you smell bad," he told the car, echoing words he'd heard Stewie use a hundred times before. "It's just that I don't want to die of asphyxiation."

"You always talk to your car?"

Baker slid his eyes sideways, grimacing at the sight of Phil Farmer's fat pink face looming in the open window. "Hello, Farmer," he said, fitting the key into the ignition and ignoring the smell of salted pork and milk that drifted off the banker. Maybe choking on fumes would be better after all.

"Come on, Phil, we'll be late." Deirdre's voice floated on the wind from somewhere behind the fat orb blocking Baker's view. Baker let go of the hand clutch long enough to shove Phil's fat head out of the way and feasted his eyes on the blue dress. The wind tucked it around Deirdre's hips and folded it into that soft place between her knees in a way that left little to the imagination. She struggled to smooth the fragile fabric, succeeding only in making the dress cling in more places; and Baker's face softened at the sight.

She grumbled something unladylike and pulled the fur stole covering her shoulders a little tighter. "Well, really," she said. "Phil, please. Can we go now?"

Phil smiled. "In a minute, doll." He didn't turn to face Deirdre when he spoke but looked at Baker and rolled his eyes. "Dames," he said under his breath, like Baker would know exactly what he was talking about. When Baker didn't say anything, Phil leaned into the car again, his face blocking the light and whispered, "You okay, pal? The whole town's talking about your dead brother and those hoodlums with the busted kneecaps. My mother nearly had a heart attack."

"I'm fine," Baker said, shoving Phil's face aside again and looking at Deirdre. She was shivering. He nodded at Phil. "She looks cold."

Phil grinned, showing his large overbite and making his chin look weaker, if such a thing could be imagined. "I'll warm her up. I'm taking her to the reception out at the country club. You know how dames get about weddings." He socked Baker in the arm. "What you got planned tonight, my friend?"

"Wedding reception."

Phil looked surprised. "Really? You're going? I figured you'd make yourself scarce after the wedding. What's the matter, no husbands to follow around with your camera?"

Baker grimaced, but Phil kept right on smiling like he thought Baker was smiling too. "Yeah, Phil," he said. "I'm going." He looked at Deirdre again. Her teeth were chattering, and Baker was growing angry at Phil's lack of sense. Baker nodded in her direction again. "Get her someplace warm." He shoved Phil's face out of the car once again and rolled the window up to discourage any further conversation.

Phil frowned as he stepped away from the car. He took Deirdre by the arm and half-led, half-dragged her across the parking lot to his mother's Oldsmobile.

Baker refocused his attention on getting the car started, making sure to offer compliments on her paint and structural soundness. The old girl turned over on the third try, and Baker sputtered out of the parking lot with relief. He followed the snow-filled tracks through town along Main Street, taking note of his darkened office as he passed. He was thankful that Edwards would be at the reception in case there was a scene. And with a marriage on the line, there was bound to be a scene.

He slowed the car, suddenly wondering if he should abandon this whole crazy plan. Destroying the dreamy illusions of a new bride was not a preferred way to pass a snowy evening. Was the payoff really worth it?

It was. He knew it was. If he couldn't do this job for his brother, then he'd do it for his mother back home to pay for the memorial service. She couldn't keep the farm going and foot the bill for Stewie's funeral...and she would insist on a church funeral even if her son had been cremated. She would also insist on a headstone in the cemetery, even though she'd scatter Stewie's ashes somewhere on the farm.

Baker pulled over and thought about it some more. He had some money set aside. Not much. But he'd send it home. He gripped the steering wheel. It would never be enough for a headstone. He had to do this job. If he could find the letters that Diana Kramer wanted, he'd send as much money as he could to his mother. For Stewie.

He pulled away from the curb and urged the car to the edge of town. When he reached Fieldcrest Road, he turned north. The wind picked up, and the wipers struggled to keep up with the onslaught of snow. The procession of wedding guests was nowhere in sight; and he accelerated a little, hoping to catch up.

Fieldcrest Road was wide, flat and paved. The Chevy protested only slightly as it nosed into the strong headwind. The snow grew heavier. It pelted the windshield, melting as it struck the glass, only to freeze into icy streaks as the wipers tried to rake it away. Baker had started out ahead of Phil and Deirdre; but it wasn't long before the couple passed him in Phil's new Oldsmobile, the nose of the giant car plowing effortlessly through the snow. Phil grinned and waved as they drove by, the glow of his enormous teeth swallowing that impossibly small chin. Deirdre sank low in the seat, the top of her head barely visible in the dark interior of the car.

Baker opened his mouth to deliver an insult through his open window and was seized with a fit of coughing for his efforts. Gas fumes seeped through the rusted undercarriage, filling the car with the stench of exhaust. He swore under his breath, knowing that even with the windows rolled down, he would stink like the Ford garage by the time he reached the reception.

He sucked the night air as he fought to stay on the road and cursed as another set of headlights came up fast behind him. He gestured for the car to pass, afraid of a stall if he pulled to the side.

Snow on the shoulder was too deep to make stopping safe.

He steered as far to the right as he dared, tensing as his wheels slid off the tarmac and ground through the snow on the shoulder. The Chevy, made of sturdy stuff, shuddered and groaned but stayed pointed straight ahead as he maneuvered it back onto the blacktop. He tightened his grip on the wheel and struggled to see through the ice-covered windshield as he waved the car around a second time. The eerie headlights held steady but slowly inched closer to the back bumper; and Baker shoved his head out the window, waving for it to pass. The bandage on his cheek was soaked, the wound beneath numb from the cold. Still, Baker thrust his face further into the wind, swallowing snow and air, somehow wishing it hurt more.

The headlights were all but touching his back bumper now. He swore again and braced himself for the impact that was sure to come. But just as the cars would have locked bumpers, the headlights veered into the left lane. Baker caught a glimpse of the car's silhouette as it reflected the glow from his taillights. Its wide tires chewed up snow and spit it out as it pulled up alongside Baker.

Even in the darkness, with snow blurring his vision, Baker recognized Barone's Packard. The sleek car stayed abreast of the clumsy Chevy, making no move to pull ahead.

"Well, shit," Baker muttered, pulling his head back inside. "This is all I need."

A second set of headlights appeared in his rearview mirror; and Baker held his breath, wondering if Barone brought company to help run him off the road. Baker checked the Packard at his left. It made no move to slow down and pull in behind or to speed up and pull around the front.

The second car crept closer. Baker watched the snow dance furiously in its headlights as it drew up to within a few inches of the Chevy's back bumper and held steady. He held his breath.

This is it, he thought. They were going to run him into the ditch and finish him off when he tried to leave his car.

Something, fear probably, sat heavily in the pit of his stomach, threatening to lunge up in a roar of anger. Baker swallowed against the force of it and narrowed his eyes in concentration.

The snow was a blinding curtain, pried open by the three cars slicing their way through its fury. The ice on Baker's windshield was a thick crust, and he switched off the useless wipers. He held the Chevy steady even as the Packard crowded the centerline, swerving dangerously close as the strong north headwind shifted for an instant, blowing from the west and sending the cars toward the right shoulder. Baker clutched the wheel and checked the rearview mirror. Just the tiniest nudge from the back car, and he'd be shoveling snow in the afterlife.

But the second car honked. Once.

Then again.

And then the driver flashed his lights. He wanted nothing more than to pass. Baker slowed to a crawl, blowing out the breath he'd been holding as the honking grew impatient.

In the left lane the Packard slowed in concert with Baker, then accelerated just enough to pass him before cutting hard into the right lane, nearly clipping the Chevy's front bumper. There the Packard slowed further; and the rear car sped past, blasting its horn.

Baker pushed his head out the window, squinting into the blizzard and watched the car until its taillights were nothing more than two red points of light poking holes in the dark. In time they disappeared altogether, swallowed by the curtain of snow.

Baker found himself alone with nothing but Barone's Packard in front of him and nothing but darkness and wind blowing snow over the deserted highway behind him.

Focusing on the distorted taillights barely visible through the ice-covered windshield, Baker reached across the front seat and opened the glove box, nodding once with satisfaction as his fingers closed around the Colt inside. He lifted it out, already relaxing as light from the dash glinted off the cold steel. "Bring it on," he mumbled to the Packard as he pulled the hammer back, smiling when he heard the satisfying click of the bullet settling into the chamber.

In front of him Barone's taillights winked in the darkness, slowing further and edging into the center of the road.

So that was the plan. Stall him in the middle of the narrow highway. There was no way to turn his heap around in this snow. But Baker was ready. He followed the Packard's lead, slowing in increments. He considered maneuvering a pass, but that would put the Chevy half on and half off the shoulder; and Baker couldn't risk a skid. One way or another, when these cars came to a stop, Baker was going to have to put a slug in the monkey driving the Packard; and he didn't want to do it from the ditch.

And then, just as the cars had slowed nearly to a stop, the lights from the Crane Haven Country Club loomed ahead of them, flinging their glow into the blizzard. The Packard accelerated and sped off, leaving Baker in a wake of snow and flying rock. He blew out another breath as he turned into the parking lot.

He urged the Chevy over packed snow and felt his heart rate slow. He'd live another night. But Barone would be back sooner or later. Baker hoped it was later. Preferably in daylight, when the cards on the table were easier to see.

Guests swarmed the entrance to the club like ants at a picnic. Baker scowled, hating the crowd, hating the music and the noise, hating his ex-wife.

Dirty snow, slashed with tire tracks, coated the ground as cars slowly disappeared under a white blanket of new snow.

"Damn," Baker muttered, assessing the mess. He'd never get the Chevy out again if he remained inside longer than an hour or two. He circled the lot, looking for a space near the exit, where higher traffic was more likely to compress the deep snow.

After parking, Baker lit a cigarette and fumbled for the emergency flask in his pocket. He sighed with relief as he pulled it out and shook it to make sure it was full. He reminded himself he didn't drink. But weddings had a way of driving him to it.

Weddings. And his job, he supposed. And his dead brother. He took a drink before stuffing the flask back in his pocket and climbing from the car. He left his trench coat and keys on the front seat, in case he needed to leave in a hurry. He stuffed his cigarettes in his front pocket and tucked the Colt in the waistband of his trousers. Then, out of habit, he scanned the lot.

A late-to-arrive couple climbed from their car, making a dash through the snow to the well-lit entrance. Baker stood silently beside his battered vehicle, wondering if the bride and groom were inside. He was about to ruin their honeymoon...possibly their entire marriage. And that realization didn't put him in any hurry to get in out of the snow.

He went over the layout of the country club in his mind, assuming the head table would be toward the back, nearer to the band

and the bar. During the war he'd made a habit of imagining the layout of a room before walking in and memorizing the locations of buildings on a map before walking down the street in any city. It was a hard habit to break. He didn't need to be so tense now. This was an easy case. Milk money. No need to be so cautious.

But there was that voice in the back of his head, warning him that something was off tonight. And the hairs on the back of his neck were standing up. He inhaled on the cigarette and blew a cloud of smoke into the night air. This feeling he had was nothing more than delayed nerves from what happened with Stewie last night. And from nearly getting run off the road by Barone's goons.

Baker chewed on the thought of Barone for a minute. The thug had two men with him last night. And Baker had ruined a knee on each. That meant Barone had called in replacements...or he was driving the car himself tonight. Baker would ask Edwards about it in the morning. The Brit knew far more about Barone than he was telling. Maybe it was time to find out if Edwards were more loyal to the mob or to his employer.

Baker laughed out loud at the thought. Like he could compete with the mob, for Chrissakes.

He finished his smoke, tossed it away and lit another one. The tingle in his neck was insistent, and he reached a hand around to smooth the hairs there. This was a wedding, for God's sake; and the only one around to ruin it was Baker. Baker, with his questions about letters from a lover.

He started for the door with angry strides; but the tingle on the back of his neck persisted and he paused, knowing he needed to pay attention to it. This feeling had never let him down before. Slowly he turned where he stood, letting his eyes rest on each car in turn. He noted the way the wind piled the snow into drifts against tires: here a little deeper, there a little fresher. He could tell which cars belonged to kitchen staff and which cars belonged to wedding guests from their location in the lot and how deeply they were buried in snow.

There were no out-of-state plates. No cars with bullet holes. Nothing suspicious. He was unaware of his hair getting soaked or the cold penetrating his tuxedo. His jaw clenched in concentration; and, until the water from melting snow on his forehead dripped into his eyes, he didn't blink. There were four sheriff's cars in the lot, all in the first row. There were no others scattered throughout the sea of parked cars. That left two patrol cars out on duty in Crane Haven. The rest of the department had come to the party.

He tossed his cigarette and lit a third, his wet hands numb in the wind. The cold pierced his tuxedo jacket and he shivered, struggling to hold the cigarette in numb lips. The smoke blew back into his face, and he squinted against the sting. He froze. There in the far corner of the lot, creeping through the gate, was the white Packard.

Barone was back. This was bad timing. But, Baker supposed, if he had to snuff a guy in the parking lot, he had to snuff a guy in the parking lot. He could track down Diana's letters tomorrow as easily as tonight. Besides, if he thought about it, he'd rather put a bullet in a guy than ruin a bride's wedding night.

He rubbed a hand over the back of his neck and wondered if Barone were really out to zotz him or if something else was going on. There was only one way to find out what Barone wanted. Baker took a drag on the cigarette and dropped it on the ground before moving with catlike grace in the direction of the Packard.

Curiosity got the best of him as he drew closer; and he squinted into the snow, trying to get a good look at the interior, keeping a hand on the butt of the Colt as he moved. He made out one silhouette, backlit by the bright lights of the parking lot. The orange tip of a cigarette glowed brighter as the driver inhaled, and Baker sensed the man's cold hatred as he trudged through mud and snow. He welcomed it. It would make it easier to pull the trigger when the time came. A few more steps and he was close enough to tell that the man in the car was too narrow in the shoulders to be Barone. The driver remained motionless, the ember of the cigarette dimming and glowing in sync with his breathing. Baker's eyes narrowed again. He felt the cold to his bones now as the snow pelted his already wet jacket and hair, melting and dripping down past the collar of his shirt. Shivering made his gun hand unsteady. And that made him angry.

He was three feet away from the car when it roared to life, its headlights switching on at the same instant. The car flew backward, its tires spraying snow and ice in every direction. Baker made no attempt to protect himself from the debris. He stood, still and angry, as the car sped away, waiting until it was out of sight before he pulled the flask from his pocket and took a deep drink. He wiped his mouth on his sleeve and turned back toward the club. He'd gotten the information he needed. He'd been close enough to make out the shape of a fisherman's pea coat and the silhouette of a flat boating hat that fishermen wore on deck. Barone had sent someone new. And that was all Baker needed to know…for now.

He put the flask away and made his way back through the parking lot toward the front entrance and hoped no one would notice he didn't have a gift.

He dripped on the floor as he entered, but the guests were too happy…or too drunk…to notice. The joint was full of tuxedoes. Had there been this many at the wedding? He'd been too busy trying not to gag on the stench of gardenias to notice. The country club carried the aroma of tobacco and scotch. Baker found it quite pleasant.

He bypassed the gift table, making only a half-hearted signature in the guest book and noting that Diana Kramer's signature was not on the list, before moving on. He'd been right about the layout. A band was onstage in the middle of playing a slow fox trot. Couples bobbed up and down as they meandered around the floor, the volume of the music and the drone of conversation drowning out the sound of their feet.

And…hello.

Baker froze as he looked at the singer for the band. She was a doll. A canary. In a red dress that shimmered like fire. She was gravity for light, and Baker watched as every ray refracted in her direction. She pulled it in and held it briefly, letting it light up her golden hair and her shiny dress, before generously shooting it back to the world in the form of a million twinkling stars dancing on her gown.

He didn't know how long he stood, captivated by the woman—by her song and its words. But he knew he wasn't yet ready to return to reality when the nudging of couples moving past him on the floor brought him back. He looked around, bewildered. Somehow he'd managed to drift halfway across the room and stood now in the midst of overzealous wedding dancers.

A sharp bark of laughter, followed by a stiff poke in the ribs, caught Baker off-guard. He spun around and found himself standing face-to-face with Phil Farmer.

"Hey, Shamus," Phil grinned, keeping his fat hand curled around Deirdre's waist. "You're in the middle of the dance floor. Where's your partner?" He made a point of looking around before nudging Baker again. "You *do* have a partner, don't you? Or do you prefer to go it alone?" His laugh ejected a plume of milk-scented breath into the room, and the jealousy Baker felt earlier turned to pity for Deirdre.

Deirdre cleared her throat and mumbled a hello as Baker flushed, embarrassed to have been caught watching the canary in the red dress. He nodded to Deirdre and turned back to Phil. "I know a guy who can help you with that chin, Farmer," he said, already pushing his way through the crowd toward the safety of the sidelines.

From behind him, he heard Phil mutter, "What's wrong with my chin?" followed by Deirdre's reassuring, "Nothing, Phil. Your chin is just fine."

Baker made it a point to keep his gaze averted from the red dress as he scanned the room for the wedding couple. At first glance, they were nowhere to be seen. For the sake of being thorough, he pushed his way around the room, hoping to catch a glimpse of the wedding dress. He made a complete circle, noting that the sheriff was sitting at the head table, enjoying his prime rib and mashed potatoes. A wedding cake stood on an elaborately decorated table in the corner near the back wall and had already been cut. Baker wondered just how the hell he managed to miss the meal and the cake. The drive out here must have taken longer than he realized.

He stood on the edge of the dance floor and helped himself to a glass of champagne from a tray carried by a passing waiter. He'd stand here awhile and hope something turned up. Like Chet and Marian. Or Edwards. Where the hell was Edwards?

The blonde singer was crooning again, and Baker sipped his champagne and let his eyes wander in her direction. She had her hands wrapped around the microphone, and Baker wondered what it would be like to have those hands wrapped around him. He wondered what Celia-Sarah was doing tonight. Then he shrugged and worked his way toward the stage.

After elbowing his way through the crowd, he found himself at the base of the stage, staring at the sparkling red dress. He looked up with a stupid smile on his face. She smiled back and winked.

Baker wondered if the erection he had would ever go away.

The song ended and the woman spoke into the microphone. "I'm going to take a break," she said. "Try not to kill each other."

Baker leaned forward and rested an elbow on the stage. The doll sat down and dangled her feet over the edge. Iridescent threads in her dress caught the light and threw it back as pink shadows on the floor.

"Got a cigarette?" she asked.

Baker reached into his pocket. He lit two and passed one to her.

She smiled, blowing the smoke out and watching it curl toward the ceiling. "Bride or groom?" she asked.

"Groom, I guess. I know his pop." He watched her lips tighten around the cigarette and felt his own pants tighten in response. "What about you?" he asked after a minute.

"Bride. Married to her brother."

Baker hid his disappointment.

The woman took another drag from her cigarette. "You live in town?"

"Yeah," he said, watching the way her eyes shimmered in the dim light of the ballroom.

She smiled. Her teeth were white and even, and her neck was long and soft. "But you don't come to the club much." It wasn't a question.

"No."

"I figured. You don't look natural out there." She nodded to the dance floor.

Baker glanced at the crowd pushing its way around in circles and shrugged. When he looked back at the woman, she was studying the flask-shaped bulge in his breast pocket. He opened his mouth to offer her a drink, but she was already moving. With long, delicate fingers, she reached for the flask. Baker held his breath and waited to explode.

She held the tip of her tongue between those white teeth as she slid the flask from his pocket. "Do you mind?" she asked, holding the flask between two fingers. "I've had nothing but dime store champagne tonight."

He shook his head. He didn't mind. Thinking. About her lips on that flask. And other places.

She lifted the flask to her lips, leaned her head back and

swallowed. The burn of the liquor made her shiver once, and her eyes brightened with the heat. For the first time she eyed the bandage on his cheek. "Interesting mask," she said, passing the flask back to him.

Baker absently fingered the bandage and said, "I'm looking for the groom."

"Ah." She nodded to his face. "He do that to you?"

Baker shook his head. "Car accident."

He knew she didn't buy it. But she didn't leave, and Baker was glad of that.

A group of men at a nearby table erupted into shouts. Baker tore his gaze from the woman to check it out. They were all in tuxedoes, of course. There were five men seated there, and Baker recognized all but one of them from around town. They were obviously drunk. Drunk and unhappy. Three of the five were exchanging heated words. Baker watched carefully. No one looked on the brink of violence.

Yet.

"What's their problem?" Baker asked.

The woman smiled, but it was bitter. "See the man on the left?" She pointed to the man Baker didn't recognize.

Baker nodded.

She scowled. "My husband." She took a long drag on the cigarette. "He's a drunk. Those men there," she nodded to the rest of them, five in all, "went to school with him. Seems they're catching up on old times."

"Your husband doesn't look too happy."

She shrugged, dropping her cigarette to the floor where Baker crushed it with his shoe. She said, "So what else is new?"

Baker snatched two glasses of champagne from a passing tray and handed one to her.

She frowned but drank it anyway. Beautiful or not, there was no way Baker was letting her drink up his entire flask.

"So where do you live when your sister-in-law isn't getting married?"

Her eyes were guarded, and for a minute he thought she wouldn't answer. After a time, she said, "We live in the city. Just here for the wedding." She smiled. "I'm doing the show as a favor to Marian. They didn't want to pay for a real singer."

Baker enjoyed hearing her speak. He liked watching the light play on the dress and cast its reflection in the floor. But he had a job to do, and in order to do it he'd have to move on. He cleared his throat. "Have you seen the groom?" he asked.

The woman's mouth turned up in a crooked smile. "You looking for trouble?"

Baker shook his head and lit another cigarette for her. "I never look for trouble."

She smiled and looked amused as she blew the smoke out the side of her mouth. "You won't find him. He and Marian left an hour ago."

Baker felt a headache start behind his eyes. "Do you know where they went?"

She laughed at that. It was deep and sincere, and he found himself smiling in response. "Are you for real?" she asked. When Baker's expression remained blank, she said, "Honeymoon." She nodded toward the head table. "But his dad's still here. Maybe he can help you."

Baker moved to leave, then turned back and looked at the table of loud men. The woman followed his gaze and smiled. "Will you be all right?" Baker asked.

She laughed again. "I'll be fine," she said. "Thanks for the drink."

Baker moved in the direction of the head table, ignoring the smiles and seductive stares of the females he passed. He was almost to the sheriff's table when a firm hand on his arm halted his progress. He looked up. "Ah, Edwards," he said with relief. A tall woman with dark hair and enormous breasts had glued herself to Edwards' side. Baker stared at her chest a moment too long before returning his attention to his friend. "I see you made it."

The woman looked down her nose. "Who's your friend, Lord Edwards?" she asked.

Baker cocked an eyebrow. "*Lord* Edwards?"

Edwards' face reddened with embarrassment, but his eyes narrowed in warning. Baker kept quiet. Edwards turned to the woman. "Just a waiter, my dear," he explained. "His father worked for my father. He comes from a long line of domestic helpers." He clicked his heels together, "Shirley Fritz, may I present Mr. Hamilton Baker. Mr. Baker, Shirley Fritz." Baker and the woman nodded to one another. Edwards said, "Shall we return to the table?"

The woman nodded, and Edwards led her from the dance floor. Baker followed, rolling his eyes. Just the same, he snatched a freshly-opened champagne bottle and two glasses from a passing tray. And when Edwards and the woman were seated, Baker made a show of pouring champagne for them. When the glasses were filled, Edwards knocked his to the floor.

"Oh dear, how clumsy of me," he said, clucking his tongue and bending over to pick up the broken glass.

Baker knelt. "Oh, please let me, Lord…Edwards, was it?"

Edwards flinched but said nothing, leaning closer to Baker's ear. He whispered, "The couple has left, sir. It seems they departed directly from the church. From all accounts they were very much in love and couldn't wait to start the honeymoon."

Baker wondered who the hell cut the cake if the wedding couple were gone. "Where's the honeymoon?"

"No one is supposed to know that."

"Right."

Edwards looked thoughtful. "Perhaps your client hasn't been truthful with you. Perhaps there is more to the letters than you were led to believe. I have questioned several guests, and no one gives any indication that the couple was unhappy."

Baker nodded. "You may be right. Head out whenever you like. I need to speak with the sheriff."

"Sir," Edwards said.

"Yes?"

"You look terrible."

Baker smiled. "Thanks." He stood to leave.

"Sir," Edwards said, following him.

"Yes, Edwards?"

"Well, sir, I've danced with the young lady." He looked over his shoulder and waved at his date. "She is very fond of dancing." He smiled to himself, then looked at Baker. "And I've promised her a ride home at the conclusion of the evening. I realize our work here is done, sir, but…it would seem a shame to take her home so early."

Baker smiled. "Have fun, Edwards."

Edwards grinned and bowed. "Thank you, sir."

Baker moved on, spotting the sheriff at the table nearest the exit. Ferrebee laughed in his usual jolly manner and spoke with guests who stopped by the table to offer their congratulations. Baker wondered, now that he was here, how to go about asking how to get in touch with Chet Ferrebee while he was on his honeymoon.

A dour-looking woman in purple sat beside the sheriff. The scowl on her face repelled any guests who might be interested in extending their congratulations to her as well. Baker fingered her for the groom's mother…the groom's *very unhappy* mother. Although she sat directly beside the sheriff, the two were as indifferent to each other as if they were in separate rooms. The woman watched happy dancing couples with obvious disdain, while the sheriff focused his attention anywhere but in her direction.

There was a tap on Baker's shoulder.

"Excuse me, please."

Baker turned. The woman in the red dress stood behind him, struggling to keep her drunken husband upright. "I needed to get him out of there before he did something stupid."

"Let me help." Baker took the man from her and hoisted him over his shoulder. The man reeked of gin, and Baker struggled to hold his breath as he carried the burden to an empty chair beside the sheriff.

Mrs. Ferrebee adjusted the bodice of her purple dress and looked like she'd just swallowed a piece of rancid meat. "Is this entirely necessary?" she asked.

Baker stood and mopped his brow. "Afraid so, ma'am. He's too heavy to carry all the way to the parking lot."

The woman in red stepped forward. "I'm terribly sorry, Mrs. Ferrebee. Jeffrey's had too much to drink and…"

When Mrs. Ferrebee would have opened her mouth to say something, the sheriff stood and put a hand on her shoulder. "It's fine, Judith," he said to the woman in the red dress. "Just fine."

Baker smiled. *Her name was Judith.*

"Detective Baker," the sheriff said, pumping Baker's hand. "Glad you could make it. How's the face?"

"Fine, sir." This was it. Ask about the letters and get it over with.

"Sheriff, I was wondering…"

But the sheriff wasn't listening to Baker. There was a crash heard even over the happy swing tune of the band as a set of side doors was wrenched open, and two deputies raced in. One grabbed the sheriff's elbow. "We need to speak with you." And they walked Ferrebee a few feet away where they spoke frantically in hushed tones.

Baker strained to hear what was being said. He was vaguely aware of Mrs. Ferrebee scowling at the sheriff, of Judith tending to Jeffrey Drake, of the band playing. But he focused his attention on hearing what was being said to the sheriff. After a minute of fast talking, the deputies raced out into the night again; and Sheriff Ferrebee, his mouth tight, his legs stiff, made his way over to his wife.

"Effie," he said to the sour-looking woman. "There's been some trouble. I have to go."

His wife didn't look happy about that, but she didn't protest.

The woman in red was saying something else to Baker, but he didn't catch it. He was in a hurry. He raced out the side doors and around the building to the parking lot. The cold stole his breath away, but he was determined to make it to his car before the sheriff left. Sheriff Ferrebee was heading somewhere important, and Baker intended to be right behind him.

Chapter 4

Baker chipped the ice from his windshield as the sheriff and the two deputies started their cars. The blizzard had let up some, but the Chevy still struggled to make it out of the snow- packed parking lot. The procession of sheriff's cars pulled out onto Fieldcrest. They turned north, away from Crane Haven. Baker followed, careful to stay well behind. The road intersected five miles later with Highway 262. There they turned east, toward the city. Snow fell in a driving fury now, the wind hurling it through the night air with a force that rattled the Chevy's frame. Baker hoped his car could weather this journey.

The patrol cars, out of their jurisdiction now, moved without lights or sirens as they crossed into the city limits. The road was clearer here, having been plowed earlier. Over the last few years, the city limits had crept farther and farther toward the suburbs and now all but touched the county line. The governor had promised a population boom after the war. So far, the city was growing and showed no signs of slowing down.

But as the city crept toward the suburbs, so did the sin; and Baker was well-acquainted with the stretch of road they traveled now. In addition to fresh new businesses and quaint houses, cheap motels and all-night bars had sprung up along this previously deserted stretch of Highway 262. "Cheater's Row," the private dicks called it. He recognized one motel and bar after another as he shook the memories from his head and pushed the car forward, concentrating on the red glow cast on the road by the taillights ahead of him.

A heavy feeling settled in his gut. With sick certainty, he knew where they were going. And he prayed for the deputies to lead the sheriff further down the road...to any other dollar-a-night motel but this one.

But the procession veered to the right, stopping on the shoulder in front of the painfully familiar dive known as The Road King Motel. Baker made a good part of his living hiding out in this parking lot, waiting for half-clad cheating husbands to step out for a smoke, allowing Baker to catch a glimpse of the dame inside. A few peeks, a few snapshots, an easy two hundred bucks. It was dirty work, but it exposed the truth. And truth was anything but clean.

The vacancy sign flashed in the darkness, offering hot showers and rooms for rent by the hour, night, week or month. Wind pelted the sign with driving snow that cracked and sparked as it struck a naked wire, then melted and dripped into a dirty puddle below.

Baker slowed to a crawl as he passed the motel, able to make out room 112 even from here. It was a year ago last September when Ginger emerged from that room, her eyes filled, first with shock at seeing him, then defiance as she grasped the hand of the lover standing beside her. Thirteen months and fifteen days had passed, and he hadn't been back since.

He snapped back to attention and surveyed the lot. Half a dozen city cop cars were scattered throughout, their red lights pulsing in the gloom. A meat wagon, its rear doors gaping in anticipation of broken cargo, had backed up to a narrow sidewalk jutting from a cement stoop that ran the length of the single story building. Baker couldn't acknowledge that anything carried in an ambulance could be living; and his heart lurched, wondering who was dead. For an agonizing second, he thought of Ginger, the hatred he felt replaced with concern. Was she all right? Was she hurt?

And then reality settled back around him. Of course she was fine. She was married last month. She had no reason to sneak around at The Road King anymore. Baker was out of her life, and she was free to sleep with her new man legally.

The sheriff's cars nudged into the drifting snow on the side of the road, the size of the drifts forcing them to park halfway on the blacktop. The road was quickly turning into a narrow corridor, walled in by snow-covered cars. There was no way Baker could park this close. He pushed the Chevy further down the highway, parking near a stand of trees just to the east of the motel.

After one more drink from the flask, he stepped from the car. The wind whipped his coat around his legs, and he sank up to his ankles in the snow. Other cars drove past him now, their tires spinning. Baker tucked his head against the wind and pushed on, nearly colliding with two reporters from The Crane Haven Gazette as they climbed from a snow-encrusted Oldsmobile, one clutching a camera, the other a notebook.

Theo Carver carried the notebook. He grinned at Baker with the self-important sneer of a reporter. "Hiya, Baker. What's all the fuss about?"

Baker shrugged. "You tell me. I'm just tailing the sheriff."

Theo clucked his tongue. "Word is this is a homicide. Does Lewis know you're here?"

They stood near a stand of trees that effectively blocked their view of the motel, and Baker stopped. If Tucker Lewis were here, then there had indeed been a homicide. And Baker would be tossed out on his ear. "Fuck Lewis," Baker said, but he detoured into the trees just the same. Theo and his partner, Mike Dawson, chuckled but kept on walking.

Baker made his way through the woods. The snow wasn't as deep here, and he moved with relative ease. His thoughts were on Lewis and Ginger, and he concentrated on forcing unwanted images from his mind. Leafless trees clawed at his coat with gnarled branches. Tears sprang to his eyes as one grazed his mangled cheek. Keeping his hands outstretched, he made his way through the thicket, careful to stay well under cover of the trees when he made it to the edge. From his new vantage point, he was able to look directly out onto the parking lot.

In all, there were four sheriff's cars lined up along the shoulder. He counted six city cop cars in the lot. The wind continued to blow snow in all directions, and every law enforcement officer on the scene was shouldering an inch of snow on the hat and jacket.

It could only be Chet Ferrebee, Baker thought, observing the animosity between the city cops and the sheriff's men. That's the only thing with enough pull to drag the fat boys in brown all the way to The Road King.

An informal argument erupted in the center of the lot between the blues and the browns. Theo Carver scribbled in his notebook while Mike Dawson snapped photos. Baker, safe in the shelter of the thicket, leaned against a tree and watched, weighing his craving for a cigarette against the desire to remain unobserved. He knew the smoke would draw attention; but if the nancies in the parking lot were going to sling jaw, Baker would need a smoke. He fingered the bandage on his face and sighed, but the breath caught in his chest as he spied Detective Tucker Lewis step from Room 102 onto the low front stoop.

Baker pushed away from the tree that supported his weight, his gut tight, his jaw clenched. In the dark cover of tangled trees, he let a trembling hand close around the butt of the Colt. Silently he eased it from the waistband of his pants, thumbed the hammer back and aimed at Lewis' head. It was a clear shot. It would never get clearer.

For an instant he was back in the bedroom, filled with morning light; and Ginger was on the bed, reaching for him. She could be his again if he would just pull the trigger. Here at The Road King, Lewis was talking calmly to the men, using his hands to make a point. Baker held the Colt steady. Steady.

A gust of wind rattled dead tree limbs together, dropping a pile of snow on the ground at Baker's feet.

"Fuck," he muttered, tucking the gun away and ignoring the shaking of his hands. When had *that* started?

Lewis, of course, was arrogantly unaware that he'd nearly been fed lead. He was lecturing the gaggle of uniforms on proper police procedure and etiquette, as if a guy like Lewis knew a fig about etiquette.

Baker didn't need to know what was being said. He didn't care what was being said. But he listened with the hope of discovering whose corpse was in Room 102. And there was a corpse. Lewis' presence assured him of that.

Baker's money was on Chet or the new wife…or both, since he didn't see either of them around.

Lewis' gruff voice carried on the wind, but Baker heard nothing about murder. It was just the standard "get the hell out of here, you county pigs" lecture. He swore he'd arrest any deputy that wasn't gone in three minutes, and then he stalked back to Room 102. The deputies muttered to themselves but headed back to their cars. All except Sheriff Ferrebee, who stood leaning against the car he'd pulled right up next to the ambulance. He rested against the hood with his arms crossed over his tuxedo jacket, ignoring the snow that covered his hair and his shoulders, daring anyone to tell him to leave.

Sheriff Ferrebee was the only man Baker had ever met who was larger than Edwards. And he smiled to himself now as the city policemen pretended not to notice the snow-covered giant in their midst.

Baker leaned against the tree again and waited. In time Lewis emerged from Room 102 and stood at the edge of the yellow tape marking the crime scene. He stared at Ferrebee and Ferrebee stared back. Baker watched as the two men regarded one another, Lewis with his hands in his pockets, Ferrebee with his arms crossed over his chest. An unspoken understanding passed between them, and Lewis stepped forward as Sheriff Ferrebee cradled his head in his huge red hands and cried.

So it was true; Chet Ferrebee was dead. Baker wondered about the bride, Marian Drake. Was she dead too? What happened? Were they dealing with a highway killer?

Baker forgot about his desire to plug Lewis. He leaned forward now, straining to hear what the detective was saying to the grieving sheriff. "I need you to stay behind the perimeter, Doug," was all Lewis said as he rested his hand on Ferrebee's shoulder. "Let us do our jobs."

The sheriff lifted his head and stared at Lewis with wide eyes, like a child who doesn't understand why he's in trouble. When Lewis put a hand on the sheriff's shoulder, Ferrebee shook it off. "My son is dead," he said, his hands shaking. "My boy."

Lewis removed his hat, revealing a cap of blonde, well-pomaded hair. Baker noted it retained the shape of his fedora nicely. "We're doing all we can, Sheriff. Please."

Ferrebee shook his head. "I know, Detective. I know." He took a deep breath and let it out before looking at Lewis again. "How is Marian?"

Lewis' mouth was grim. "She's in bad shape," he said, "but alive. The paramedics are with her now." He excused himself and made his way back to the stoop and into Room 102.

Sheriff Ferrebee stood rigid, the rhythmic clenching and relaxing of his scaly fists the only evidence of his turmoil. Baker was dying to get more information, but he wasn't ready to risk being seen by Lewis. From the cover of trees, he scanned the lot for his favorite city cop, smiling when he spied the stocky frame and round face that belonged to his friend, Sully Castle.

Sully was a hard-core flatfoot but would, with the right sort of encouragement, divulge information regarding certain cases. Sully stood, braced against the wind and driving snow, on the far end of the lot, his hands cupped around the cigarette he struggled to light.

47

His round face was red from the cold.

Baker stepped out from the shadows and strode across the lot as if he had every right to be there. The snow swallowed the sound of his feet as he approached his friend. "Sully," he said in a low voice.

Sully stopped fiddling with his lighter and looked at Baker. His features settled into a frown. "Aw, Christ, not now, Baker, huh? I'm on a job here."

Baker looked around. "You're watching yellow tape. That's not a job, Sully; it's a waste of taxpayers' money." Baker pulled out his own lighter and touched the flame to Sully's smoke. "Besides," he continued. "You owe me."

"Shh, not so loud. You trying to get me canned?" He turned and looked Baker full in the face. He pointed to the bandage. "Sheesh, what happened to you? You working a case here?"

Baker stuffed his hands in his pockets, wondering if the wind would ever die down. "Car accident," he said. "And yeah, I'm working a case. I've got a tingle it may be related to what happened to the sheriff's kid, but it's too soon to tell." He jerked his head toward the motel. "Clue me in."

Sully cast a nervous look around at the other uniforms manning the perimeter. "All right," he said, "but if I spill, you got to back off. I mean it."

"Sure, Sully."

Sully took a drag on the cigarette, letting the smoke escape in a dark cloud as he spoke. "Right. Okay. So the sheriff's kid gets married today, to a real hot dish."

Baker rolled his eyes. "I ate that news for dinner." He jerked his head toward Room 102. "What's cookin' in there?"

Sully's face was hard. "The kid's dead. New wife beat up pretty bad."

"How'd he get it?"

Sully blew smoke into the air, watching as it drifted into the night. "Somebody strangled him."

"And her?"

Sully looked back to Baker when the smoke was gone. He shuddered. "Beat her half to death. She's a mess."

"Jesus."

"Yeah."

"Anything in there?"

"Like what?"

Baker shrugged. "Like mail. Letters, papers. Anything like that."

Sully shook his head. "Nah. Nothing like that."

"So why did they stop here? Weren't they supposed to be going on some sort of mysterious honeymoon?"

"You get a look at the lady?"

"Yeah," Baker said.

"Could you wait 'til the honeymoon to make your marriage official-like?"

Baker supposed he couldn't. He shook his head. Some wedding night. At least he hadn't been the cause of disaster for the married couple. Someone else took care of that job for him. He nodded his thanks to Sully and moved in the direction of the trees again, careful to stay out of sight of Lewis and the sheriff. When he got to the edge of the lot, he moved into the trees and worked his way toward the motel porch. He pushed through the woods and exited on the hot side of the perimeter, two feet from the motel's sidewalk. "Stupid bulls," he mumbled, straightening his coat and scraping the mud from his shoes on the gravel.

He stepped onto the sidewalk with silent feet and moved toward the motel room door. A pile of rubbernecking Blues blocked the entrance, making it impossible to catch a clean look. So he stood at the edge of the crowd and tried to blend in. When a paramedic hurried from the room in the direction of the ambulance, Baker stopped him.

The paramedic, his arms cradling a tray of bandages and bloody towels, looked at Baker. "Yeah?"

"You working the scene?"

The medic held up the tray. "What the hell does it look like, pal?"

"There any letters in that room?"

"What?"

Baker said, "You know, letters? Envelopes? Stamps? Dear Bill? Love, Helen?"

The man shook his head, his face an unusual combination of confusion and pity as he walked away.

"Yeah, same to you, pal," Baker said, leaning against a post and trying to light a cigarette. It was windy and his lighter wouldn't catch. He cocked it once, then again. Nothing. He shook it, trying to coat the sparker with fuel and was about to cock it a third time when a steady flame appeared an inch from his bandaged cheek.

"Let me help you with that."

Baker looked up into the face of Detective Lewis. With hooded eyes that barely concealed the smoldering hatred he felt for the man, Baker touched his cigarette to the flame. He inhaled deeply, blowing the smoke into Lewis' face. "Thanks," he said, imagining the bullet he'd almost fired scattering Lewis' tiny brain all over the parking lot.

"Don't mention it," Lewis answered, shredding the fantasy and pocketing the lighter.

"Looks like you've got a crime scene here." Baker gestured to Lewis' coat pocket. "And a nifty lighter unaffected by wind. I gather that's one of the perks of making deals with the devil."

Lewis smoothed his mustache. "It's a Zippo. And get out of here, Baker."

Baker smiled but made no move to leave. "Rumor has it someone off'd the sheriff's kid."

"I'm not at liberty to discuss anything with you, *Mr.* Baker."

"That's Detective Baker. And I'm not asking for information. The fact that you're here implies murder. The fact that the sheriff is here looking like someone expunged his son implies that someone probably did just that. I'm guessing Chet's wife didn't get zotzed, but she's likely had some blood drawn."

"You have all the answers, Mr. Baker. Tell me more."

Baker shrugged and jerked his head in the direction of the ambulance. "The meat wagon's still here. 'Round these parts, dead people ride in hearses."

Lewis bowed. "Very good. I see you've been reading Sam Spade again."

"Careful what you say to me, Lewis, or I might not let you have any of the credit when I solve this case."

"Have you suddenly developed new skills, Baker? Skills that allow you to solve real crimes?"

Baker let his gaze wander up and down the motel's sidewalk. "It's got to be pretty rough, Lewis, you being here for a murder and all. I imagine this place holds some special memories for you."

Lewis' eyes flashed. "If you were any kind of a detective, you'd have caught me and Ginger long before you did."

Baker's heart stopped, and his fists clenched involuntarily. He forced his face to remain impassive, but he knew some of the color drained from it.

Lewis smiled, knowing he'd hit a nerve. "She says 'hi,' by the way. We'll send you a wedding picture when we get them back from the photographer." He examined a fingernail. "We'd have gotten them sooner, but we were so busy with the honeymoon. You know how it is."

Baker opened his mouth to speak, but the world had stopped. His heart had stopped. He fought suffocation as he waited for it to start again. He felt it as it pumped. Once and then again. Air passed from his chest, out his mouth and into the night. He sucked it in again with greed. The wind had dried his eyes, and he blinked to bring the world back into focus. There. He was fine. He looked at Lewis and when he spoke, his voice was steady. "Did I ever tell you about the time Ginger gave me the clap?"

Lewis' face darkened. "Beat it, Baker, or I'll haul you in."

Baker held his hands up in submission. "I'm going. I'm going. I'll just head over here and observe from outside the lines, Lewis. You can't arrest me for that."

Lewis shook his head but was unable to hide his rage. He shoved a uniform out of the way as he stalked back into 102. Some of the motel's usual guests wandered drunkenly from their rooms clad in wrinkled suits and half-zipped dresses. They shivered in the cold, shielding their faces from Mike Dawson's camera, and answered questions for the police.

Outside the perimeter, Ferrebee waited with poorly controlled hostility. After a few minutes, he shook his head and wiped a meaty hand over his face. Baker moved in that direction, wanting to say something...anything. But that was a bad idea. Ferrebee would wonder about his being here. Maybe not tonight, but soon; and Baker wasn't ready to sing that song just yet.

"Sheriff." The woman from the wedding, the singer in the red dress, Judith—her name was Judith—was there, her husband's tuxedo jacket draped over her shoulders, her feet swallowed by enormous boots. The red dress peeked out from beneath the coat that hung to her knees.

Sheriff Ferrebee turned to stare at her.

"I just heard," she said. "Wally told us. My God, where is Marian?"

Ferrebee's expression faltered a bit as he stared at Judith. After a moment, he collected himself and lurched with unsteady strides toward 102, shoving the blues out of his way. A short, squat officer, *probably a rookie*, Baker thought, stepped in front of the giant sheriff. "Hold it, pal," he said.

Ferrebee towered above the cop, his eyes narrowed. But in the usual father-like way he had, he put his hand on the man's shoulder. Baker looked around for Wally Sims, the deputy who'd spread the news to Judith. He was nowhere in sight.

"Inside," Ferrebee said, letting Judith brush snow from his hair and shoulders.

"You'll catch your death out here," she said. "Let's wait in the car. I'll stay with you."

"I want to see my son," Ferrebee said, his voice thick with emotion.

"I think it's best if we wait here, Sheriff. We need to let the police do their work."

But Ferrebee was beyond listening to reason. He clenched and unclenched his fists, as if working up the nerve to do something. He paced restlessly back and forth as Judith watched. Baker too watched from a safe distance. Back and forth, back and forth. Ferrebee's movements were almost hypnotic in the snow. Then, without warning, he lunged. He sprang forward and ducked under the yellow tape with surprising agility. Once on the other side, he stood for a minute, bewildered. Then he said, "I'm going in, son."

The shorter officer hitched up his belt and nodded in sympathy. "I can't allow that, sir. Detective Lewis' orders."

Ferrebee backed up a few steps, his face a curious mixture of confusion and anger. The officer allowed his shoulders to slump in relief, thinking he'd just managed to pacify the biggest man he'd ever confronted. But Ferrebee had no intention of leaving; and the shorter officer was unprepared when the sheriff lunged forward like a charging bull, his heavy fists whistling through the cold air.

The cop ducked one swing, then another, his eyes wide with the knowledge that the situation was about to get *really* out of hand. He swung a few times himself, his miniature fists not fazing the half-crazed sheriff.

Judith ducked under the perimeter. "Sheriff, stop, please," she called; but another officer held her back, his hands lingering too long on her chest as he grabbed her from behind.

Baker moved to help her; but Sully was there, restraining him. "Lewis'll lock you up and throw away the key, Baker. Stay here; I'll get her."

Sully moved forward, gently taking Judith from the pawing officer's hands. "Better wait in your car, Miss," he said, tipping his hat.

Judith didn't need to be told twice. But she had no intention of heading back to the highway for her own car. She climbed into the passenger seat of the sheriff's car and watched.

Back on the sidewalk Ferrebee faced half a dozen cops, his fists connecting with one or two. The smaller cop took a shot to the jaw and dropped like a sack of wet sand. The others surrounded Ferrebee, jumping at him from all directions. Two clung to his back like infant primates, the sheriff oblivious to the burden of their weight. Three others swung at him from the sides and front as frightened motel guests edged back into their rooms.

"Break it up," Lewis yelled, his face red with fury as he stepped into the midst of it. "Break it up now."

Ferrebee brushed the two officers from his back like a couple of spiders.

"He's resisting arrest," one said as he fell to the ground.

Lewis ignored that.

So did Ferrebee. "I want to see my son," he said, his breathing ragged, his hair hanging in wet tendrils around his face.

Lewis waved the others back to their posts and took the sheriff aside, careful to step over the cop that had been knocked cold. "Look, Doug," he said. "I can't. Chet wouldn't want you to see him. Not like this. Let us do our job. Go home to Effie. She needs you."

The sheriff's jaw remained tight, but his eyes softened. "Can I see Marian?"

Lewis looked out over the lot, studying the tire tracks in the snow. "She's not as bad as we thought at first. She's talking. She's not making much sense, but she's talking. The paramedics think she's stable enough to move." He looked Ferrebee in the eye. "You can see her at the hospital. For now I need you to stay out of the way. That's not a request. Any more funny business and I'll arrest you."

There was a commotion at the door, and the paramedics emerged wheeling a gurney. A white sheet covered Marian Drake, and the ambulance driver hurried to cover her with dark gray blankets.

Baker craned his neck to get a look at her, catching only a glimpse of her raven black hair.

Judith climbed from the car and watched, crying softly, as the stretcher was loaded into the ambulance.

Once Marian was settled inside, the paramedics returned to help the beaten cop off the ground. He was angry but awake, and they insisted he come along to the hospital with them for evaluation.

"Hell," Ferrebee said, watching the ambulance make its slow departure. Then he motioned to Judith, and the two of them climbed into his patrol car and followed the slow- moving ambulance into the heart of the storm.

A few minutes later Ollie Tate's wagon pulled in. "Took you long enough," Lewis shouted from the doorway.

"Take it easy," Tate yelled back, squeezing himself from the front seat. "Had another call in the city. Stabbing."

Lewis didn't care. "Get in here. We need you to get your pictures done so we can get him to the morgue."

"Hey, I am the morgue." Tate pushed people out of his way as he ducked under the tape and strode to the sidewalk. "Where is he?"

Lewis ushered him into the room, and Baker frowned as the pair disappeared into the dim yellow glow. The groom, the only source for the letters so far, was dead, his wife badly beaten. Baker was nowhere close to finishing this job for Diana Kramer. It was time to annoy someone.

He set his shoulders and approached the yellow tape with a grin. Once there, he paced back and forth in plain view of the uniforms. Back and forth, back and forth. Now hopping on one foot, now skipping. Now whistling. After a time, Sully meandered over.

"Baker," he nodded.

Baker continued to pace. Back and forth. Back and forth. "Sully," he said. Lewis watched from the motel room, scowling.

"What are you doing?" Sully asked. "You here to arrest me?"

"No. I'm here to warn you that you're starting to bug Detective Lewis. This is his crime scene. He's trying to keep it low-key, if you get my drift."

"I get your drift, Sully. But I'm not anywhere near the crime scene." He skipped a little, back and forth. "I'm outside the perimeter."

Sully didn't bite. "I already told you all I know, Baker. Strangled. Beaten. He's dead. She's not. End of story."

"Technically, my good man, that's just the beginning." He hopped on one foot.

"Jesus, you're starting to sound like that windbag who works for you."

Baker froze. "Good Lord, you're right. Hmm." He shook his head, then began pacing again.

"Stop, just stop. Tell me what you want."

Baker looked toward the motel, satisfied to see Lewis' scowl deepen. "I want to know if anyone knew about the letters."

"Christ, I told you. There weren't any letters in there."

Baker leaned in, his face serious. "Someone hired me to find letters that were mailed to the groom. You know my guarantee. If I don't find the letters, I can't keep the retainer. I need the recovery money, Sully. Things are tight right now." He couldn't bring himself to mention Stewie. Not here. Not tonight.

Sully backed up, shaking his head. "No can do, pal. Last time I helped you I ended up behind a desk for six months."

Baker resumed pacing again. After a moment, he stopped short in front of his friend. "Sully, Sully, Sully. Do these boys know about you and that little hatcheck girl at the Palms? What was her name? Edna? Elsie?"

"Stop. Okay? Just stop."

Baker snapped his fingers. "Ellen. That's it." He looked around and raised his voice. "Any of you boys met Ellen? She's a real dish." He whispered to Sully, "Isn't she Detective Lewis' niece? I've got some pictures from that night we all went to that place in the city. You remember? That little bistro?"

Sully sighed and lifted his hat to scratch his head. "Fine. You win. Just go, okay? Get outta here. I'll stop by when I've got something."

Baker grinned and moved back to the trees. "Until then, darling," he called.

Chapter 5

By morning the clouds were dark with the inevitability of more snow, and Baker's cheek ached with the threat of bad weather. By the time Sully arrived to spill what he knew about the Chet Ferrebee murder, Baker was digging in his desk for more aspirin and wondering if he would hear from Diana Kramer today. There was a gnawing fear in his belly that she might somehow be involved in this mess.

"A swarthy police officer to see you, sir," Edwards said, opening the door to the inner office.

Baker scowled at the interruption. "Where the hell is the aspirin, Edwards?"

Edwards kept his face impassive, but Baker thought he saw the hint of a smirk playing around his mouth. "I'm sure I don't know," Edwards drawled. "You had it last."

Baker slammed the drawer shut and rested his aching cheek in the palm of his hand. "Well, send him in, man. I haven't got all day."

Edwards' lips twitched, but, "Very good, sir," was all he said

Sully loped in, scowling; his shoulders were hunched in frustration. "Gee whiz, Baker. Why's your guy always got to insult me?"

Baker's cheek was biting now, a maddening combination of itching and pain. "What, Sully?"

"Your guy. I heard him. He called me swarthy."

Baker shook his head. "Just his way, Sully. What've you got for me?"

"Not much." He assessed Baker's face. "How's the cheek?"

"Better all the time."

"What the hell happened, anyway?"

Baker shrugged, not wanting to think about it. "Car accident. What have you got for me?"

Sully nodded like he didn't believe that for a minute and consulted a small notebook he pulled from his coat pocket. "Chet Ferrebee was strangled with the bed sheet. It was tied in a special knot. Like the fishermen use to dock their boats, only with an extra twist to make it impossible to untie."

Baker thought about Barone and his men and their tendency to conduct business with boatmen, using riverboats for moving various types of cargo. He kept his expression impassive. "Any leads?"

Sully shrugged. "None. But Chet put up a helluva fight first. Knuckles bruised and bloody, face bashed in." He shook his head. "Somehow the killer managed to get behind him. That's how he was able to tie the knot around Chet's neck." Sully tapped his pencil on the notebook and thought for a minute. "Maybe Ferrebee was stunned or unconscious. I can't say. But old Ollie Tate had to cut the sheet off. There was no way to untie that knot."

Baker considered this. "What about the wife?"

Sully nodded and looked at the notebook again. "Funny thing, that. She can't remember a thing about the attack. She's a mess but says she doesn't know who did it to her. And she put up a fight too."

"She still in the hospital?"

Sully shook his head. "Get this," he said, leaning forward and sticking the notebook back in his pocket. "They're sending her to the loony bin on account of she can't remember anything." He leaned back in his chair and lit a cigarette. "Can you beat that? The dame lost two fingernails." He held up the first two fingers on his left hand. "Ripped completely off. A lady gets knocked around like that, and she can't say who did the knockin'. That's nuts is what that is."

"Maybe she got hit on the head."

Sully frowned as he blew out a cloud of smoke. "Doc says, 'No, just punched in the face a coupla times is all.'"

"Is all," Baker echoed, lighting a cigarette of his own. "What asylum?"

Sully shuddered. "Crane Haven's Place of Restoration. Sounds like a funeral parlor."

Baker's mouth was tight when he answered, "Yeah. Why didn't they send her home?"

"How the hell should I know? Afraid the killer might come back for her, maybe? I can't see as how she's any danger to him. She can't even remember her wedding."

It was obvious Sully had more to say, but Baker had heard enough. He stood, walked Sully to the door and shook his hand.

Sully shoved his hands in his pocket and rocked on his heels. "So," he said, "was this helpful?"

"Sure, Sully, sure," Baker said, already heading back to his desk. "Edwards will show you out."

Edwards appeared at the door and took Sully's arm. Sully shook him off. "Say, Baker," he said, "any chance of getting that picture of me and Ellen back?"

Baker didn't answer as Edwards led Sully away. He stared out the window, not seeing the people or cars as they passed in front of him, and thought of Stewie. By now Baker's little brother had been cremated and was on his way back to Cedar Rapids. Baker wondered if Ginger had written to his mother as he'd asked. Baker hadn't phoned home, hadn't written a note, hadn't made any effort to contact the woman who raised him. Who the hell was he to tell Ginger to write a note when he hadn't so much as called?

"Interesting fellow," Edwards said, striding into the room and recalling Baker to the dim office. He carried several suit jackets. "These just arrived from the cleaners, sir. Miss Deirdre brought them over while you were occupied with Mr. Sully." He disappeared into the closet.

Baker slumped into his chair, cradling his cheek in his hand again. "I need to go to the sanitarium on the edge of town," he said.

Edwards returned from the closet carrying two of the clean jackets and four ties. A distasteful expression lined his mouth and eyes. "The sanitarium, sir?"

Baker nodded. "It appears I'll have to talk to the widow if I want to retrieve Chet's love letters. That is, assuming Miss Diana Kramer didn't murder him and skip town."

Edwards was thoughtful for a moment as he examined the suit jackets he held. "What mood do you wish to convey to the widow?"

"I need to look...empathetic."

"Very good, sir." Edwards held up one of the jackets. "You shall wear tweed. If woven properly, it can be a very empathetic fabric." He laid the jacket over a chair. He looked at the four neckties he'd brought from the closet. "But you'll need a different tie. None of these will work. Something dark blue, I think." He walked toward the closet.

Baker swiveled in his chair and looked out at the dark clouds, wishing the ache in his cheek would disappear.

Crane Haven's Place of Restoration was an old Victorian house that loomed above the town from its perch atop a steep hill three miles away. In the summer the hill was a carpet of bluegrass and wildflowers, offering a welcome respite for the weary mind. Now as Baker urged his ancient car up the narrow road covered in frozen mud and alighted on the even muddier drive that approached the house, he thought it resembled the desolate castles used over and over again as settings in the romance novels Ginger was always reading. He scowled and parked his car, swearing loudly as he stepped out and slipped on a patch of dirty ice.

He picked his way over the ruts in the lot with care, not wanting to fall and ruin the stolen suit Edwards had taken such pains to assemble for him today. The house was well-cared-for; and, despite the name, the appearance of the establishment was inviting. A wide verandah lined the front of the house. Worn wooden rocking chairs were strategically placed to offer the best views of the town below. Baker made his way up the steps and paused near the front door.

A plaque to the door's right read:

Crane Haven's Place of Restoration
Built 1848 as farmstead of Russel and Esther Snow
Donated upon their deaths to the City of Crane Haven
Restored and Converted to House of Restoration in 1922

Baker stepped into the dimly-lit vestibule, wincing as the outer door blew shut, trapping him in that awkward place between inside and out. He shivered briefly, hating how the sound of his breathing was artificially loud in this small space, and pulled his coat more tightly about him. Then he pushed through the inner door and immediately choked on the air. Raw sewage. No other stench held the same revulsion. It drifted through the halls of the old mansion, settling in a putrid invisible cloud in the lobby, clinging to his clothes, working its way into his nose and mouth. He coughed delicately, reaching for the navy blue handkerchief in his breast pocket.

He considered returning to his car and heading back to the comfort of his office; but he was here to see the widow, and he had every intention of doing so. Keeping the handkerchief over his mouth, he looked around.

Other than the stench, the old building was immaculate. Dark wood floors were polished to a sharp gleam, furniture was tasteful and elegant and gray winter light drifted in through filmy curtains. A long mahogany counter that served as a desk for the nursing staff ran the length of the foyer; and Baker approached it cautiously, searching the ceiling for evidence of dripping waste.

"Problem with the pipes?" he asked the nurse behind the desk. Her nametag read "Enid."

She shook her head. "No one knows for sure. You get used to the smell after a while." She frowned when she noticed the bandage on his face. "Fight?" she asked.

"Car accident. I'm here to see Marian Drake."

Enid's frown deepened. "Are you with the police?"

"Friend of the family." Sweat broke out on his upper lip as the lie slipped out.

Enid didn't notice. She shook her head and clucked her tongue. "That poor girl. The more family she has around her now, the better." Enid gestured to a guest book on the counter. "If you'll sign in first, please. Then you may join the rest of your party in the women's parlor."

Baker nodded his thanks and picked up a pen. The guest register was thick and dusty and quite old. He resisted the urge to flip backward through the book and peek at names of visitors through the years. Instead he studied this morning's entries. Sheriff Ferrebee's name was on the bottom of the list. Above his signature, Judith and Jeffrey Drake's names were scrawled on the same line in the same feminine hand. The drunk and the singer. Baker's heart skipped.

Judith was still here.

With her husband.

Someone had signed in before the Drakes, but the name and the time had been scratched out. He studied the entry for a moment, holding the book to the light.

"Is something the matter, sir?" Enid asked.

Baker showed her the book. "Someone signed in on this line but scratched it out."

Enid inspected the ledger. "Hmm. That's interesting." She held the book to the light, turning it back and forth. "I can't make out the name." She handed the book back to Baker and smiled. "Someone probably signed in on the wrong page." When Baker looked confused, she said, "Each patient has his or her own page. It helps us keep track of who is receiving visitors and who isn't. Dr. Rogers feels that family support is crucial to recovery. I'm sure someone signed in on Marian's page, realized they made a mistake and scratched out the signature before signing in on the page belonging to the correct party."

"I see," Baker said, studying the scratches in the page. They were deep and jagged; as if someone wanted to obliterate the name, not just erase it. He signed his name under Sheriff Ferrebee's and asked Enid to point him toward the ladies' parlor.

The parlor, as it turned out, was not a parlor at all; and, after entering and taking a couple of steps, Baker retreated to the door again to make sure he was in the right room. Once assured, he entered a second time, stepping lightly, as if any sound might bring the women of the ward running toward him in a homicidal frenzy. His feet were nearly silent on the shining wood floor.

The stench of sewage was not as strong here, and he lowered the handkerchief. He moved three steps deeper into the room and found himself between two rows of white metal tables three deep. Each table was surrounded by six metal chairs. He turned slowly. Where were the deep armchairs and overstuffed sofas? Where were the shelves of books? Where was color? Here, as in the vestibule, Baker's breathing was artificially loud; and he brought the handkerchief to his mouth again to silence himself.

There were four patients in the room. One worked on a sewing card, using an enormous plastic needle to string yarn in and out of holes big enough to put a thumb through. She smiled and muttered to herself with each stitch. Another woman worked on a drawing done entirely in red crayon. A third sat silently, staring out the window at nothing.

Baker swallowed the revulsion he felt even as he acknowledged his hatred of this place and its people. He could feel Ginger's memory, fighting to get through; and he was tempted to give in and let it wash over him. But Ginger never solved anything. Even when she'd belonged to him, she couldn't take away the disgust he felt at doing his job.

He nearly laughed aloud. Years ago his mother had wanted him to be a dentist. She was obsessed with clean teeth. But Baker had been unable to stand the thought of touching other people's mouths. "I'd feel dirty all the time," he said. He sniffed again, nearly choking on the stench of the sewage, then pressed the handkerchief more tightly over his nose and wondered if his mother was as disappointed in him as he was in himself.

He spied Marian Drake-Ferrebee at a table next to the bank of windows along the back wall. She sat with her head bent forward, her black hair hiding her battered face. And beside her was Judith.

Baker's breath hitched when he saw the singer again. She'd been watching him, mentally recording his assessment of the room. He wondered if he passed her test. "Well," she said with suspicion in her eyes. "We meet again." Her voice was like honey on a cracker, sweet but with a hint of salt. Just looking at her made a mouth too dry to whistle.

"Mrs. Drake," he said.

Sheriff Ferrebee, his face tight with grief, turned his red-rimmed eyes in Baker's direction. "You two know each other?" he asked. But his eyes were glazed, and Baker decided not to remind the man that he was present when Baker helped Judith get Jeffrey into a chair at the reception last night.

Judith wasn't quite as insensitive. "We met last night," she said, laying a protective arm over the widow's shoulder. When she looked at Baker, her eyes were cold. "This is Marian," she said.

Marian made no move to acknowledge that she'd been touched, let alone introduced.

"Hello, Marian," Baker said, feeling uncomfortable and wondering where Effie Ferrebee was.

The widow didn't respond.

Judith jerked her head in the direction of the windows. "You remember my husband from last night, don't you? Say hello, Jeffrey."

Jeffrey stood with his back to the room, gazing out at the barren ground and the trees beyond. He did not respond to his wife's voice, nor did he turn to greet Baker. And Baker was relieved.

"What can we do for you, detective?" the sheriff asked, his vacant eyes clearing for the moment. "You're not working with the city cops on this, or Lewis would've told me."

"Detective Lewis?" Judith leaned forward. "You work with Detective Lewis?"

"Not if I can help it," Baker said.

Ferrebee swiped a big hand over his face. "Baker here is private." He addressed Judith, but his eyes never left Baker's face. "He photographs cheating spouses."

Judith made a face and slid her eyes in Baker's direction. "Then what's he doing here?"

"Exactly my question," Ferrebee said.

Baker pulled a pack of cigarettes from his pocket and offered one to the sheriff before opening his lighter. Ferrebee declined. Baker watched Marian as he spoke to Ferrebee, "I'm not working with the police." Marian made no movement as he spoke. Her head remained tilted forward, her chin nearly resting on her chest. Baker could make out a purple mass of bruising behind her hair, but not enough of her face was visible to offer details of facial features or eye color. He gave up and looked directly at Ferrebee. "I sure am sorry about your boy." And he meant it.

The sheriff regarded Baker with a look bordering on hostility. Raw grief lay below the façade. And that made a simple job like finding love letters tedious indeed. "What do you want, Baker?" Ferrebee said at length.

Baker cleared his throat and thought about saying that for starters, he'd like to sit down. But he didn't figure that would go over too well. So he offered what he hoped passed for a smile. "I'd like to talk to Mrs. Ferrebee."

Judith's arm tightened around Marian. "I don't think so, *Detective*." She spat the word as her eyes flashed blue in the too-bright room. "She's done nothing but answer questions since last night. She's exhausted."

Baker kept his smile in place. He took a drag on the cigarette and crossed to the far side of the table and looked out the window into the snow beneath. He felt like an ass, but money was tight and he needed to bury his brother. He blew a cloud of smoke toward the ceiling and turned to look at Ferrebee. "I can talk to her here in front of you, Sheriff, or I can come back later."

Judith bristled. "We'll tell the nurses not to let you in."

Ferrebee stared at Baker, regarding him with animosity. Baker's tactics were well- known. He'd find a way inside to get the answers he needed. And Ferrebee knew it. Baker watched Ferrebee's eyes as the old man debated the wisdom of letting Baker question the widow alone. "Shit," he muttered. "Won't do any good, Judith. He'll find a way." Then he shook his head. "All right, Baker, take your shot. But I warn you that if you upset her, I'll come after you."

"Sheriff?" Enid stood at the door, her white shoes spotless, the stench behind her overwhelming. "The station is on the line for you. They tried to get you on your car radio."

"Damn incompetents," he said, rising. "I'll be right back." He looked pointedly at Baker. "Judith will tell me everything."

Baker waited until the sheriff was gone before pulling out a chair. Its metal legs grated over the black floor. He ignored the hateful look Judith directed toward him as he sat down and told himself it didn't matter that they would be enemies now. He was an outsider driving a spear into the breast of a helpless woman. He knew it and Judith knew it. He'd been in this position a hundred times. Maybe more. Wasn't it supposed to get easier with time?

He thought about the flask he'd left at the office and wished he hadn't decided to stop drinking again.

He took his time crushing out his cigarette and lighting another. When Judith began to squirm impatiently, he spoke. "Marian," he said, watching her closely. When she didn't respond, he tried again. "Mrs. Ferrebee, I need to ask you some questions."

Slowly she lifted her head. And the curtain of black hair parted. As her face became visible, Baker forced himself to remain expressionless. But it was difficult to keep from recoiling as he viewed the full extent of her injuries. Her left eye was swollen completely shut, the left side of her jaw was blackened and swollen, the lower left side of her mouth crusted with dried blood. He met the stare she offered with her unmarked right eye and nodded once as he studied the rest of her face. Other than a slight cut on her cheek, the right side of her face was unmarked. Baker made a mental note. The assailant was right-handed. Her neck was also clean, he noted.

He looked back to her open eye; green, he noticed, and fringed with long, dark lashes. "Do you have a cigarette, Detective?" she asked. Her voice was soft and breathy but confident. Not what he expected.

Keeping his own cigarette clenched between his lips, he pulled out the pack and helped her to hold it to her lips between bandaged fingers as he lit it. Her hand shook as she inhaled deeply.

Baker nodded at her hand. "I heard about your fingernails," he said, looking from Marian to Judith.

Judith cocked an eyebrow.

Baker cleared his throat, thinking that if he could just talk about something simple, maybe they wouldn't hate him so much. "It's just that I know how important fingernails are to a dame—I mean lady," he said.

Judith's eyebrow remained elevated.

Baker cleared his throat and gestured with the cigarette. "I used to be married, you see; and," he chuckled, "when she broke a nail, the whole building knew about it. We lived in these apartments over on Fifth..."

Both women stared at him now, their expressions bewildered. He stopped speaking and cleared his throat again. Then he said, "Mrs. Ferrebee..."

"Marian."

She didn't seem hostile. So far, so good. "Marian, I've been hired to find some letters."

She shrugged Judith's arm from around her shoulders and, smiling, leaned back in her chair, causing the thin hospital gown she wore to rise to mid-thigh. Her smile was seductive. "I don't know anything about any letters," she said.

Judith straightened Marian's gown and took the cigarette from her. "You don't smoke, Marian," she said, crushing it out. To Baker, she said, "Who hired you?"

"I'm not at liberty to say," Baker told her.

"You don't look like a detective," Marian said, smiling and shifting in her chair so the gown could rise up again. The look in her eyes was cold, emotionless; and for some crazy reason, Baker thought about the hostility used to scratch out the signature in the guest book.

He studied Marian Drake-Ferrebee for a long moment. "You don't look crazy," he said at last, wondering where that thought had come from.

Marian jerked as if she'd been slapped and stared at her lap again. Baker regarded her, wondering…

"What about these letters you're looking for?" Judith asked.

Baker kept his eyes on Marian. "I'd like to ask Mrs. Ferrebee these questions, if you don't mind."

Marian rose from her chair. On silent feet wrapped in white slippers, she walked to the window farthest from her brother and stared out at the trees.

From the doorway the sheriff cleared his throat. "I need to go to the bank," he said. "That Farmer kid's gone and got himself stuck in the vault again. I'm the only other person in town besides his mother who has the combination, and she's at the church for quilting today." He walked to Marian and put a hand on her shoulder. "I'll see you tomorrow," he said. When he spoke again, Baker noticed the dark circles under the eyes still red with grief. "Detective," he said, "I'll be in touch."

Baker nodded and turned his attention back to Judith, who sat with her arms wrapped around herself, frowning. "This is important," he said, wondering why he felt the need to explain himself to her.

She snorted. "To whom?"

He ignored that and looked at Marian. "Marian. Please. Your husband was in possession of some letters. The person who wrote them wants them back."

Marian kept her back turned and said nothing.

Judith stood up, glaring at Baker. "What the hell is wrong with you?" she hissed.

Jeffrey moved then, turning from the window and grinning stupidly as if the whole scene unfolding in front of him were delightfully entertaining. Then he pulled a flask from his pocket, toasted the room and took a deep drink.

Baker returned his attention to the table. "Why is Marian here, Judith?"

Judith sat down. "To recover. To remember what happened." She made a helpless gesture with her hands. "And for protection."

"From whom?"

Judith shook her head. "I don't know."

Baker raised his voice to be sure Marian heard. "I'm not here about the murder, Mrs. Ferrebee."

Marian turned to look at him. "I don't have any letters," she said.

Judith nodded. "There. You see? She doesn't have any letters. Now go away."

Baker wasn't discouraged. "Maybe your husband hid them somewhere, Marian. Maybe in your house? Would you be willing to let me take a look?"

Judith stood again, slamming her hand on the table. The woman with the sewing card started to cry. "Who hired you?" Judith demanded, her voice a hoarse whisper.

An orderly hurried over to the crying woman, and Baker knew he was about to be tossed out. He met Judith's stare. "I'm not at liberty to say."

"What's in the letters?"

"I'm not at liberty to say that either."

"This is growing tiresome, Detective." She opened her mouth to say something else, but Marian interrupted her.

"I'm feeling quite ill now, Judith," she said.

Judith rushed to her side. "Lean on me," she said, steering Marian away from the windows. "I'll take you upstairs to bed."

Baker rose. "Let me help you. Which room is hers?"

Judith pushed his hand away. "I'm not at liberty to say."

The orderly managed to calm the crying woman but glowered at Baker, who shrugged and followed Marian and Judith from the room. He stood in the foyer and watched as they climbed the wide staircase to the rooms above. Marian leaned heavily on Judith's arm.

Baker looked down at the tweed jacket Edwards convinced him to wear and frowned. "Empathy, my Aunt Fannie," he muttered, strolling over to the guest book. He held the book to the light again and peered closely at the scratched-out name. The first letter was a "D." Diana Kramer? He looked around. Enid wasn't at the desk, and the orderly hadn't followed him. He was alone for the moment. Carefully he pulled the page from the book, folded it and tucked it in his pocket. He wanted to return to the parlor to ask Jeffrey about the letters but knew the orderly was still inside. And Jeffrey was drunk and likely incoherent.

Shaking his head, Baker left the parlor and found his way back out the main entrance into the cold, fresh air.

Chapter 6

Edwards was gone when Baker got back to his office, which explained why Leadfoot Barone was sitting with his feet propped up on the desk, dripping mud and snow everywhere. Baker was preoccupied with thoughts of Diana Kramer, the widow and the elusive love letters. He was in no mood to deal with Barone.

"That's my chair," he said, closing the door and hanging up his hat.

Barone smiled, dropped his feet and wiggled in the chair. "It squeaks," he said, his voice oddly muffled by the bandage covering his cheek. "I know a guy who can look this over if you want."

Rage flared behind Baker's eyes, but he tamped it down and met Barone's stare. "Where are your goons? Don't they follow you everywhere?"

Barone frowned. "Here and there," he said. "There's two still in the hospital with bum knees, thanks to you." When Baker was silent, Barone continued. "This is just a social call," he said. "Nice and peaceful." He rose and gestured to the door leading to Edwards' office. "Don't you have a secretary? Where is she?"

"It's a 'he' and obviously he's gone."

Barone's brow rose in surprise, and his wide lips spread in what passed for a smile. "A man, you say?" He shoved his hands in his pockets and walked to the front of the desk. "I didn't figure you for one of those funny boys," he said.

Baker kept his feet firmly planted but watched every move the gangster made. "Beat it, Barone," he said, "before I finish what I started the other night."

Barone raised his hands in submission and perched on the edge of the desk. He pulled cigarette papers and a tobacco pouch from his jacket pocket and set to work rolling a cigarette with his nimble fingers. "No need to get riled, Detective," he said, keeping his eyes on the task of rolling the smoke. "This is a friendly visit, remember?" He licked the edge of the paper, smoothed out the cigarette and clamped it in his lips while he fished for his lighter. "I find myself in need of your services," he said. Baker opened his mouth to speak, but Barone held up a hand which clasped the lighter he'd just found.

"Hear me out," he said, flicking the lighter and touching the flame to the cigarette. "I'm willing to erase the debt your brother owes me in addition to paying you full price for your services. Provided you can be discreet, of course." He pocketed the lighter, the cigarette papers and the pouch of tobacco and regarded Baker with his beady eyes.

Baker casually pulled the gun from his shoulder holster and pointed it at Barone. "How's about I plug you and then everybody wins?"

Barone laughed, spewing yellow smoke into the room. The brand of tobacco he used smelled terrible, and Baker made a face as the stench reached his nostrils. "I could have killed your brother," Barone said. "But I didn't."

Baker re-holstered his gun and moved behind the desk. He opened a window, letting frigid air fill the room. "Who did?"

"Someone with long arms and a bad temper. That's all you need to know." Barone began to pace, gesturing with the rancid cigarette as he moved about the office. "Sometimes the Philadelphia boys like to see how far they can reach. Your baby brother met up with the son of one of 'em in Atlantic City a while back. Borrowed from me to cover the loan and then went and borrowed from them again."

"And you graciously extended his credit."

Barone stopped pacing and smiled. "No. I didn't. Your brother was dead the minute he borrowed the second thou from those guys."

"You're telling me the guys from Philly whacked him?"

"It's what I'm telling you."

"I don't believe you."

"Doesn't matter. It's the truth." He stopped pacing and regarded Baker for a minute. "But I'll tell you this: working with me is the only way to make certain you don't end up like your brother."

"Is that right?"

Barone smiled. "They'll come for you, Baker. Stewie couldn't keep his mouth shut about his rich detective brother up in Crane Haven, New York." He looked around the office, shaking his head. "He may have exaggerated about the rich part, but the Philly boys won't care. They'll take what Stewie owed them out of your flesh." He let that sink in for a minute. "Unless, of course…"

"What? I go to work as a hit man for you? I beat up little old ladies and take their purses? I smuggle diamonds up my ass?"

Barone laughed loud and long. Then he sat down and crushed out his cigarette. He pulled two thick cigars from his pocket and handed one to Baker before lighting his own. "You amuse me, Detective." He puffed on the cigar until a cloud of yellow smoke surrounded him. Baker wondered how the man could stand all the different types of tobacco without turning green. "I want you to find my sister," he said.

Baker gave a bark of laughter.

Barone nodded as he leaned back in his chair. "You put two of my best men in the hospital, Detective. I don't take kindly to that. Now, ordinarily I'd have them tail Christina. However, since they are now out of commission for a time, I am prepared to hire you and to provide you with protection from the Philadelphia Syndicate."

"I'm already on a case."

Barone waved his hand. "Surely there is someone who can help you with this task. Your secretary perhaps?"

"How do I know I can trust you?"

"This is business. A fair transaction. I don't fig on transactions."

Baker cocked an eyebrow. "I'll consider it," he said.

The office door creaked open. "Is everything all right in here, sir?" Edwards stood in the doorway with dry cleaning draped over his arm. "I heard voices." He froze when he saw Leadfoot.

Barone too was frozen for a moment. Eventually he found his legs and stood, playing with the cigar. "You," he breathed.

"My, my," Edwards said, amused. "Larry Barone." He took a step into the room and laid the dry cleaning over a chair. Then he removed his suit jacket and laid it on top. Rolling up his sleeves, he advanced toward Barone. "What are you doing here bothering my employer?"

Barone backed up, sitting hard on the desk when he could go no further. He held up his hands. "Now, look, Dagger, this is legitimate business. I'm here to hire a dick to help me with my sister, that's all."

Baker leaned back in his chair and regarded his secretary with amusement. "Dagger?" he asked.

Edwards shrugged and rolled his eyes before turning his attention back to Barone. "What's going on with Christina?" he asked, his hands relaxing only slightly.

"She's missing."

Edwards took a step back before coming forward and grabbing Barone by the lapels. "Did you order the hit on Stewie Baker?"

Barone laughed out loud and Baker watched, mesmerized, as Edwards' face softened; and then he too started to laugh.

"You think I'd be dumb enough to show up here after ordering a hit on the dick's brother?" He laughed again and pulled out another cigar for Edwards.

"Ah," Edwards said, passing the cigar under his nose and smiling with satisfaction.

Barone moved over to inspect the dry cleaning. "Nice," he said, inspecting a pair of pants. "Pockets O'Hurley?"

Edwards shrugged. "I'll never tell."

Baker wished he had a cup of coffee.

Edwards regarded Baker. "We will, of course, take the case," he said.

Baker shook his head. "I've agreed to nothing."

"But sir, you must...Christina is like a sister to me."

"How do I know this guy didn't zotz Stewie?" Baker asked.

Edwards' mouth was grim. "Because he says he didn't."

"And gangsters never lie," Baker said.

"Look here," Barone said. "I said I didn't. That means I didn't. I never lie about business. If I off'd your brother, I'd own it. I own any job I do."

Baker scoffed...but believed him.

"Look," Barone said, pulling a picture from his wallet. "She's been seeing one of the guys from the docks. Paul something-or-other. I didn't pay much attention because I figured she's young, she's wild, she's trying to show me a thing or two." He passed the picture of a pretty young blonde to Baker before continuing. "I tried to introduce her to nice guys, you know? Honest businessmen." He shook his head. "But she says to me that they only go with her because they're scared of their businesses burning down if they don't make her happy. Can you believe that?"

Baker was silent.

"We'll find her," Edwards promised. "Where was she last seen?"

"How the hell should I know?" Barone said, standing and pacing again. "The guy had a place out at the lake. A cabin or something. I had Frankie follow her out there once to make sure the chump she was keeping time with was treating her good."

"Can Frankie take me out there again?" Edwards asked.

Barone glared at Baker. "He could if this mook hadn't shot up his knee. But he'll tell us how to get there."

"I still haven't said we'll take the case," Baker said.

Barone and Edwards stared at him for a long moment.

"Okay, fine," Baker said. "You pay three days in advance. And no funny business, like having me followed on icy roads."

Barone laughed. "You mean Phil Merrick."

"Who the hell is he?"

Barone shrugged. "Works on the docks. Small time knuckle bruiser. Good with his fists. Good with a gun."

"Why did he follow me? He almost got me killed."

Barone shrugged. "He was supposed to invite you for a meeting, but Phil gets a little carried away with the cloak-and-dagger stuff."

But Baker was thinking of the knot around Chet Ferrebee's neck. "Is this Phil character capable of murder?"

Barone shrugged. "Sure, he could kill a guy, but only if I told him to. He don't whack nobody without permission from me."

"You give him permission lately?"

Barone smiled. "Not lately."

"He good with knots?"

Barone scowled. "Hey, what is this?"

"You want our help with your sister, you'll answer the question."

"Yeah. He's a genius. Is that it?"

Baker nodded. "Yeah. Give Edwards the advance. He'll drive out to the lake and check things over."

Barone buttoned his coat. "I'll go with him."

Baker shook his head. "I suggest you stay out of our way. It'll make things easier."

"How will I know when you've found anything out?"

"Edwards can get in touch with you."

Barone scowled but agreed.

By three that afternoon the office rent had been paid, Edwards had twenty bucks and Baker had twenty-five plus a new coffeepot. Now he sat with his feet propped on the desk, smoking a well-deserved cigarette, and read from Chaucer.

At 3:15 Edwards opened the door. Before he could speak, Baker held up a hand. "Listen to this, Edwards, *to count her vices, every one, exceeds my wit...*" He shook his head. "Does that sound like my ex-wife or not?"

"It does, sir."

Baker closed his book and laid it aside. "Any luck with the lake?"

"Some. I'll fill you in later. Sheriff Ferrebee is here to see you."

Baker leapt to his feet. He smoothed his jacket, straightened his tie and slicked his hair.

"Shall I show him in?"

Baker nodded, remembering the way Judith had to help Marian up the stairs that morning and wondered if the widow's condition had worsened. If it had, he would be blamed. Of that, he was certain.

Ferrebee's appearance had not improved since morning. If anything, the giant man looked smaller and slightly feeble. Baker rose and shook his hand. "Would you like a cup of coffee, Sheriff?"

"No thanks, son." Ferrebee waved him away and took a chair. "Let's get to the point." His voice was low, his eyes hard. "I want to know what you're up to." He rubbed his red hands together, sloughing dead skin onto his dark trousers.

Baker poured himself a cup of coffee and stalled for time. Ferrebee had always been hard to read. His slow movements and gentle face tended to lull people into thinking he was ignorant or indifferent to the goings on in Crane Haven. But Baker knew from experience that Ferrebee could be cold, calculating and violent when needed. Baker weighed the pros and cons of revealing details about his case to the large man sitting in his office. In the end he decided to be cautious. "I have a client," he said, taking a drink of coffee.

The sheriff gave a sad laugh, furiously working his dry hands together. "I gathered that, son. I want to know about these letters you're searching for."

Baker sat down and leaned back in his chair. "I'm not at liberty to discuss that."

Ferrebee laughed again, his voice raspy from too many years of cigars. Then his face grew serious, and he passed a cracked hand over his tired eyes. "If you were to ask people what they think of me, Detective, over half of them would say I'm a pushover." He leaned forward, resting his arms on his knees, and stared at the floor. "Maybe I am."

Baker listened, the coffee cup resting against his lower lip.

"Chet planned to run for sheriff next year, once he and Marian got settled. He'd be a natural choice for the office, and the town would have elected him in a heartbeat." His eyes misted and he rubbed angrily at them. "Effie and I were going to retire out to the lake." He looked at Baker, his eyes dark and sad. "I've got a cabin out there. It's where I taught him to fish."

Baker twisted uncomfortably in his chair. "Look, Sheriff..."

"It's bad enough my boy's been murdered and there are no suspects in custody." His eyes bore into Baker. "But now you come along with your story about letters, bothering his widow, who can't remember a thing about that night."

"Sheriff, I didn't mean..."

Ferrebee held up a hand and sighed. "Oh, I know, son. I know. We've all got our jobs to do." He shook his head. "I've always tried to respect what it is you do, Detective. I haven't approved of it, but I've always tried to respect that you perform a service of sorts to our community. But now you're troubling my family...at a very difficult time."

Baker nodded. "Yes, sir."

"How much would it take to make you stop this?"

Baker's heart hammered against his ribs, and he was sure his voice pulsed with the force of it when he spoke. "What?"

"If I offered you five hundred bucks, would you leave it alone?"

Baker fumbled for his cigarette case, wondering about the case and this man sitting across from him. He lit his cigarette and stared at the sheriff through the smoke. "That's a lot of money."

Ferrebee shrugged. "I've got a little set aside."

Baker closed his eyes, felt his gut clench and said, "I can't, Sheriff. I've made a commitment. I have a client and I intend to fulfill my obligation."

"Have you stopped to think the letters could be linked to the killer?"

Baker nodded. "Of course." He set the cigarette in the ashtray and concentrated on the thin trail of smoke that curled toward the ceiling. "If I nose out the letters and they cast a glow on your son's murder, I'll call."

The sheriff leaned back, letting a sigh escape his huge body. "I guess I can't fault you for having integrity, son. But I would ask a favor of you."

"Okay."

"Try to keep this thing quiet. I don't know what these letters are. But I don't want them to hurt Marian. And I'd like to keep my son's name in good standing."

"I'll do my best, but Marian may be wise to where the letters are. I may need to talk to her again."

"What if I help you?"

"Excuse me?"

"I can get you into Marian's house. Her brother and Judith are staying there for the time being. They'll be here until things settle down...." His voice broke. He took a moment, then cleared his throat. "There's the funeral to be arranged. And Marian is having a hard time. They thought they'd stay on awhile. Chet was going to live in the house with Marian. His things are there. Maybe the letters are with them."

"You'd let me look?"

Ferrebee shrugged. "Judith won't like it; but when I help her see that the sooner we get this over with, the sooner we can let Chet rest and help get Marian well, I think she'll cooperate."

"What about Jeffrey?"

The sheriff laughed, and this time it was sincere, a real belly-shaker. "He's a drunk. Has been since high school, only he was better at hiding it back then. As long as he's got a bottle, he doesn't care what goes on around him."

The sheriff stood and shook Baker's hand. He turned back and smiled as he opened the door, allowing Edwards, with a glass to his ear, to fall inwards.

Edwards hurriedly stood, reclaiming his dignity. "Will there be anything else, sir?" he asked.

Baker's face was grim. "No, thank you, Edwards. You may show the sheriff out."

Ferrebee scowled. "Six o'clock, Baker," he said. "I'll pick you up out front. I don't think that car of yours could make it."

Baker's face reddened, but he managed a feeble wave.

Edwards showed Ferrebee to the door and was thoughtful when

he returned to Baker's office. He rested his hands on the back of a chair and chewed on his lower lip. "Why do you suppose the sheriff is so cooperative?"

Baker took a sip of his coffee and rubbed his chin. "Well, let's rehash this. He offers me a bribe. He knows I won't bite, but he offers it anyway. And when I say 'no thanks,' he gets busy with being helpful."

"Yes, but why?" Edwards wondered.

Baker set his coffee cup down and lit another cigarette. "To keep his fingers in the dirt is my best guess. And to keep me in his sights."

"Well," Edwards nodded. "There is that, I suppose."

Baker leaned forward. "Look. The fact that Chet Ferrebee might not be the golden boy everyone thought he was has poked a big hole in the sheriff's office. Ferrebee Senior and his deputies are itching to patch it up. And they don't want to do it alongside the city cops."

Edwards nodded but said nothing.

"Ferrebee will play nice with Lewis to keep it all smooth, but my guess is he thinks I'll get lucky with the letters."

"And find the killer that way?"

Baker shrugged. "Who knows? But I'll take Ferrebee's help if I can get it, and it will piss Lewis off." He rubbed his hands together. "This day keeps getting better and better."

Chapter 7

At 5:30 that afternoon, Baker and Edwards had yet to agree on a suitable necktie.

Edwards had a soft spot for paisleys.

"Paisleys are for church and funerals, Edwards. This is a search for missing letters. I want the blue and gold striped."

Edwards sniffed and turned away. "Then you shall have to tie it yourself. I will not be held responsible for your appearance if you choose to ignore my advice."

The sharp ring of the telephone cut off Baker's retort. Edwards shoved the three paisley ties he held into Baker's hands and picked up the receiver. "The Baker Agency," he said. "How may I be of service?"

Baker carefully laid the paisley ties over the back of a chair and entered the closet to search for the one he wanted. "Ah hah," he said, spying it.

"Yes, Miss Kramer," Edwards said as Baker emerged from the closet, waving the tie above his head. "Detective Baker is here now, and I know he would be happy to speak with you." He put his hand over the mouthpiece. "Diana Kramer for you, Detective."

Baker made a half-hearted attempt to knot his tie before grabbing the phone. "Miss Kramer," he said. "We've been wondering about you. Where have you been?"

Edwards, grumbling under his breath, fussed with the crooked tie. "You never do this right," he muttered.

"Beat it," Baker hissed.

"I'm sorry," Miss Kramer said, "I thought Mr. Edwards said you'd take my call."

"What? Oh, yes, he did. I'm sorry, Miss Kramer." He slapped Edwards' hands away. "I was talking to someone else."

"In your office?"

"No. Never mind. It's fine now."

Edwards left, his face sullen.

Baker returned his attention to Miss Kramer. "Where have you been?" he asked.

Diana paused and Baker closed his eyes and listened to her

breathing, wondering if she were a murderess. "I'm sorry to have been out of touch. But with all the publicity following Chet's death, I didn't feel I could risk a phone call."

"Yes. Chet's death." Baker sat down, propped his feet on the desk and fingered his tie. "You didn't have anything to do with that, did you?"

The sound of her breathing altered, grew ragged. And when she spoke, her voice was thick with tears. "I swear to you I didn't, Detective. I only want the letters. I stayed away as long as I have for my own protection and out of courtesy for his family."

"Courtesy? Or fear?"

Diana was silent for a moment. "Both."

"What are you afraid of?"

"His wife."

"She's locked up."

Diana laughed. "Nevertheless, I don't think she approved of me."

Baker pulled out the paper he'd swiped from the sanitarium's guest book and studied the scratched-out signature. He held it under his desk lamp and scrutinized the name. If he held it just right, he could make out what appeared to be a letter "D" but nothing else. "Did Marian know about you?"

Diana sighed. "In a manner of speaking, yes."

Baker squinted at the name on the paper and decided to gamble. "So, what did she say when you visited her at the sanitarium?"

There was silence on Diana's end. Only the hum of the live line let Baker know she hadn't hung up. At last she said, "You've been to see her, then?"

"Come on, Doll. You knew I'd go. It was a logical place to start looking for the letters. I've got the guest register with your name on it."

"I scratched it out."

"I'm a detective."

She laughed. It was bitter.

Baker said, "Why are you afraid of Marian Ferrebee?"

"Marian Drake."

"They got married, Angel. Check the records."

"Chet didn't love her. He loved me." But her voice was quiet now, as if she weren't quite sure if this were true.

Baker let that sink in. He leaned back in his chair and lit a cigarette.

When Diana spoke again, her voice was soft. "Did she say anything?"

"About what?"

"About me."

Baker hesitated. "No," he said slowly, wishing like hell Diana Kramer was sitting in front of him so he could read her expression. "She didn't mention you."

"Did you mention me?"

"No. Although now I wish I had. Maybe she would have opened that pretty mouth and started to sing."

"No luck with the letters, then?"

"None." He closed his eyes and took a drag on his cigarette. "But I'm still on it. I've got an appointment tonight with a potential lead." He pulled a pad of paper close. "How's about I give you a ring when I'm done? I can give you the skinny. Where are you staying?"

She hesitated. "I'll call you. Tomorrow."

After she hung up, Baker sat for a few moments, staring at the phone. Something felt off. Why all the mystery with this dame? Why did she hire him and then confront the widow herself? And why did she refuse to give him so much as a phone number? "Edwards," he called.

"Yes?" Edwards said, poking his head inside.

"Do you still see that telephone operator? What was her name? Rosella? Roseanne?"

"Rosemary Marsh, sir."

Baker snapped his fingers. "Rosemary. That's it. Do you still see her?"

Edwards delicately cleared his throat. "Not since her father caught us in a compromising position on her mother's sofa, sir. I have not been welcome there for some time."

"Edwards. I'm shocked."

Edwards had the grace to blush. "I assure you, sir, it was not my doing. Miss Marsh is a very strong and…robust young lady. And she seemed to enjoy my accent a great deal."

Baker frowned. "Hmm. Well, I need you to start seeing her again."

"Sir?"

"I need to know where Diana Kramer is holed up, and I don't want to go through the cops. Miss Marsh can trace the call better than they can anyway."

"Ah. Very good, sir," Edwards said, rubbing his hands together. "All in the line of duty. You can count on me."

Baker stood up. "Good. Now, if you'll excuse me, the sheriff will be here any minute; and I don't want to keep him waiting." He strode to the door, setting his hat atop his head.

"Sir," Edwards called him back. "We didn't discuss the Barone case. I need to tell you what I discovered at the lake."

"Later, Edwards. I don't want to keep the sheriff waiting."

Chapter 8

The widow's house was tucked a hundred feet from the road at the end of a muddy lane. Even in the darkness the white paint appeared dirty against the fresh snow that tried to bury it.

"This is it," Ferrebee said, in no hurry to leave the car. He switched off the ignition and rested his enormous hands on the wheel. "This is where Marian lives." He looked in the direction of the house, but Baker sensed his eyes were focused on something far away.

Baker played with the burning cigarette held between his fingers. "Marian lived here alone?"

"This is the Drake family palace," Ferrebee said with a half-smile. The house wasn't anything resembling a palace. It was a tiny cape cod with a sagging front porch and two tiny dormers jutting out from the second floor. "Marian and Jeffrey were raised here, but Jeffrey moved to the city after he got married. He and Judith come and visit sometimes. But usually Marian drives to the city to see them." He focused on the house, and this time Baker knew he saw it for what it was…a dump. "Chet planned to fix it up," the sheriff said. "He had big plans for this place. You can't see it now, but it has a nice backyard."

Baker nodded, but he thought the house was beyond help. It needed to be bulldozed. He thought about Jeffrey moving to the city and leaving his sister here alone. What did Marian do for money? He let his gaze move through the snow to the dim light spilling from the front rooms. "Does Jeffrey get along with his sister?"

The sheriff shrugged and twisted in his seat to meet Baker's gaze. "Can't really say. He's always been quiet. I think he likes that bottle more than people, just like his daddy."

They sat staring at the house, watching snow fall from the sky in fat, wet flakes. It collected on the roof of the house and the top of the sheriff's car, which was filling with cigarette smoke. Baker cracked a window to watch it escape into the night air.

When the silence stretched and Ferrebee still made no move to get out of the car, Baker said, "What about their parents?"

Ferrebee was far away again, his face lined with grief and dark shadows. His mental absence made Baker feel lonely. At length Ferrebee shook off his thoughts, and his face relaxed. A little. "Old Pete ran off early in the depression. Gave some cock-and-bull story about getting out of the fishing industry and finding full-time work in the Midwest. He left and never came back. Jeff never forgave him for that. Their mother, Norma, toughed it out with them. Died of cancer six years ago next January."

Baker looked at the house, thinking of Marian in the middle of the woods by herself; and disgust for her brother bubbled to the surface again. A dame ought to have protection. Someone to watch out for her.

As if reading Baker's thoughts, Ferrebee said, "It's safe enough out here, son. This is a good town, full of good people. And Marian liked her privacy."

Baker raised an eyebrow at that, and Ferrebee chuckled. "She wasn't one for letting others know her business."

"Chet was close to her," Baker said before he could stop himself. "So I guess he knew her business."

Ferrebee's face darkened. "There's Judith at the window," he said, finally climbing from the car. "We'd better get in there. I'm sure she'll make us eat some supper."

Reluctantly Baker stepped into the snow. A north wind whipped through the lane. Its appearance was sudden and cruel, as if the devil himself threw a switch the second Baker's feet touched the earth.

Baker usually loved the smell of a winter's night. The aroma of wood smoke mated with the scent of snow, weaving a nostalgic cloak that draped him in the secure memories of his childhood in Iowa. But there was no nostalgia in this cold place. There was the sad knocking of dead tree limbs in the darkness. There was the stench of molding hay and dead livestock and a hundred other rotten smells.

"It's just sulfur deposits," Ferrebee said, noticing the stricken look on the detective's face.

No, Baker thought, *it's Hell.*

Judith stood just inside the front door with a halo of yellow light dancing around her golden hair. She didn't belong here among the stench and the filth.

No one did.

"Come in, Sheriff, you'll freeze out there."

Baker smiled and removed his hat as he stepped inside, ignoring the fact that she ignored him.

"I've got dinner just about ready," she said. "Jeffrey is having a cocktail in the living room. Why don't you join him?"

Baker hadn't realized they would be having dinner, and he thought about apologizing for not bringing a bottle of wine; but Judith wouldn't look in his direction, so he kept quiet and followed Ferrebee through a dark and empty parlor into the next room. There Jeffrey stood at the radio, fiddling drunkenly with the knobs. A weak fire burned in the ancient fireplace, casting a sickly yellow glow in the dimness. The furniture was threadbare and obviously decades old. The surfaces of the tables and chairs were clean but gave off an underlying odor of dust and mold that drifted throughout the house. Baker coughed delicately as he let his eyes wander around the room. There were no photos on the shelves, no pictures on the walls, nothing to indicate that a family had once occupied this space. The house had the air of one abandoned, left empty for years. Baker's neck tingled, and he absently rubbed a hand over the tiny hairs that stood on end. Unconsciously he stepped closer to the fire.

Jeffrey looked up with glazed eyes and smiled upon discovering he had company. "Glad you could join us, Sheriff Fairberry," he slurred. Baker wondered if he deliberately mispronounced the sheriff's name, or if he were just drunk. There was an underlying malevolence in the look he cast in Ferrebee's direction. Jeffrey let his eyes slide to Baker. "I see you've brought a friend." His lips pursed in an expression of acute distaste.

"This is Detective Baker," the sheriff said. "You met him this morning."

Jeffrey shrugged, returning his attention to the radio in the corner. "I can't get this blasted contraption to work," he said. "Nothing but ads for Chesterfield cigarettes." He threw his hands into the air and walked away. "Pity too. *The Bickersons* starts in half an hour."

"Want me to have a look at it?" Ferrebee asked.

Jeffrey shook his head. "Forget it," he said, holding up his glass. "Help yourselves, men. The bar is over there." He gestured to a wooden sideboard stocked with three bottles of cheap wine, a half-empty bottle of brandy and several bottles of gin, one of which was nearly gone.

84

The sheriff poured himself a small brandy, then held the bottle up to Baker, who shook his head.

"So, Detective," Jeffrey said. "To what do we owe the honor? Here to search my sister's things, no doubt. I'm afraid the police were already here." He rose and crossed to where Baker stood, staring him in the face. He stood inches shorter than the detective, and his frame was severely thin and angular. He smiled with his mouth wide open, allowing the stench of booze and the underlying odor of rotting teeth and gut drift into the room.

Baker took a step back and coughed.

Ferrebee cleared his throat. "Actually," he said, "we're here to have a look around. If it's all right with you, of course."

Jeffrey tossed his drink back and dropped into a chair, waving his hand indifferently. "Of course, the mysterious letters. I wasn't paying much attention when you dropped by this morning, Detective." He laughed bitterly. "But Judith gave me an earful on the way home, so I'm well-informed now." He rested his head against the back of the chair and closed his eyes. "Well-informed indeed. Feel free to look anywhere you like."

Ferrebee smiled but it didn't reach his eyes. He rubbed his giant, red hands together; and flakes of skin fell onto the faded rug. "I knew you'd agree," he said. And the way he said it made Baker's neck tingle.

After a few moments, Jeffrey stood and staggered to the bar to pour himself another gin.

"Marian could use a sober brother at a time like this," Baker said, thinking of the widow alone in this dismal house.

Jeffrey laughed out loud and then turned to look at him. "Really?" he said, wiping the back of his hand across his nose. "What would you know about it?"

Baker shrugged. "I know there's something eating you."

Ferrebee cleared his throat. "Pour the dick a drink, Jeff. He's wound a little tight this evening. Guess we all are."

Jeffrey stared at Baker with fire in his eyes. "Help yourself," he said, returning to his chair.

Baker filled a glass with gin and added a splash of soda. It wasn't scotch but it was 80 proof, and that was good enough. He tossed it back and fixed another before glancing at Ferrebee, who sat staring at his shoes, the brandy in his hand forgotten, his thoughts a million miles away.

Jeffrey leaned his head against the back of his chair and closed his eyes. Baker swallowed the lump of lonely in his throat and wondered about the secrets between these two men. He could smell it like a bad egg and knowing he'd never get them to spill it willingly gnawed at his gut.

He was the enemy, an outsider hired by a woman who would do nothing but hurt this family. He drank the gin and grimaced. Always, always his job was like lifting a rock, only to recoil in horror at what crawled out from beneath. So why did he do it, he wondered. The money wasn't great. Wives didn't fall on their knees in gratitude when he handed over black-and-whites of their secretary-pawing husbands. Too often they cried and beat on his chest demanding, "Why, why, why?"

He swallowed again and Ginger was there, in his mind, asking him why he tried so hard.

"Because truth is all there is," he told her once. "And the world doesn't feel right if we don't all know the truth."

"Ugh, please," she said. "You sound like a minister. It's not like these men and women say they're going bowling, and then they don't. They don't say anything. They just go and make love with someone who happens to be someone other than their spouse. If you don't say anything, then it's not a lie."

Baker looked at her, and at that moment he loved her more than anything. "But they break vows. And that is a lie, Ginge."

She smiled then. "I'd never lie to you."

Even then, he didn't believe her; but he said, "I know," making him a liar too.

So here in Marian Drake-Ferrebee's living room, he poured another drink and accepted the bitter silence offered by Jeffrey and the sheriff. He would do this job. At least no one could call him a quitter.

After a time, Judith called them to dinner. Jeffrey stood on trembling legs and led them down a long hallway to a small dining room lit by a fire in a freshly-cleaned fireplace. Baker suspected the cleanliness was a result of Judith's handiwork.

"We're informal here, men," she said. "Sit anywhere." Judith took a seat at the head of the table and passed steaming dishes filled with roast beef and potatoes and corn.

"This smells heavenly," the sheriff said.

Judith smiled graciously, taking care to avoid looking in Baker's direction. He sat next to her, angry at how aware of her nearness he was. He studied the delicate bend of her elbow, the graceful way her hand held her knife. He noticed the way her throat moved when she swallowed.

The party of four ate in silence for a time. At last Baker cleared his throat and said, "This is quite good."

Judith met his eyes and nodded. She hadn't smiled, but she hadn't looked away. And that was something anyway.

Jeffrey ate very little, apparently preferring his drink to solid food. The sheriff ate in silence, looking only at his plate. When Judith excused herself to start dishes, Baker was relieved. He pushed his chair back and carried plates to the kitchen. Judith accepted his help silently, not looking at him, but not shying away when his arm accidentally bumped hers or when he reached around her to place the butter on its high shelf in the kitchen pantry.

He left her to wash and dry on her own, aware he'd lingered in her presence too long already. He found the sheriff in the living room staring out at the snow. Jeffrey lay on the sofa, passed out.

"It's piling up out there," Ferrebee said with a touch of sadness in his voice. "We'd better get to looking through those boxes."

Marian's bedroom was on the first floor just off the kitchen. They had to walk past Judith to get there, and she froze at the sink as they passed. Her back was to them, and the image of her face was reflected in the dark glass of the kitchen window. Baker met her stare, flinching at the open-mouthed distortion of her expression in the imperfect glass. Did she really hate him as much as her reflection showed, or was it just a trick of the light?

He looked away and moved into the bedroom behind Ferrebee. The furniture in the room consisted of a sagging double bed covered by a faded chenille bedspread and a simple wooden chest of drawers with an oval mirror hanging above it. A small bedside table held a faded of photo of Marian, Jeffrey and an impossibly thin woman Baker assumed to be their mother, Norma Drake. There were no other photographs in the room. No teenage trophies or ribbons adorned the walls. No books lined the shelves. There were no women's magazines here. Just like the living room, this bedroom held no personal effects.

Baker wandered to the closet and opened the door. The usual dresses and sweaters hung here. Marian's wardrobe was drab, consisting of faded dresses nearly out of fashion, sensible shoes and one navy blue dress of a more modern style Baker assumed was for church. A matching hat rested in a box on the shelf above, and Baker recognized it as one from Deirdre's shop. Other than the single hatbox, there were no other boxes or cartons stored in the closet. Baker tapped along the edges of the walls, looking for a secret compartment or door. The walls were solid.

As he turned to leave, a photograph, obviously torn from a high school yearbook, caught his eye. It had been taped to the inside of the closet door and a dozen hatpins had been stuck through the six faces in the photo, making it impossible to recognize anyone. As he peered closer, he could make out the jeans and sneakers below the punctured faces and recognized them as belonging to high school boys. The words in the caption were clear enough to read, but Baker didn't take time to examine it more closely. He checked over his shoulder to make certain Ferrebee wasn't watching. With as much care as possible, he removed the pins from the photo, dropped them on the floor and shoved the picture in his pocket.

"Anything in the closet?" Ferrebee asked as Baker stepped out and shut the door.

"Nothing. Just clothes." The lie, even one so small, made Baker sweat. He was unable to meet Ferrebee's eyes.

"Must have put the boxes upstairs."

They moved through the kitchen again, through the living room and up the narrow staircase that smelled of dust. The second floor consisted of a full bath and two bedrooms. The larger of the two bedrooms contained a set of twin beds with a bedside table tucked between them. Two suitcases rested neatly against the far wall. The closet door stood open, and Baker spied the red dress Judith had worn to the wedding reception hanging beside the rest of her dresses and skirts. *This was where she slept*, he thought and wondered for a moment which bed she used, which pillow she rested her head on at night.

"Here they are," the sheriff called from the next bedroom.

The second upstairs bedroom was obviously the one Marian and Chet had planned to use. Several football and track trophies, obviously Chet's, sat atop a mirrored bureau. Photos of the couple had been placed atop a second chest of drawers beside the closet. This bed was in no better shape than any of the others in the house, but it was good enough for newlyweds, Baker supposed.

A scattering of boxes had been carelessly piled at the foot of the bed; and Ferrebee stood in the middle of the mess, looking lost. "That's everything he brought over," he said. "I helped him unload the car myself." He rubbed a thick hand over his face and sat on the side of the bed looking weary. "I don't think you'll find any letters here, son."

Baker shrugged. "Maybe I'll get lucky." He knelt and began sifting through the boxes.

The first box was filled with dirty laundry, and Ferrebee smiled when he saw it. "That boy wore every lick of clothing he had before he'd finally bring it to Effie to wash," he said. "Guess he was counting on Marian taking over for him."

The second box held more high school trophies, some family photos and three yearbooks. Baker considered the yearbooks and wondered if the photo in his pocket had been ripped from one of them as he half-heartedly looked through the remaining boxes for Diana's letters. When his search uncovered nothing further, he sat back on his heels and sighed. Picking up the yearbooks, he sat on the foot of the bed next to Ferrebee and began turning pages, quietly searching for a photo that matched the one he took from Marian's closet or evidence that the photo came from one of these.

"I loved my son, Detective."

Baker stopped looking at black-and-white photos of happy teenagers and regarded the sheriff.

Ferrebee's eyes filled. "I know that isn't the thing to say out loud. Effie scolds me for the way I am." He wiped his eyes. "But I did love my son, Detective. And I want to find out who killed him. But I'll do whatever it takes to protect my family and my family's name."

Baker only nodded. Any reassurance that his family wouldn't get hurt in this would have tasted a lie. Baker had lied once tonight.

Besides, the rock had already been lifted. There was nothing to do now but see what crawled out from under it.

He turned a page in the yearbook he held in his lap. There it was. It had to be. The shoes, the position of the legs. It matched the photo he'd taken from Marian's closet. The photo was one of six boys, including Chet and Jeffrey, with their arms casually slung over one another's shoulders. Baker recognized them as the group making all the noise at the wedding reception. They wore blue jeans, sneakers and toothy teenaged grins. Why would Marian shove hatpins through a photo with Chet in it? Baker showed the yearbook to the sheriff. "He looks happy here."

Ferrebee nodded. "Chet was a good boy. He would have made a great sheriff."

"I recognize all these men. They live in town." Baker tapped a face in the photo. "Isn't this man a deputy?"

"Wally Sims," the sheriff said. "He delivered the news about Chet to Effie and Judith after I left the reception so suddenly."

Baker snapped the yearbook closed, his heart pounding. "I think I'll hang onto this for a while. I'm ready to go now."

Chapter 9

Edwards was bleary-eyed and unshaven, and his cheek sported an ugly black bruise.

Baker cocked an eyebrow. "Morning, Edwards. Rough night?"

Edwards tried to scowl; but the bitter expression turned wistful as he said, "Miss Rosemary is every bit as robust as I remembered, sir."

"Mm-hmm. She do that to your mug?"

"It was her father."

"Really. And you let him?"

Edwards cleared his throat. "Yes, well, I didn't want to damage our case by humiliating him. And any effort to defend myself would have resulted in his injury."

Baker nodded. "I see. And I suppose you're right. How do things stand with Rosemary?"

Edwards allowed himself a cautious smile. "She feels I was treated dreadfully, which has worked to our advantage. Happily she finds me irresistible."

"Fine." Baker returned his attention to the yearbook photo he'd been studying since last night.

"Is that something to help with the case, sir?" Edwards asked.

"I hope so." Baker studied the intact yearbook photo of Chet and his five friends, comparing it to the one Marian hid in her closet. The caption read, "Chet Ferrebee, David Holden, Wally and Bertie Sims, Jeremy Watts and Artie Pfeiffer prepare for the Christmas dance. Jeffrey Drake decides to lend a hand."

The youths posed comically in front of a half-decorated Christmas tree in the middle of a school gymnasium. Five of the boys posed with ornaments in their hands and toothy grins on their faces. Jeffrey Drake stood off to the side, one hand in his back pocket, the other grasping Chet Ferrebee's elbow. Baker wondered what happened the instant after the snapshot was taken. What did they say to each other? Where did they all go when they were done decorating the tree? But the photo was just that, a snapshot in time. He suspected if any of the boys remembered that particular dance, the images had faded with time. He pulled the yearbook closer and examined the smiling faces.

David Holden was thin in the way teenage boys are thin. He had a sunken chest and an enormous Adam's apple. His long angular teeth took up half of his face. Next to Holden was Jeremy Watts, wearing a Santa hat and looking anything but merry. The sheriff had told Baker that Watts played football in high school. "He was good," Ferrebee had said. "His father saw to that." Jeremy's frame dwarfed the Christmas tree; but rather than hold himself in arrogance with regard to his size, he hunched forward in awkward self-consciousness. Baker pursed his lips, remembering his own awkward teenage years and said, "God, I hated high school."

Artie Pfeiffer stood next to Jeremy. His nose, large enough to cast a shadow, begged for ridicule. "Poor guy," Baker muttered. Pfeiffer's dark hair was clipped close, and the thick glasses he wore did nothing to hide his severe case of acne.

Wally and Bertie Sims stood off to the side. It was obvious they were brothers and equally obvious that neither was a leader of the small band of boys. They stood close together, arms slung lazily over each other's shoulders. Baker studied the picture carefully. Other than an inch in height, the boys were nearly identical. Baker already knew Wally was a deputy. He hadn't seen him at the reception or the murder scene; but he knew from Ferrebee, as well as from what he overheard from Judith, that Sims was the one who delivered the news of Chet's death to Effie and Judith.

He turned his gaze to Chet Ferrebee and Jeffrey Drake, frozen in that awkward pose that made it appear as if Jeffrey was trying to tell Chet something—or give him something from his back pocket. "Jeffrey Drake lends a hand."

"Edwards," Baker said, leaning back in his chair, "doesn't David Holden run The Diner?"

"I believe so, sir. Excellent food."

Baker grabbed his hat and coat and tucked the yearbook under his arm as he strode to the door. "Guess I could treat myself to breakfast for a change."

He stepped out into the blustery November wind, easily swallowing the four blocks to the diner with his long strides.

The Diner, which was what Holden's father named it three decades earlier, was crowded; and Baker elbowed his way to the counter for a seat. The waitress was busy refilling cups with hot coffee but nodded, smiled and made her way over when Baker signaled.

The writing embroidered on the pocket hugging her enormous breast said her name was Betty. She set a mug in front of him and filled it to the top. As she moved away, Baker touched her arm. She looked back, eyebrows raised and smiled. "Are you getting fresh with me?" she asked.

She was twice his age, but Baker smiled anyway and shrugged. "Any chance of talking to David Holden this morning?"

She looked at Baker's hand resting on her forearm, then back to him. "Sure," she said. "But we're in the middle of the breakfast rush right now." She checked the coffeepot-shaped clock on the wall behind her. "It'll be another half-hour or so."

Baker nodded. "I'll have toast and eggs when you get a minute," he said. When Betty moved on, he looked around the diner. He'd lived in Crane Haven for almost two years. When he and Ginger first moved here, they'd gone out to meet people and make neighborly visits. After she left, Baker had no desire to meet new people or seek the company of others. He'd failed in the worst way a man can fail. He'd lost his woman to another man. What few acquaintances he had made dissolved over time until to people he'd once considered friends, he was nothing more than a familiar face on the street.

Even here in this crowded diner, he was just another guy eating his breakfast. Betty set a plate of eggs in front of him, and he smiled his thanks. But he couldn't get his mind off Ginger. What kind of detective misses the signs that his own wife is cheating? What kind of man lay with a woman night after night without realizing she'd been sleeping with someone else? He looked around, watching couples sip their coffee and read the morning paper. What kind of secrets did they keep from one another? Could those secrets destroy a marriage? Chet Ferrebee was cheating on Marian Drake before they'd even walked down the aisle. What a chump.

Baker finished his eggs and swiveled on the stool, resting his elbows on the counter behind him and letting his coat fall open in the front. On the street outside new cars drove by. *Everyone had a new car*, he thought. All he could do right now was hope the Chevy made it another year.

The bells over the door jingled as Sheriff Ferrebee and Detective Lewis walked in. They nodded at Betty and took a booth near the front. Baker's jaw tightened. He lit a cigarette, picked up his coffee cup and meandered to their table.

"Morning, gentlemen," he said.

"Mr. Baker," Lewis mumbled, studying the menu.

Ferrebee cleared his throat. "We're discussing Chet's case," he said, rubbing his hands together. He looked like he hadn't slept since it happened.

Baker nodded and declined the seat the sheriff offered. "Any luck with the investigation?" he asked.

A muscle in Lewis' jaw clenched, and Baker knew there had been no progress. Lewis glared at him and asked, "You ever solve a murder?"

Baker set his cup on the table and took a deep drag on his cigarette. "Not usually my thing."

Lewis gave a bitter smile. "No, I suppose not. You're more the divorce and infidelity type."

"I suppose."

"Finding lost things."

"On occasion."

"Who are you working for now?"

"I'm not at liberty to say."

Lewis smiled again. Betty showed up and took the breakfast orders. As she left, Sheriff Ferrebee twisted uncomfortably in his seat. Baker sighed and clapped Lewis on the back. "Well," he said, picking up his mug, "if you need any help solving this murder, you know where to find me."

He made his way back to the counter again and picked up a discarded newspaper while he waited for David Holden and wished like hell he could hear what Lewis and Ferrebee were jawing about.

At 9:30 the crowd in the diner thinned out. Baker caught the waitress' eye. "More coffee?" she asked, already tipping the pot over his mug.

"Please. The eggs were perfect."

"Family recipe of David's. You still hungry?"

Before Baker could answer, she said, "I'll bring you some more toast, on the house." She disappeared into the kitchen and returned with four slices of toast and a glass of milk. "Eat up," she said. "We just toss it out after the rush anyway." She looked at him for a moment. "And you have a nice face." She patted his arm and winked. "David will be right out."

Baker couldn't help but smile...and think of his mother with an ache in his chest. Stewie's ashes had been shipped. Money for the funeral had been wired, thanks to Edwards. There was nothing more Baker needed to do for his brother. Except stay alive, but that was more for himself and, he supposed, his mother. She wouldn't take kindly to another mob-related death in the family.

Across the room Lewis and Sheriff Ferrebee ate their breakfast. As Betty passed again, Baker touched her sleeve and nodded toward the pair. "They come in here every day?"

She shrugged. "Only the last two, since the deputy was killed." She clucked her tongue. "Poor Sheriff Ferrebee. Such a sad thing to happen."

Baker nodded.

"I'll take it from here, Betty." David Holden stood at the counter, mopping his perspiring face with a damp dishtowel. Baker studied him, mentally comparing the man standing before him now with the man from the photo. Holden had filled out since high school. He remained thin, but it was no longer the skinniness of youth. Now he possessed the leanness that comes from hard work, hard booze and an endless supply of cigarettes.

Holden dropped the dishtowel on the counter, poured a cup of coffee and lit up. "Christ, I hate mornings," he said, walking around the counter to perch on the vacant stool next to Baker. "They're the worst. Lost my second cook a week ago."

"Mmm. That's rough," Baker said, sipping his coffee.

Holden slid his eyes and regarded Baker with curiosity. "You're the detective, right?"

Baker nodded.

"Betty says you want to talk to me." Holden was the type of smoker who held the cloud in his lungs for as long as he could, releasing it very reluctantly, so that when he spoke, it was slow and pinched. His sentences ended in a great sigh of smoke billowing from his mouth and nose. When he took a breath for the next sentence, the cigarette was there, filling his lungs, slowing his speech and getting him through the next few words.

Baker nodded. "I understand Chet Ferrebee was a friend of yours."

Holden breathed in and held it for as long as he could. "I still can't believe Chet's dead," he said, letting his sentence end with a whoosh before taking his next big drag. "We were friends since grammar school." He scratched his chin and examined the cigarette, no doubt wondering how it got so short after only two sentences. Then he shrugged, inhaled again and with hooded eyes said, "I don't know anything about any letters."

"Funny, I didn't ask about any letters."

"You will." *Whoosh*. He inhaled again.

"What if I say I don't believe you? About the letters."

Holden crushed out the dying ember of his cigarette and lit another. "Doesn't matter," he said. "I don't know a thing." He let his gaze wander to Ferrebee and Lewis on the other side of the room. "Sheriff Ferrebee's a good man," he said. "He doesn't deserve to have his son's reputation destroyed." *Whoosh*. "Not over some dumb letters, anyway."

Baker took a bite of toast and washed it down with milk. "That may be," he said after a minute. "But I've been hired to find the letters, and I deserve to get paid. The rent is due. You know how it is."

Holden smiled. "Not my problem."

Baker shrugged. "I saw a high school picture of you last night," he said.

"Really? How'd I look?"

"I couldn't tell. Marian Drake had shoved a hat pin through your face." Baker stood, well aware of the stillness that had settled over David Holden and pulled a business card from his pocket. "If you change your mind, give me a call."

Holden set the card on the counter and forgot to inhale from his cigarette before he spoke. "Who hired you?"

"I'm not at liberty to say."

Holden unfolded his thin frame from the stool and, ignoring Baker, disappeared into the kitchen.

"Well, well, well," Detective Lewis said, shoving Baker back onto a stool and taking the one David Holden vacated for himself.

Baker looked around. "What did you do with the sheriff, Lewis?"

Lewis lit a cigarette and signaled Betty to bring him some more coffee. "Unlike you, Mr. Baker, the sheriff has a job that pays. He likes to show up on time."

Baker clenched his teeth and watched as three more customers paid and left. "Aw, gee, Lewis. Look at that. You're scaring off customers." He drank some milk. "You're bad for business."

Betty approached with the coffeepot.

"Half a cup, Doll," Lewis said.

She rolled her eyes and made a face but filled the cup.

When she'd gone, Lewis said, "Ferrebee's shitting a brick over these letters you're looking for."

"That's funny. He's been very helpful with my investigation."

"He's concerned maybe the letters have something to do with how his son got dead."

"Not my problem."

Lewis gripped his cup until his knuckles were white. "No. Your concern is getting paid."

Baker took a bite of toast and shrugged.

"Let me spell this out for you, Mr. Baker," Lewis hissed.

"Detective Baker."

"Let me spell this out for you, *Mr.* Baker. I'm handling this murder investigation. If you uncover any evidence in this sideshow of yours, I expect you to share it with police. Do I make myself clear?"

Baker said, "Tell Ginger her ex-brother-in-law is dead. She should send a note to my mother." He shook his head. "Mom always liked Ginger. Go figure."

Lewis opened his mouth as if to say something cruel, but he closed it again and remained silent. After a moment, he stood, dropped a bill on the counter and left.

"I hate that guy. He giving you trouble?" Baker looked up to see David Holden standing at the counter again with a smoldering cigarette cradled between yellowed fingers.

"Nah," Baker said. "He's good for a laugh."

"He's like one of those punks we'd hang over the toilet in the locker room. You know what I mean? The kind that just don't know when to keep their big mouths shut."

Baker nodded. Holden was twitching about something, and Baker had an inkling it was Lewis that set him off. Holden stood at the counter, his eyes watching his fingers trace a design in spilled sugar. Baker almost felt sorry for the man. Whatever secret he was thinking of sharing was eating him up.

Baker ate his breakfast, watching Holden smoke and trace letters in the sugar. More customers paid and left. The breakfast rush was over. And the diner was empty at last. Baker finished his toast, lit a cigarette and sipped coffee while he waited for Holden to come to a decision about telling what he knew.

Finally Holden sighed. "Betty," he said, "I've got some shelves that need stocked in the back."

Betty was stacking clean coffee cups on a shelf under the counter. She turned and glared at him. "That's not my job."

Baker couldn't see the look Holden gave her, but it did the trick. She stalked off to the back muttering, "I've quit better jobs than this."

When she was gone, Holden took a drag on his unfiltered and leaned over the counter. "You didn't say the cops were after the letters too." *Whoosh.*

"As far as I know, they aren't."

"Yeah, but if they're nosing around, it's just a matter of time, you know?" *Whoosh.*

"A matter of time?"

Holden shook his head. "Until they find the letters." He made an "X" in the sugar. "We were young and stupid, you know? We never should have trusted him, but we did."

"Trusted who?" Baker's neck tingled, and he tried like hell to follow what Holden was saying.

"Look," Holden said, "I can't talk now. I'll try to come to your office later. You're on Main, right?"

Baker nodded. "Across from the bank."

"Right." He leaned forward. "I know things. Things that should be left alone. Things that would hurt some of us if the cops found out. You know?"

"Yes." No.

"I've seen the letters."

Baker's neck was on fire. "Where?"

"Here. Chet had her mail them to me."

"Why?"

Holden was shaking now, watching out the window. "So no one would get wise, I guess."

"Where are they now?"

Holden shrugged. "It's anybody's guess. As soon as a letter came in, I turned it over to Chet. I never liked it, him cheating on Marian like that." His eyes were sad. "She deserved so much better." *Whoosh.*

"Maybe Chet just had a pen pal."

Holden raised an eyebrow.

Baker laughed. "Okay, maybe not."

"Marian was happy. She hadn't been happy for years. Chet promised her the world. For a long time, it looked like he meant to give it to her. Then this Diana Kramer dame wanders into the picture."

"You've met her?"

Holden shook his head. "No. Never even saw a picture of her. But she stayed at the Ferrebee's lake house, I think."

Baker grinned. "My, you're a fountain of information all of a sudden."

Holden shrugged. "Cops are sniffing. Better for you to find these letters quietly than to let the city boys get wind of anything to do with Diana Kramer."

Baker didn't ask David Holden to elaborate. For some reason, he was afraid of what he might find out...like he was working for a killer, for example.

He paid his bill and left the diner more confused than before...and decidedly more nervous.

Chapter 10

When Baker returned to the office to make notes on his conversation with David Holden, Edwards was ready with a change of clothes. He held out a blue wool suit and a starched white shirt for Baker's inspection. "I presume you will be driving to the sanitarium again today, sir."

"You presume correctly." Baker nodded at the suit and sat heavily in his desk chair.

"I suggest we pursue a more elegant appearance today." Edwards ran a lint brush over the dark fabric of the jacket. "Will you be meeting Miss Kramer as well?"

Baker frowned. "No. I'm trying to intimidate the widow's family into giving me the information I need."

Edwards beamed. "This suit will work wonders for you. May I suggest a red handkerchief for the breast pocket? It will make them putty in your hands."

"Sure, Edwards. You're the boss."

"Very good, sir." Edwards disappeared into the closet and returned with a red handkerchief that he placed on the side of the desk. He set a plain white handkerchief on top of it.

Baker picked up the white handkerchief. "What's this for?"

"Considering how elegant you will look in this suit, and with the possibility of succeeding with intimidation, it is possible one of the ladies will be moved to tears." He cleared his throat. "Naturally it would be better if you had something other than a scandalous red handkerchief to offer."

Baker stared at Edwards. "Then why take the red handkerchief at all?"

"Because it looks wonderful."

Baker stared at a moment longer, then turned his attention to the notebook on his desk. He began to jot notes from his conversation with David Holden.

Edwards finished brushing the suit before speaking again. "Barone called while you were out," he said at last. "He wonders about progress on finding his sister."

Baker looked up and set the pencil he was holding on top of the notebook. He didn't want to discuss Barone. Despite Edwards' assurance that Barone had nothing to do with Stewie's death, Baker couldn't bring himself to trust the man. And there was still the matter of this so-called Philadelphia syndicate to consider. Barone said working with him would give Baker protection from the syndicate. What the hell did that mean?

He shook his head. He didn't have time for this right now. But he had taken the case of Barone's missing sister, and he needed to treat it as he would any other case. He pinched the bridge of his nose and groaned. "I suppose you'd better give me your report, Edwards. What have you got so far?"

Edwards took a seat, leaning forward and resting his arms on his legs. "I got directions to Barone's lake house from Frankie. He's healing nicely, by the way."

"Hmm."

"The cabin isn't much. And there's no evidence that a woman was ever there. But I did find some mail." He laid two envelopes on the desk.

Baker examined them. "There's nothing in these."

"Stealing mail is a federal offense. I brought you the envelopes so you'd have the man's name."

Baker cocked an eyebrow. "Jerry Mulligan. This is from Crane Haven College."

"Perhaps he was a student."

"Mmm." The other envelope had no return address. Baker slid them across the desk to Edwards. "I don't suppose you recall anything about the contents of these."

"I didn't feel right reading another man's mail."

Baker rose and began to undress, carefully laying his slacks, jacket, and shirt over his desk chair. He pulled on the clean shirt and tucked it into the dark pants. "Did you give this information to Barone when he called?"

"I told him the full name of the gentleman in question. I also said we would continue to look around the docks for any clues regarding his sister."

Baker allowed Edwards to fix his tie and shoved the second handkerchief in his pants pocket before putting on his overcoat.

"I'm afraid you'll have to scour the docks on your own,

Edwards. I've got to find these letters."

"Understood, sir."

"Do you plan to see Miss Marsh again?"

Edwards smiled. "At the earliest opportunity."

The stench within the sanitarium hadn't changed. The same fetid cloud of rot and despair hung in the air, clinging to Baker's hat and coat. He pictured the look on Edwards' face if ever the Brit walked into this foul place. What sort of rancid expression would his friend wear in the midst of such gloom? He pulled the spare handkerchief from his pocket and covered his mouth and nose.

Enid was behind the desk again, her own mouth covered with a scarf she had tied behind her head. Her eyes narrowed when she saw Baker, and it was clear she was not happy to see him. "You again," she said.

Baker sighed and put on a tight smile. "Good morning to you too."

Enid's shoulders were rigid. "I understand you upset Marian Ferrebee yesterday."

"That was not my intention."

Her eyes were cold. "It's against my better judgment to let you in to see her today, Detective."

"Detective? I guess you found out who I am."

"Judith Drake told me."

"Ah."

"She also told me that the sheriff wants you to be permitted to ask Marian questions, provided you don't upset her."

"Mmm."

"However, I intend to fill Dr. Rogers in on the situation as soon as he comes in. And if he feels your presence is counterproductive, you will have to leave."

"Fair enough," Baker said, tiring of the subject. "Tell me something: how do you stand the smell?"

Enid pursed her lips but said nothing and moved away.

Baker signed the guest register and headed to the ladies' parlor.

The parlor was every bit as gloomy as it had been yesterday. The same lost souls were scattered throughout. The bright lights bleached the room of all color, giving it an unreal quality. Baker wondered about heaven, if it were as white and sterile as this. And did it smell as bad?

Judith and Marian sat across from one another at a table close to the windows. Judith met Baker's eye as he approached and frowned.

Baker pretended it didn't hurt. "Where's Jeffrey?" he asked. A forced smile creased his hard face.

Marian, her head bent over her chest, chewed on a strand of her hair and giggled. "He didn't come," she said. "He's hung over."

"Marian," Judith said with a warning in her voice.

Marian shrank into herself, and Judith's expression softened. She looked at Baker and said, "He couldn't come." Then she tapped the table in front of Marian until the widow looked up. Judith winked and said, "He's hung over." The women laughed together, and Marian brightened a little.

Baker took a deep breath and sat in the chair next to Judith. This had two advantages. First, he could read Marian's expression as he asked questions, provided she looked up occasionally. The second reason, which he was loath to admit, was that he wanted to be near Judith. She radiated warmth and softness in this too-bright room. In a selfish way, he wanted the comfort she gave, whether it was given willingly or not.

Clearly Judith did not feel the same way about him. The three sat in hostile silence for a few moments, which bothered Baker, until he determined that this was probably the best way to get questions answered. Under normal circumstances, he preferred the baseball method of interrogation. Throw questions out and wait to see what got tossed back. When that approach failed, sit in silence. Eventually someone would start to talk. Someone would give him something useful. He'd just have to wait.

He'd tried the baseball method with these dames yesterday. They had called foul, and he figured that was their right. Now he'd be silent. Their manners dictated they tolerate his presence. Their desire to have him disappear would dictate their conversation. In the end they would tell him what he wanted to know because that alone was the surest way to get him to go away. And oh, how they wanted him to go away. He sensed it in Marian as she sat with her head bent forward, chin on her chest, waiting for the floor to swallow her. He felt it in Judith, like a radio transmitter, hot loathing conflicting with what he knew to be good and patient in her. It hurt him and he hated that it hurt him. But still he sat.

At last Judith spoke. "Have you found anything out?"

He closed his eyes at the sound of her voice. She smoked today. The cigarette between her fingers was circled with her lipstick. He waited a minute longer before speaking. He knew that what he had to say was mean, maybe cruel. And it would be directed at Marian. He'd had to wait for someone to speak. Judith opened the door. And he knew it was only because she wanted him gone. And now he would hurt the helpless Marian, and Judith would hate him for that as surely as January followed December.

Baker steeled himself. He looked at Marian with eyes like flint and said, "Seems your husband was having an affair." He waited, feeling the silence in the room expand and let his vision tunnel to a single point: Marian Ferrebee. How she reacted would tell him what he needed to know.

She lifted her head slowly, her hair parting and falling away from her face. It was in that position that she froze, her eyes wide and her mouth fixed in a silent "O."

Judith was more prompt and predictable with her reaction, and Baker braced himself for the heat of it. She leapt from her chair, the force of her movement knocking it to the floor with a resounding clang. "How dare you!" she said, her voice shrill. "Get out!"

Baker's heart pounded against his ribs, causing his head to throb and his mouth to dry up. He stared at her with a coldness he did not feel. "I'm not leaving until I get what I came for."

He pulled his cigarette case from his pocket and took his time removing a smoke. He lit it and slowly laid the lighter on the table before offering the case to Marian. She shook her head and looked at her hands.

Baker leaned back in his chair and studied the widow. Diana Kramer said Marian knew about her. That didn't make what he was doing any easier. He inhaled deeply and blew a cloud of smoke into the air. He made his face hard. "Letters from an unnamed woman made their way to a Mr. David Holden, a friend of Chet's." He leaned forward. "You know him?"

Marian shook her head.

"That's funny. He was at your wedding. And I found this picture in your bedroom." He pulled the photo full of pinholes from his pocket and laid it on the table in front of her.

She looked at the picture for a long moment, and Baker watched her face. There was shock there initially, but it turned to something else after a minute…disgust maybe? Or hatred? Or fear? Baker couldn't be sure what emotion flickered across the widow's face. It was unlike anything he'd seen before. Beside him Judith crushed out her cigarette and balled her tiny hands into fists. She watched Marian with a mixture of wonder and fear.

At last Marian met his eyes. She nodded. "I know him," she said, staring at the photo again with her good eye. "I know all of them. Does that make you happy?" She shoved the photo across the table as if she couldn't stand the sight of it.

Baker took another drag on the smoke and picked up the picture, careful not to bend it as he returned it to his pocket. "As I was saying," he said, "Mr. Holden held the letters for Chet and turned them over, one at a time, over a period of a year or so. As Mr. Holden no longer has the letters, I have to assume they are somewhere in your possession, Mrs. Ferrebee." He leaned forward again, hating himself. "Or are you back to being Miss Drake now?"

Judith hurried around the table to Marian's side, drawing the widow into a protective embrace and piercing Baker with her cold stare. "You can go to hell, Detective."

Baker ignored her, his eyes boring into Marian, studying every move, every breath she took. He leaned back, holding the cigarette between his lips and squinting at her through the haze that drifted into his eyes. Funny how she was more believable from this point of view. "My sources tell me Chet's family had a house at the lake. Apparently he kept her secluded out there so no one would get wise. I expect they had lots of romantic weekends together." He took the cigarette from his mouth and laid it in the ashtray. "Tell me something: did Chet go fishing a lot? Go out of town on business? Sheriff's outings? Maybe you found out about his mistress, Mrs. Ferrebee. Maybe that rubbed you wrong."

Marian rocked back and forth in her chair, the movement knocking Judith's arms away. Judith stood to her full height and let hatred fill her eyes. Baker felt something in his chest crush under her stare. "What are you suggesting, Detective?"

"You know what they say, Judith." His voice was steady.

"No, Detective, what do they say?"

"Hell hath no fury." He let his eyes slide to Marian, wondering what would happen to her after this visit. Things were going to start crawling from under rocks now, and he hoped he had the stones for it. He ground out his cigarette, stood and donned his coat. "When you want to talk about the letters, give me a call." Then, nodding to the two women, he turned and walked from the parlor with a calmness he did not feel.

Judith caught up with him in the vestibule, her cheeks red with fury. She shoved him against the wall and let the inner door swing shut. There they were shielded from the nurses' desk as well as the front porch. Now, as before, Baker's breathing was too loud in the small space; and he was far too aware of Judith's soft body pressed against him.

"Why, Mrs. Drake," he said, hoping his voice didn't betray the emotion he felt at being this close to her. "Enid will talk."

Judith pushed against him again. "How much is she paying you?" Her eyes were blue ice.

The warmth of her hands penetrated Baker's coat. He ignored the feeling. "I'm not at liberty to discuss..." He stared at her lips, unable to finish the sentence.

She slapped his face. "How much?"

Baker grabbed her wrist. "Watch yourself, Mrs. Drake. You don't want to make me angry."

Her eyes widened in fear for an instant, but the look disappeared and was replaced with the hatred Baker recognized all too well. "I'll double it," she said. "Whatever she is paying you, I'll pay double. You find those letters and bring them to me."

Baker's eyes narrowed, as if seeing her for the first time. "Very interesting. What's in it for you, Mrs. Drake?"

Her arms relaxed and Baker released his grip. She blinked and rubbed the place where he'd touched her. "May I have a cigarette?"

Baker took two from his case, lit them both and passed one to her. A man in an overcoat stumbled into the vestibule from outside, stomping the snow from his boots. He eyed the couple curiously before pushing his way into the foyer.

When he was gone, Judith blew out a cloud of smoke and said,

"Marian is a child. Even before all this happened, she was just a child." She took a step away from Baker and looked out the foggy windows on the front door. "There has always been something queer about her. Aside from Jeffrey, she is the only family I've got. I feel protective of her. There is nothing in it for me, other than keeping a vulnerable woman from further harm."

"You and Jeffrey never had kids?"

She laughed but it was sad. "I will never have children with Jeffrey, Detective. I can't stand the thought of it." Her eyes grew serious. "Marian is a kind soul. And there is something that torments her."

Baker scoffed. "Imagine that. A woman who sees her husband killed is tormented."

"Then you don't believe she did it? In there, you said..."

"I haven't ruled anything out, Mrs. Drake. I'm just saying she witnessed something violent, and maybe that has a little something to do with her mental state. Truthfully I just want the letters."

"You've stopped calling me Judith." Her eyes softened, and she took a step closer to Baker.

He watched her, amused.

She took another step, smiling now. "Tell me," he said, his voice raspy with the desire he was having trouble controlling, "do you believe the stuff you shovel?"

Her eyes flashed like quicksilver, and she drew her hand back to slap him once more. But Baker was quicker. He dropped his cigarette and grasped her wrists, spinning her around and pinning her against the wall.

Judith's eyes widened in fear, but he ignored that. "I warned you not to make me angry," he said, studying her trembling mouth. "Not so tough now, are you?"

Her chest heaved with ragged breaths; but Baker was staring at her lips, the way she held the bottom one with her teeth. It had been too long since he'd kissed a woman. He'd kissed the redhead a few nights ago. But she wasn't real. Not like this.

How long they stood in that dim world between the stench of sewage and the raw cold of winter, he couldn't say. At last he leaned down and kissed her with ferocity he could no longer contain. She kissed him back, moaning softly as he pushed her into the wall with his body. Baker traced the outline of her mouth with his tongue, savoring the way she trembled against him as the kiss deepened. He felt her fingers slide around his neck and tangle in his hair. He heard her moan his name, but it was lost to the roaring in his ears.

He pulled away before his heart exploded.

Judith's eyes were wide, her lips swollen from the kiss. "Do we have a deal?" she asked.

Baker straightened his tie. When he spoke, his voice was soft. "Hell, no." He pushed through the outer door and into the cold, wondering if he would ever respect himself again.

Chapter 11

The office was cold and dim, but Baker stripped naked anyway and lay down on the cot atop the rough gray army blanket. He'd thrown Chaucer back on the shelf and opened Poe again, which was a more accurate reflection of his mood.

He lost himself in the book, ignoring the chill that crawled over his skin—whether from the story or the cold room, he couldn't say. His mind wandered to the case every so often, and the chill of his flesh was replaced with searing heat as he remembered Judith and her touch. She was married, for Chrissakes, and he'd kissed her...making him as bad as Ginger.

He swung his long legs over the edge of the cot and fingered the bandage of his cheek. Snow was piling up on the windowsill, and he wondered how long it had been falling this time. Main Street businesses had been closed for hours; and the sidewalk in front of his office was dark, save for the weak glow coming from the pharmacy's Christmas display next door.

On the way home from the sanitarium, he'd picked up a bottle of bourbon. He didn't know if he'd sleep this night after what he'd done. He'd kissed another man's wife, the very thing he detested most in the world; and he figured if that wasn't worth getting drunk over, nothing was.

But he hadn't yet made up his mind about drinking the bottle. Baker had a tendency to see things when he drank. Specifically he had a tendency to see Ginger. So he'd done all he could tonight to avoid opening the bottle. He'd hung his suit back in the closet. But his pajamas were at the cleaners (damn Edwards, anyway), which was why he was naked. He'd washed the cut on his cheek and replaced the bandage. He'd made more notes on the case. And he'd thought about Judith Drake and her lips...as well as other parts of her anatomy. And he hated himself for it.

The sad truth of the matter was that he didn't think he'd sleep tonight without a shot...or twelve.

Swearing loudly, he gave in and opened the bottle. No need to bother with a glass tonight. No one here cared about etiquette. He opened his book and tried to read; but he kept thinking of the Drakes, the widow, Sheriff Ferrebee and David Holden. He looked down and read a passage aloud: "I never saw any set of reasonable people so thoroughly frightened in my life. They all grew as pale as so many corpses..." The line was from *The System of Dr. Tarr and Mr. Fether,* and he'd been trying to move to the next paragraph for the better part of ten minutes.

He closed the book and tossed it on the floor before drinking deeply from the bottle and reclining on the cot. His plan was to drink as much as possible as quickly as possible in order that he might simply pass out and avoid seeing unwelcome images of his ex-wife. It was a trick he'd used during the first few months after she left, but it got old fast. After a night of heavy drinking, morning came, as it always did, and he found himself groggy and unable to concentrate. So he gave up the bottle and focused on his job.

Until this case.

He brought the bottle to his lips as he reclined, spilling some on his chest. He shivered and wiped the spill with his pillowcase. He'd send the bedding to the laundry, and no one would be the wiser.

An image of Ginger floated, unbidden and undesired, in front of his face. He wasn't drinking quickly enough. "Scram," he said to her; but she didn't listen and he wasn't entirely certain he meant it anyway.

He could see the apartment they shared. He knew it stood empty now, but in his mind it was new and fresh and filled with things the two of them shared. He could see the two plants on the window ledge, green and full in the sunlight. Ginger hadn't taken them when she left. Neither had he. Were they dead yet?

He was with her now on the sidewalk outside of city hall, talking to the street vendor. Ginger showed off her wedding band; and the man said, "New bride needs a new plant." So Baker bought two.

Ginger smiled, her nose wrinkling. "Our first kids," she said. "Twins."

Now Baker groaned and drank from the bottle. He propped himself on pillows and stared at the snow. But Ginger floated before him, looking like a schoolgirl, blocking his view of the street. He loved that she wore her hair unfashionably long and loose. It suited her. His chest clenched at the memory and he drank again. The bottle was half-gone. *Isn't it funny,* he asked himself over and over again, *that a man who trails cheating spouses for a living was blind to his own wife's affair?*

He hadn't eaten anything since breakfast, and the bourbon burned like fire in his belly. He curled up on the narrow bed and waited for the burning to ease. When his gut relaxed, he leaned back on the pillows again and looked for Ginger's face. But she was gone. Now Judith Drake floated in front of him, a perfect apparition of what he could never have. The vision before him was pale and beautiful with pink on the tip of her nose from the cold, hair the color of honey and eyes like blue sapphires. He smiled drunkenly. "I kissed you today," he whispered in the dark. But the memory made his chest hurt again with a feeling he was too drunk to recognize as loneliness. He set the bottle on the floor beside the cot and lay back, folding his arms under his head. Eventually he fell into a dreamless sleep.

When he awoke, snow was falling in a great fury outside his window. He was cold. He was still naked. But these things were not what awakened him. He lay still, keeping his breathing deep and even, as if he were still sleeping. The world outside his office window, beyond the blowing snow, was black. The Christmas display was no longer lit. And the streetlights were out. Darkness lay on him like a velvet shroud. He closed his eyes to the blackness, letting his other senses sharpen in response.

He was not alone. The feeling was intense and the knowledge indisputable. His head pounded from the bourbon, and he berated himself now for his lapse in judgment. It was impossible to hear above the rushing of blood in his ears.

He stilled his breathing further, keeping his eyes closed and sensing his office around him. The closet was to his left and just behind him. He sensed the door was closed and let his attention continue to trace its invisible path around the room. The desk was in front of the window. The cot was in front of the desk. A slight displacement of air sighed in the dark; and he leaned his head to the right, letting the most primitive of his senses seek it out.

He stilled his body further, forcing his heart to slow until his pulse became a slow thud in his ears. After another moment, he heard it, the softest rustle of paper from Edwards' office, no more than a whisper in the skilled hands of the one who searched there.

He rolled from his cot, feeling vulnerable in his state of undress and cursing the squeak the narrow bed gave as it released his weight. He sensed the tensing of the intruder in the next room and crouched, waiting for another sound. Silence stretched endlessly. In the dark he felt for his gun on the floor under the cot. His fingers brushed it silently; and just as silently, he lifted it and eased the Colt from its holster, the rub of leather against metal a scream in the night. He waited a minute, then two, then ten.

Finally on silent feet, he moved to Edwards' door, the gun raised in front of him. The search at Edwards' desk was frantic now. Baker thumbed the hammer as he touched the doorknob.

The attack came from behind. As his world exploded in a million stars and he collapsed on the floor, he cursed himself for failing to consider a second intruder. The world turned white, his head a core of pain crushed by the entire universe. At last darkness encircled him. As it opened its mouth and swallowed him whole, he felt nothing but relief.

Through the cover of his eyelids, the morning light was blood red. Baker lifted a hand and traced the lump on the back of his head. It was as big as an orange and crusted with blood. He opened his eyes and moaned as the light stabbed his brain. As he moved his hands to block the sun from his view, he realized he was wearing pajamas. He lifted his head and assessed his condition. He lay in the middle of his office floor, covered with the gray army blanket. Someone had dressed him and covered him after the attack. He closed his eyes and moaned again, humiliated that he'd been seen in such a state.

Nauseated, he rolled to his hands and knees, leaving a bloody stain on the wood floor where his head had rested. Fresh blood, warm and thick, dripped down the back of his neck, soaking the pajama shirt he wore. He stood, staggered to the bathroom and was violently ill. When he was done, he splashed cold water on his face and scanned the floor for the bottle of bourbon. It was overturned and empty. "Shit."

The outer door opened and slammed. Baker winced at the sound and waited for the tirade that would follow Edwards into his office like a bad smell. Baker leaned on the sink, stared at his reflection in the mirror and listened. There was the sound of Edwards' shoes as they moved deliberately over the black and white tiled floor of the outer office. There was the pause in the stepping as the Brit undoubtedly surmised the damage done to his desk. The unmistakable angry stride to Baker's door came next. Edwards stormed in, the force of his entrance throwing the door against the filing cabinet with a crash.

Baker met him outside the bathroom door. Edwards assessed the blood dripping down his employer's pajama shirt, looked at the bloodstain on the floor and pursed his lips together. "I see you've ruined another shirt."

Baker looked down at the pajama shirt. "It's not mine," was all he could think to say. "I don't know where it came from."

Edwards showed no concern for Baker's condition. "I'm sure you're aware that intruders broke the glass on my door last night. It's all over the floor. And I won't begin to tell you about the state of my desk." He pointed an enormous finger at Baker. "But it has been searched; I'll tell you that much. And just look at you." He shook his head.

Baker made his way to the cot and sat down, holding a wet cloth to the back of his head. There he closed his eyes, wished for a cigarette and a cup of coffee and waited patiently for Edwards to finish his rant.

Edwards crossed to the closet and began searching for a clean suit. "I'm fairly certain I can guess what happened, sir," he said. "You were intoxicated and thinking about that woman."

"My wife," Baker growled.

Edwards poked his head out of the closet, his eyebrows raised and his cheeks red with anger. "Your ex-wife, if you please." He disappeared again. "But I was referring to Judith Drake, whom you seemed so taken with at the reception the other evening." He emerged from the closet carrying an armload of suits. "But I'm getting off the topic. As I was saying, you were intoxicated and passed out."

"Fell asleep."

"Passed out, sir. I'm certain of it. And after you passed out, two men..."

Baker stared at him with raised eyebrows.

113

"Oh, don't be ridiculous, Detective. Of course there were two. You haven't reached a level of such incompetence yet that you could be rendered unconscious by just one."

Baker wasn't sure what to say to that. "Hmm."

"Right. So two men sneak into the building, break my window, which you don't hear because you are passed out. One sneaks in here, discovers you and stands watch to make sure you don't wake up. The other searches my desk. You hear him, get up, draw your gun and get struck on the head."

Baker pulled the wet towel from the lump on his head and looked at it, wondering if Deirdre would be able to get the blood out. "Very good, Edwards."

Edwards held up one suit after another, finally nodding. "I think you should wear black today. It matches your mood." He pointed at the pajamas. "Miss Deirdre wants those back when you've finished with them."

Baker nearly choked. "Deirdre?"

"Yes. She heard a crash last night and came to check on you. Said you were naked. And I really must insist that if you are determined to become an exhibitionist, we move our offices to a back street, sir."

Baker moaned and held his head. "I've bled all over these pajamas."

Edwards waved his hand. "That's neither here nor there. Deirdre said they were old and abandoned. Someone dropped them off as laundry and never returned to pick them up."

But Baker wasn't paying attention. All he could think about was returning the pajamas to Deirdre and knowing that she'd seen him naked and beaten. Of all the ways he wanted a woman to see him, drunk, naked, bloody and passed out on the floor were nowhere on the list.

Edwards put the suit he'd selected in a garment bag and handed it to Baker. "May I suggest, sir, that you go to your real home and take a shower?"

Baker stood, took the bag from Edwards and nodded weakly.

He carried the suit in one hand and his car keys in the other, wincing as he stepped from his office onto the front sidewalk. Even the deep gray of the sky was painful as it penetrated his sensitive eyes. In his haste to cover them, he missed seeing Judith Drake approach and ran right into her.

"Pardon me," he managed to say over the rumbling in his ears. He left the office directly in the pajamas, his trench coat and bare feet; and he blushed furiously as he realized Judith stood before him with her brow creased in amusement. Ice cold cement burned holes in his heels and he tried to hop to avoid the pain, only to set his head to throbbing and his stomach to churning.

At least Judith seemed equally embarrassed, and that was some small comfort. "Detective," she said, "are you all right?"

His jaw clenched, and he tried not to think of his cold feet. "I'm fine. Are you looking for me?"

"You don't look all right," she persisted, covering her nose with her hand. "And you smell like you slept in a bowl of vomit."

He squeezed his eyes shut, willing the world to stop spinning. "Yes, well…if you'll excuse me."

She touched his arm as he moved away. "I stopped by to ask if you've given any further thought to my offer for the letters."

Baker unlocked his car and tossed the suit inside. "I can't figure out what's in these letters," he said. "Seems to me everyone wants them." He stared at Judith, considering her for a long moment. "Seems to me they're worth more than money." He climbed in and started the car.

"Wait," Judith said, putting her hand on the door, "where are you going?"

Baker glared at her, and she flinched as she realized he had no intention of answering and stepped away from the car. When she was out of striking distance, he turned his attention to the Chevy. "I don't want any bullshit," he said. "Just start up and get me the hell out of here." For once, the car obeyed and he roared away from the curb, ignoring the way the road slipped in and out of focus.

Halfway to his apartment, he pulled over and was sick on the side of the road. When there was nothing left in his stomach, he stretched out on the front seat, letting his bare feet dangle out the door and rest in the snow.

Everyone wanted the goddamned letters. He was betting that's why his office was searched last night. The only other case he had going right now was Barone's, and Barone wasn't the sort to sneak around. If he wanted to search, he'd blast his way in, hold Baker at gun point while he dug through drawers and make as much noise as necessary. That left the letters as the reason for the search. So whom did the letters affect, really? Chet had an affair. Big deal. That made him a jerk. It didn't make him a target for a hit, did it?

Baker's eyes felt heavy and his head pounded. If he fell asleep here on the side of the road, he might get mugged. Or worse, one of Ferrebee's boys would see him and tell Lewis. Reluctantly he pulled his feet back into the car and drove the rest of the way to the Bliss Street Apartments on Fifth.

He pulled into his old parking space and ignored the sting of nostalgia that bit him on the ass. His spot hadn't been used in awhile and was buried beneath a fresh blanket of snow. He pulled in as far as he could, pushing the drift out of his way with the door as he climbed out. He sank in the snow up to his knees; but he only shrugged, no longer able to feel his feet. The path to the front entrance was neatly shoveled and free of ice. His feet were red and burned furiously by the time he made it to the second floor.

The apartment that he and Ginger had shared was in the rear. Ginger liked the view from the rear. "From here we don't look out onto the main road," she said. What she really meant was that it was easier for Lewis to get in the windows without being seen.

The apartment had the smell of emptiness and neglect. Usually after a day's work, he came home to the aromas of hot food and Ginger's perfume—smells he associated with home. He didn't recognize this place any more. The plants were gone, which meant Ginger had been by some time during the last three months. She'd left a couple of his suits in the closet…old, out-dated numbers that Edwards would as soon destroy as look at.

The bed was neatly made too. Baker never made the bed. She must have done it when she came to get the plants. Out of habit, he looked for a note, swallowing disappointment when he realized there was none.

He showered and dressed in the black flannel suit Edwards wrapped for him. Then he stood for a long time and stared at the bed, wondering if he could afford to take a nap. His head throbbed and, underneath the nausea, the first stirrings of hunger had started. Maybe he could nap here awhile and make his way to The Diner for a meal, once he woke up.

In the end he knew he couldn't lie on the bed he shared with Ginger...the bed she'd been unfaithful in. And knowing that helped him make his decision. He pulled the old suits from the closet and the apartment key from his pocket. When he reached the main floor, he knocked on the super's door and waited for an answer.

"Yeah?" The super was a thin man with thick black hair and large ears. A soggy cigar spewed yellow smoke into the hallway.

Baker swallowed the bile that rose in his throat. "I'm moving out," he said. "Apartment 2B."

The super studied him for a minute. "What happened to your face?"

"Car accident."

The super didn't believe him. "The apartment clean?"

"It's clean. It's empty. You can have it back."

The super scrawled out a check. "I don't have time to inspect it right now. If there's any damage, I'll want some of this deposit back."

Baker nodded and tucked the check into his pocket before walking back out into the snow.

Chapter 12

Baker sat in his car and studied the yearbook photo. He'd rattled David Holden's cage and could only hope, for now, that Holden would keep his word and seek Baker out so they could jaw in private.

The guys in the photo were all still local with the exception of Jeffrey Drake, and all worked in town. Artie Pfeiffer ran the Used Car Emporium. Bertie Sims and Jeremy Watts worked at the Ford garage. And Wally Sims was a deputy. Baker's stomach wasn't up to dealing with a used car salesman; and he knew he'd run into the deputy sooner or later, so he pointed the Chevy in the direction of the garage, hoping to catch Bertie and Watts between jobs.

He stopped by the only other bank in town and cashed the deposit check from his ex-landlord. He had nothing against the Farmers who ran the bank across from his office, but he knew Phil would be nosy about the check and Baker wasn't in the mood. He planned to mail the money home to his mother. He hadn't phoned her since shipping Stewie home and knew an envelope of cash would be a sorry substitute for his voice, but he wasn't up to talking to her yet.

He exited the bank and climbed into the car, already cold. The Chevy protested as he tried to start it, whining and giving a shudder loud enough to turn heads. Baker swore with enough venom and volume to carry across the street and punched it in the dash. He ignored the shocked stares he received from pedestrians and told the car if it didn't start, it was going straight to the junk heap.

Once the Chevy was idling at a dull roar, Baker coaxed it forward. He dry swallowed two aspirin and coasted across town, wondering about the letters the whole time. Even if Sims and Watts knew nothing about Diana Kramer, they were on Marian's list of enemies. She hadn't shoved hatpins through their faces for the fun of it. It couldn't hurt to ask what they knew.

The Ford Garage was a hollow shed held together with rusted walls made of corrugated metal and a sagging tin roof. It sat, sulking, behind Ken's Full Service Station, doing its best to hide from any potential customers. Shep Smith ran the garage. He was an old man who hated everyone, especially his wife, who made him keep the garage running because the Smiths needed some sort of income.

Baker didn't frequent Shep's place. Something about a man making a living according to the dictates of his wife made Baker nervous. Plus, he generally avoided garages on principle alone. Mechanics had a tendency to ogle over his car, wanting to tear it apart and sell it for scrap.

It was mainly for safety reasons then that he left his Chevy at Ken's in the hands of a pimply attendant with a voice like a broken victrola record. The kid scoffed when he saw the car but pocketed the fifty-cent tip Baker gave and promised to shine her up the best he could.

Potholes filled with ice were scattered like mines throughout the Ford Garage's ancient gravel lot, and Baker avoided stepping in them as best he could. The garage had four bays and all were closed up tight against the November chill. No light was visible through the grimy windows, so Baker cupped his hands and peered inside, wondering if they were closed.

He couldn't see anything; but after a minute, the tinny sound of a radio drifted out, along with the noise of power tools and dropped wrenches. Shep's was open for business. Baker sidestepped mud-filled potholes and made his way to the office, which served as a pass-through to the garage itself when the bay doors were closed. Old Shep would be sitting inside like a fixture…the inevitable troll under the bridge. And the thought gave Baker pause. Baker hated Shep and had forgotten until just this minute that he'd have to deal with the slovenly man.

Baker paced around the lot a couple of times and smoked two cigarettes in an attempt to dull his senses before opening the door. He thought about lighting a third but realized he was wasting time. He opened the grimy door and stepped into the office. Shep sat at his greasy desk in his greasy coveralls, chewing on a greasy cigar.

"Thought you was going to stand out there all day," he said without looking up.

Baker made a face at Shep's bent head. "I thought about it."

Shep laughed a little at that and looked up. "The smoke help?"

"Not really."

He laughed again. It was a laugh filled with phlegm; and after a minute, it changed into a raspy cough that turned his head the color of a rotten plum. When he caught his breath again, he said, "It'll cost you new brakes."

"What will?"

"Whatever it is you want."

"How do you know I want something?"

Shep shrugged. "I may be fat and bald, but I ain't stupid. New brakes."

"I'd rather have new tires."

"We'll compromise. You can talk to both of my mechanics, and I'll let you buy both brakes and tires."

"That's a compromise?"

"I gotta make a living."

"Done," Baker said, feeling pissed at the world and heading for the door leading to the garage bays.

"Hold it," Shep said. "Not so fast. Car first, then you can talk."

Baker returned to the desk and looked down. "I had a bad night, Shep."

Shep laughed. "Do I look like I give a shit? Brakes and tires first."

Baker grabbed Shep by the collar and hoisted him out of the chair, ignoring the look of fear that spread to his eyes. "Now, I'm a man of my word, Shep," he said, pressing his nose against the fat man's. "And you're a greedy pig. I'll talk to your mules now and bring my car around later." Shep worked his mouth like he wanted to say something, but Baker gave him a shake. "Keep quiet, you. And if you try to stop me again, I will feed you your pecker."

He tossed Shep back in the chair and smoothed his coat. "Do we understand one another?"

Shep nodded mutely.

"Good." Baker turned and entered the garage.

The stench of grease and gasoline nearly knocked him over as he stepped from the dirty office onto the cement floor of the first bay. The radio he'd heard from outside continued to grind out its tune, but Baker couldn't make out who was singing. Two large Plymouths sat in the garage, their guts strewn here and there over the floor. Sims was tangled up with the farthest one, pulling a part out, putting a part in. *Surgery for cars*, Baker thought.

Sims spotted him, pulled his head out from under the hood and wiped his hands on a grimy rag. "Help you?" he said.

"You Bertie?"

The man's eyes narrowed. "Depends on who's asking."

Baker stared without blinking. "I'm a friend of Diana Kramer's."

Bertie flinched. It was quick; and if Baker hadn't been eyeballing for a reaction, he might have missed it. But Bertie recovered quickly, masking his jolt by rubbing his chin. "Diana Kramer. Can't say I've ever heard that name."

Baker was too pissed to be amused. "Word is she knew your pal, Chet."

Sims looked at his shoes and was silent so long that Baker thought he wouldn't answer. Finally he said, "Chet was a good man. Didn't deserve what he got."

Baker gave a half-smile and pulled out his cigarettes. "So I've heard." He lit one and offered the pack to Bert. "What about Jeremy Watts?"

Bertie didn't want a cigarette. "What about him?"

"He around?"

"He won't know nothing."

"Guess I can find that out for myself."

Bertie's eyes shifted to the back of the garage. "He's not here right now."

Baker wasn't in the mood for games, but he wasn't in the mood for a fight either. He knew Watts was around, but this wasn't the time to push his luck. "When will he be back?"

Bertie scratched his chin again. "Tell you what. We get off at eight o'clock tonight. Usually we go for a beer at Lenny's. How's about we meet you there at nine?" He gave a meaningful glance in the direction of the office. "It's a little awkward to talk here."

Baker kept his expression flat. "I'll be there," he said, knowing he was being set up. He dropped the cigarette and crushed it with his shoe, wondering how many would jump him tonight at the bar. He hoped his head was up to another bashing.

The pimply-faced kid had the Chevy shined up by the time Baker got back to Ken's. Baker made a note on the pad he kept in his pocket, reminding himself to bring the car to the Ford Garage the day after Thanksgiving for new brakes and new tires…provided he was still alive.

The kid laughed a little as he handed Baker the keys. "Good

121

luck, Mister," he said.
    "Mmm."

Artie Pfeiffer started a used car emporium fifteen years ago, after graduating from high school. The second he got his diploma, his parents moved to Atlantic City, where the roulette wheels where shinier, leaving the family trailer to Artie. Artie borrowed a truck from Chet Ferrebee and hauled the trailer into town. Together they parked it on one of the two empty lots across from Doogan's Chevrolet and put up a sign that said "Artie's Used Car Emporium." The first car Artie sold was the 1931 Ford he stole from his parents after hitching to Atlantic City and finding it parked three and a half blocks off the boardwalk...with the keys in their usual place under the driver's seat.

    Mr. and Mrs. Pfeiffer, along with the Atlantic City Police Department, chalked it up to another desperate act by a desperate citizen affected by the Depression. They didn't even bother looking for the car. Artie cleared one hundred bucks on the sale and bought two more cars with the profits. Over the years the business grew, gradually encompassing the second vacant lot across from Doogan's Chevrolet. Artie sold more cars in one month than Doogan did in six.

    The trailer remained in the middle of the first lot in the exact spot Chet Ferrebee helped haul it with his truck all those years ago. It was still rusted and full of holes, but Artie had put up a sign that flashed "ARTIE'S....ARTIE'S....ARTIE'S" in bright red across the trailer's front window. Below that, in solid glowing blue, the sign read: "Americans Buy Cars Here." During the war—a time of rationing, blackouts and the cessation of all new car manufacturing—Artie was there...as American as apple pie, ready to sell a Ford, Chevy or Plymouth to any patriot with red blood coursing through his veins. Artie made car buying seem like a patriotic duty during the war. Poor Doogan ate a lot of dog food during those years.

    Artie himself burst out the battered front door of the trailer as Baker chugged up in his Chevy. "Hello, hello," he called, his hand outstretched to grasp Baker's in a firm grip. "You've come to the right place, my good man." He stared at the Chevy, and Baker could see the glee in the little man's face. "And not a minute too soon. Looks like you are more than ready for a change in vehicle. What model year are you interested in?" He laughed. "Anything would be new compared to what you drive now. Am I right?" He nudged Baker in the arm.

Baker struggled to light a cigarette in the wind. "Actually," he said, leaning against the hood, "I just wanted to ask you a few questions."

Artie's face transformed. The open and friendly features became closed and angry. "You a cop?"

Baker shook his head.

Artie's eyes narrowed and his lips pursed. He thrust a finger into Baker's chest. "Now see here," he said, "I've never once cheated on my taxes. I've told you people that over and over again. I refuse to answer any more questions about fiscal year 1944. We were at war, for Chrissakes. War, man. Rubber was scarce. Was I supposed to ignore the ration orders regarding rubber and put brand new tires on every car that came in?"

Baker held up his hands. "Easy there, fella. I don't care about your taxes." He handed Artie a business card. "I'm interested in finding a woman named Diana Kramer. Thought you might know her."

Artie scowled. "Why would I know her?"

"Thought you were friends with Chet Ferrebee."

"Yeah, so?"

"Chet was friends with her."

Artie frowned. "Chet's dead."

"He ever mention her?"

"No. Never."

"You sure you don't know her."

"I'm sure. That all?"

Baker nodded. "Thanks for your time."

Artie started back to his office then turned and called out to Baker, "Hey, Mister."

Baker paused in the act of getting into his car, the cigarette clenched between his teeth. "Yeah?"

"Be careful who you ask about that woman." He looked over his shoulder, as if afraid someone might sneak up on him. "Some people might get upset."

"Thought you didn't know her."

"I don't know her. I don't want to know her. And if you know what's good for you, you'll follow my example."

Baker nodded and climbed into his car, the lump on the back of his head pulsing angrily, the sutures in his cheek burning fiercely. He needed to think. And when a man needed to think this early in the morning, it made sense to have a big plate of eggs and a hot cup of coffee.

The smell of bacon drifting into the street from The Diner's kitchen was overpowering, and Baker fought a wave of nausea as he pushed his way inside and elbowed his way to a stool at the counter. The tinkling bell over the door cut through his head like a knife as patrons came and went in the morning rush. His tongue was thick and dry, and he signaled Betty for a cup of coffee the minute he sat down. She set down a glass of water and two aspirin beside his mug and gave him a wink. "You look rough this morning."

Baker nodded and swallowed the aspirin. It was his second dose in as many hours, but what the hell. He'd brought the yearbook in with him and opened it now, staring at the familiar photo. "Jeffrey Drake lends a hand." He'd asked Jeffrey about the letters, true. But he hadn't asked him about Diana Kramer. If Diana *was* somehow involved in Marian's life, surely Marian's own brother would know something about it.

"Eggs today, Detective?" Betty stood on the other side of the counter with her order pad.

"Yeah. A couple. And some hash browns."

"Sure thing." She leaned over and looked at the yearbook photo. Her perfume was too strong. "Isn't it amazing how these kids grow up?" She looked at Baker. "Of course, you're no older than any of them, but I can remember back in the day when they used to come in here after school."

Baker tapped Jeffrey Drake's image in the photo. "Did he come in too?"

She snorted. "Jeffrey Drake? No. Never. He and his sister kept up the house after their father left. Their mother, God rest her soul, worked at the school, helped with lunches and that sort of thing. I think she cleaned classrooms too." Betty shook her head sadly. "No. Jeffrey and that sister of his spent all their time at home, trying to grow corn from a patch of moldy weeds. They were the poorest family in town. But Marian...she was by far the prettiest girl." She ripped the order from the pad and clipped it to a line strung across the kitchen's pass-through window. "Order for you, Dave. It's for the detective."

Holden's face appeared at the window. "Coming right up."

Baker smiled and lit a cigarette while Betty refilled his coffee. "Don't look now," she muttered, "but here comes that cop from the city."

Baker could tell by the way her face clouded that she was referring to Lewis.

"You look lovely this morning, Betty," Lewis said, sitting on the stool next to Baker. "Bring me a cup of that, would you, Doll?"

Betty gave a tight smile and filled his cup before busying herself with other customers.

"How's your case coming along, Baker?" Lewis asked, eyeing the yearbook. "Find anything yet?"

Baker took a drag on his cigarette, turned and blew smoke into Lewis' face before slamming the book closed.

Lewis' smile stopped just short of his eyes, mirroring the hatred Baker felt for him. "Thought I'd warn you to watch out for yourself. Some folks are mighty upset about you poking around for these so-called letters."

Baker shrugged. "A job's a job." He laid his smoldering cigarette in the ashtray.

Lewis laughed. "Yeah, I guess to a slob like you, that's the truth." He stood, fished the cigarette from the ashtray and dropped it in Baker's coffee. "By the way," he said, "thanks for the wife."

Baker's punch was so fast that Lewis still had the smirk on his face when the fist struck his jaw. Lewis stumbled backward and upset a table, dumping coffee and eggs all over the two old men seated there, before regaining his feet and lunging at Baker with a clumsy right hook. Baker deflected the blow with relative ease and sank his other fist deep in Lewis' gut. Lewis dropped to his knees with a loud, "Oof," his face pale.

Baker righted the upset table, picked up the dishes that had been knocked to the floor and sat on the stool again. His head throbbed, and the slice in his cheek was starting to itch. He rubbed the bandage, wanting to tear it off and scratch, scratch, scratch. He gained control of his urge and lit a fresh cigarette as Betty set his plate of food on the counter. "Better eat before this gets cold," she said, like nothing unusual was happening in The Diner.

Grimacing, Lewis rose to his feet, cradling his jaw. "I'm watching you, Baker. This whole town is watching you. You're turning up stones that should be left where they belong…in the mud at the bottom of the river."

Baker turned and picked up his fork, setting the fresh cigarette in the ashtray. "Tell Ginger I want my plants back."

Lewis left without another word.

"He's something," Betty said, refilling his coffee.

Holden offered to give the men at the upset table a free breakfast. "That's okay, son," one of them said. "It's nice to see two young fellas mixing it up on occasion. Reminds me of my youth." His friend agreed and the two of them shadow boxed with one another as they left.

Holden stood across the counter and lit a cigarette. "Detective Lewis is a snake," he said in his tight voice. *Whoosh.*

Baker nodded. "Sorry about the scene. I'll cover the breakfasts."

Holden seemed tense as he shook his head. "Forget it. What's with you two anyway?"

Baker shrugged. "Our cases overlap at the present." He took a bite of eggs. "Plus, he married my ex-wife."

"Ah," Holden said, trying to sound casual but not quite succeeding.

"We hate each other. That's all. It's no big deal."

Holden took off his paper hat and scratched his head. "I'm not so sure about that."

"About what?"

"What he said about leaving stones unturned."

"Yeah?"

"He's right. Some things should be left in the past." Holden tapped the yearbook. "And that Christmas is one of them."

"Why?"

Holden's hands shook, and he looked around the diner with the caution of one who is used to being watched. "I can't tell you," he said, the acrid smoke from his cigarette congealing into a heavy cloud that hovered over the counter. "Even if I wanted to, I couldn't. But I will tell you this: not a day goes by that I don't wish I was able to live that year over again." *Whoosh.* He wiped a hand over tired eyes. "Don't fight in my diner again," he said, heading back to the kitchen. "It's bad for business."

And that was the last thing Baker ever heard David Holden say.

Chapter 13

Despite the tussle with Lewis, Baker felt nearly human as he left The Diner. Other than some bruised knuckles, he was in good shape. He looked out his car window with a rare genuine smile on his face. He examined his knuckles, kissing them loudly after a minute. "Well done, boys," he said, noting that his hand smelled like Lewis' aftershave lotion. A good scrubbing would take care of that. He looked down and noticed egg and bacon grease on his pants. Edwards would have a fit about that; and Baker swore softly, knowing he didn't have time to return to the office to change. He needed to talk to Jeffrey, and the place to find him was the sanitarium.

Sunlight punched jagged holes through the clouds here and there, melting snow on the road. The freshly washed Chevy was soon caked in mud; and the smile Baker showed to the world after leaving The Diner disappeared, replaced by the usual hard look he wore.

It was slow going up the muddy road to the sanitarium. The Chevy's bald tires spun and stuck once or twice, but the old girl chugged along; and in the end Baker made it into the lot, swearing when he stepped in mud up to his ankles. He shook the muck from his pants and looked around. His Chevy was the only car in the lot, and he wondered if it were before visiting hours. He checked his watch. 10:30. He was fine.

As he pushed his way into the foyer, he understood the reason for the empty parking lot. The stench was worse than yesterday. A different nurse stood behind the desk with a kerchief tied around her mouth and nose. Her nametag said "Nancy." She glared at Baker. "You'll want to cover your face," she said. "The smell is a little harder to get used to than yesterday."

Baker's eyes watered. "Has anyone thought to call a plumber?"

She rolled her eyes. "Well, aren't you a genius? Of course, we've called a plumber." The starched nurse's hat she wore slid forward over her eyes and for a moment, she disappeared. "They can't find the problem," she said, pushing the hat back with a pudgy hand. "They spent half the morning looking for a leak. I don't know what I'll do if I have to keep working in this sewer."

Baker sighed and pulled out a handkerchief, pressing it to his nose. The guest register lay open to Marian Drake-Ferrebee's page, and he studied this morning's entries with interest. When he felt the eyes boring into the top of his head, he looked up.

"You're that detective, aren't you?" Nancy asked. Baker couldn't see her mouth; but from the look in her eyes, he could tell she was frowning.

"I suppose so."

Her eyes narrowed and she began to nod. "Oh yes. You are. I can tell." She shook a chubby finger at him. "Enid warned me about you."

Baker pulled the handkerchief away from his face long enough to offer an insincere half-smile. Then he turned his attention back to the book and ignored her. The sheriff hadn't visited yet. Judith and Jeffrey signed in at 9:00 and were still here. He flipped backward to yesterday's visits and searched for Marian's guest page. He easily found his signature from the morning, along with Judith's and Sheriff Ferrebee's. There were no other visitors until last night. At 7:30 a guest signed in, but the name had been scratched out in the same manner Diana Kramer had scoured hers from the book two days ago. Baker clenched his jaw and frowned. While he had been seated next to Judith Drake and eating the dinner she prepared, Diana Kramer had been here, calling on Marian.

He absently touched the bandage on his cheek and blew out a sigh.

Nancy lifted her head, her eyes suddenly wide with curiosity. "What is it?" she asked, leaning over the book. "Do you see something? Is it a clue?" She tried to pull the book closer to her; and after a minute, Baker let her take it.

"I don't see anything suspicious," she said.

But Baker was already walking away. He didn't look back as he strode toward the ladies' parlor, even as Nancy called after him. His angry strides rang through the halls, causing orderlies to turn and stare as he passed. As he pulled open the thick wooden door and stepped inside, he barely registered the presence of Jeffrey, standing drunkenly at the windows. He barely registered Judith and her cold beauty as she cradled Marian against her shoulder. What he did notice was that the widow was weeping bitterly.

His steps faltered as he moved closer but only slightly and only for a minute. He approached the widow's table with a mixture of pity and curiosity. His gut clenched a little at the state of her misery, and he gave himself a mental shake. A crying dame was no reason to get squeamish. At the table he cleared his throat as he sat down across from the women. He could wait a while longer before talking to Jeffrey. Right now he needed to hash out what was going on during these visits from Diana Kramer.

Judith regarded him with cold indifference, her full lips pushed tightly together as she spoke. "You look better than you did earlier," she said, absently stroking Marian's hair. "I trust you're feeling better as well?" Her tone implied she couldn't care less.

Baker met her gaze and was satisfied when she flinched from its hardness. "Someone knocked me out last night," he said, watching her for any sort of reaction. "My guess is they were looking for the letters I asked you about yesterday."

Judith's face shifted for an instant, and Baker scanned her features to interpret the expression; but Marian leaned into her just then, crying harder. Pity rose in Baker for an instant, but he forced it down and slammed his hand on the table. He loomed over the women and when he spoke, they shrank from the coldness in his voice. "I want to know who Diana Kramer is, and I want to know why these letters she wrote are so important."

Judith swallowed and hugged Marian closer. "Leave us alone," she said. Her voice was hard, but there was fear behind her eyes. "Why must you continue to come here? We've told you all we know."

Baker sat back in his chair, his face relaxing a fraction. "Look, lady, I got beaned in the head last night; and I'm not happy about it. If this tomato," he gestured to Marian, "knows anything about these damned letters, she needs to tell me." He pinched the bridge of his nose and stepped back. "Because I'm getting really tired of looking."

Judith stroked Marian's hair and looked at Baker with cold eyes. But Baker could only think of the fire he knew burned beneath the surface of that stare. He gave her a crooked smile; and she looked away, a deep blush coloring her face.

Baker pulled out a chair and sat down, letting his coat fall open in front. He kept his hat pulled low over his eyes, refusing to give in to the etiquette that dictated he remove it in the presence of ladies.

People were more intimidated if he looked at them from under the brim. He shifted his eyes to Marian and leaned forward. "What did Diana Kramer say when she stopped by last night, Marian?"

Judith jumped as if slapped. She let go of the widow and looked at her as if she didn't know who she was.

Marian ignored that and looked at Baker. The swelling in her left eye was down, but the sclera was red as blood. Her jaw was still swollen, giving her lovely face a grotesque, lopsided appearance. She regarded Baker with curiosity; and for an instant, she shifted, transformed into the seductress she was on that first day. She opened her mouth, and Baker figured she was going to ask for a cigarette again. But something, maybe it was just a trick of the light, *something* shifted again; and she became scared and helpless once more. Her eyes, as inhuman as they looked with the blood swimming through the sclera on the left side, were wide and scared and...innocent. "Diana won't leave me alone," Marian said. "She says I have the letters. But I don't." She turned to Judith and grasped her hands. "She frightens me." Judith pulled the widow into her arms again and stroked her hair, as she looked at Baker with questions in those big blue eyes.

But Baker wasn't watching Judith. He was studying the widow, wondering things about her that he couldn't put into words. "Where can I find Diana Kramer?" he finally asked.

Marian shook her head, turning her face into Judith's shoulder. Her voice was muffled as she cried, "I don't know. I don't know."

Baker looked at Judith. "Tell the nurses not to let Diana Kramer in if she shows up again. And it would be best if you spent as much time here as possible." He looked at Jeffrey. The man's back was rigid as he stared out at the woods, and Baker wondered how much of what went on the drunk absorbed. "Ladies," Baker said, nodding, "if you'll excuse me."

He rose and walked to where Jeffrey stood, leaving Marian to the comfort of Judith. Baker was still their enemy, but perhaps now they realized the importance of finding the letters and the danger posed by Diana Kramer. And Diana Kramer *was* dangerous...he felt it in his gut.

Baker shoved his hands in his pockets and stood at the window next to Jeffrey. Jeffrey hadn't shaved. He hadn't bathed. He was like a radiator, circulating the stench of stale gin and an unwashed body in a five-foot radius. For a moment Baker wondered if Jeffrey could be the source of the stench in the sanitarium but just as quickly dismissed the idea. As bad as Jeffrey smelled, he wasn't ripe enough to stink up a building this size.

They stood in silence for a minute, those two, side by side, and stared at the field of snow sloping down to the woods. At length, Jeffrey turned and regarded Baker with haunted eyes. "What do you want?"

Baker watched a cardinal hop from branch to branch on a dead tree. "I want to get paid, Jeffrey," he said. "Nothing more or less noble than that. I want to eat and pay my rent and enjoy a good slice of steak."

Jeffrey laughed a little at that; and Baker couldn't help but notice the weakness in the effort, the way the breath barely misted on the cold glass. Baker wondered if Jeffrey Drake were dying, being consumed from inside him by pain that only gin could numb. At length, Jeffrey said, "The sheriff won't let you look for these letters much longer, you know."

"Why?"

Jeffrey shrugged. "That boy was all he loved in this world. I'm sure Ferrebee has no intention of letting you ruin his memory." He swiped a hand over his face, and Baker saw that it trembled with the need for another drink.

"I won't drag anyone down on this. You have my word. I only want to return the letters to Diana Kramer."

Jeffrey blew out another one of those feeble breaths; and this time, it didn't make the slightest fog on the glass. After a minute, he started to cry, his shoulders shaking in huge, convulsive sobs. Marian and Judith looked up, and Baker could see in their faces what he was beginning to understand to be true.

"You know her, don't you?" Baker asked, not really expecting an answer. "You know she's dangerous. Tell me how to find her."

But Jeffrey didn't answer. He stared out the window and wept.

"Remove that suit immediately, sir," Edwards ordered. "What will people think when they see you? Tell me you haven't let anyone see you like this."

Baker grimaced. The goose egg on the back of his head still pulsed, and the gash on his cheek itched like a rotten foot. "Not so loud, Edwards." He slumped in his chair and tried to light a cigarette while scratching his cheek at the same time. "Plenty of people saw me, and no one said a word. And may I remind you that you picked this out."

"When I chose this suit, it was in perfect condition." He clucked his tongue and examined the stained pants as Baker stood with the cigarette clenched in his lips. "Bacon grease and eggs. This will never come out. And you look as if you've been in a brawl."

"Mmm." Baker tossed the suit coat to Edwards and slumped in his chair in his boxers and shirt with the fedora still perched on the top of his head.

"Tell me you didn't fight with Detective Lewis?"

Baker smiled.

"Assaulting a police officer is a criminal offense."

Baker held the cigarette in his lips again and took off the hat while he loosened his tie. "He started it."

Edwards ignored him and began searching through the closet for a clean suit. "We're changing to gray, sir," he called.

"Yes, fine. Whatever you say." Baker stood and stared out the window as he finished his cigarette. And he thought about Deirdre. Once again, his beautiful neighbor had come to his rescue. Last night she'd cleaned him up, put him in pajamas and covered him with a blanket.

And she'd seen him naked when she did it. His face flushed red with the thought. He didn't know whether to thank her or kill her. He didn't want to face her at all, but he'd have to. He needed to find out if she'd seen or heard anything last night.

"I've cleaned up the glass from the door, sir," Edwards said, holding a gray wool suit.

Baker nodded at the suit and accepted the trousers Edwards passed to him. "And?"

"And I found some blood. Not enough to indicate a large cut, but enough to suggest that the perpetrator was injured to a degree that would require bandaging."

Baker tucked his shirt in and slipped into the soft wool suit jacket. "So I'll keep my eyes peeled for a bandaged wrist. Anything on Miss Kramer? Did she call?"

"No, sir."

"How's things with Rosemary Marsh? Any luck with getting a trace set up?"

Edwards fingered his black eye and gave a delicate cough. "A work in progress, sir."

Baker frowned and opened his mouth to say something when they heard the sheriff's voice from Edwards' office.

"Anyone here?"

Edwards excused himself to greet the sheriff as Baker smoothed his tie and sat behind his desk.

"I heard about the break-in last night," Ferrebee said as Edwards showed him in and left, pulling the door shut behind him. "A couple of my men came over earlier today to check things out. How's your head?"

Baker shrugged. "Still attached."

"You file a report yet?"

"Not yet. I'll get around to it. What can I do for you?"

Ferrebee leaned forward, rested his enormous arms on his knees and stared at the floor. He was unshaven and haggard. His eyes were swollen with grief or fatigue...or both, Baker supposed. Ollie Tate had released Chet's body, and the funeral had been scheduled for two days from now.

With a pang that brought tears to his eyes, Baker thought about Stewie. Had his mother scattered the ashes yet? Or had she buried the box in the family plot at the cemetery? Baker was ashamed of his cowardice. He'd made no effort to contact her. She hadn't called him either, but he hadn't really expected her to. She'd collect Stewie's ashes from the train when it rolled in, nod her thanks to the baggage man as she signed the claim and then stoically walk the mile back to the farm, carrying her son's remains.

Baker would call her. Soon.

Ferrebee sat in his own world; and Baker wondered how long they had sat like that in silence, with no sound but the November wind whistling past the windows. Would Chet's death have been easier to take if there had been another son or a daughter to help spread the grief around? Was Baker's own mother less distraught because she knew that, no matter how big a disappointment he was, she still had another son out in the world somewhere? Or did she wish it had been Baker who'd had the slug buried in his brain and not Stewie.

"Effie wants me to invite you to dinner," Ferrebee said at length. And then, when Baker stared at him, unblinking, he said it again, "Effie wants me to invite you to dinner. She insists, actually." He was looking up now, the skin around his eyes so far beyond red it had turned purple. "This business about Chet is troubling her a great deal. She wants you to know he was raised to be a good boy." The sheriff slumped again. "He was a good boy."

Baker shifted in his chair. "No one questions how he was raised, Sheriff."

"Maybe not you, son. But there are those that are passing judgment." For an instant anger flashed behind his old eyes. "My family's name is being dragged through the mud because of this letter business. People say the letters and the murder are connected."

Baker's tongue thickened just a little. "Are they?"

"How the hell should I know?" The sheriff stood and paced around the office, running his red hands through his thick hair.

Baker shrugged. "I'm just asking."

Ferrebee stopped and stared, his face helpless. "Why can't you just leave it alone?"

Baker wanted to say it was because the truth needed to come out one way or another. He wanted to say that he'd already taken money for this job and that he'd already used that money to pay off debts. But in the end, it wasn't Ferrebee's business. So he said nothing.

After a while, the sheriff sat down again. "This Diana Kramer. She's your client?"

Baker nodded. That much was obvious. He could no longer hide behind his "I'm not at liberty to say" chant.

"Christ," Ferrebee said. "Isn't it enough that my son is dead? Now this horrible woman wants to ruin his memory." He rubbed his hands together.

Baker lit a cigarette and studied the sheriff through half-lidded eyes.

After a time, Ferrebee stood and began to pace again. After a moment, he looked at Baker with something that may have been a smile; but it was really more of a grimace, and for some reason, it sent a frisson of cold fear through Baker. "We'll just have to convince you at dinner tonight to give the whole thing up, won't we?" He sat again and Baker recoiled from the hard look in the man's eyes. "Will you come?" Ferrebee asked.

The hair on Baker's neck stood up; and he hesitated a moment before saying, "I'll be there."

When Ferrebee was gone, Baker pulled the phone to him and dialed the operator. The faint voice competed with the static on the wire. "Hello," the operator said. "Hello?"

"I'd like to call long distance. Cedar Rapids, Iowa."

"One moment, please."

It took the operator longer than a moment to patch the call through; but when Baker heard the soft voice in Cedar Rapids, Iowa, say, "Hello?" he smiled.

"Hi, Mom," he said.

Chapter 14

His mother cried, and Baker wondered when men got used to that…their mothers crying. Was there a magical age that made a man mature enough to take it? Because Baker hadn't reached it yet. The instant he said "Hello," she started crying. Then she thanked him for all he'd done to make sure that Stewie made it home to her…home to where he belonged. There would be a graveside service, she said. And Stewie would have a marker in the cemetery next to his father. But the ashes would be spread on the farm in the back pasture.

Baker wondered at his mother's choice of Stewie's final resting place but said nothing. Even if he'd wanted to point out that Stewie's remains would only get worked into the mud and buried under cow manure and urine, she wouldn't have heard. She was too busy crying and thanking him.

He hung up, feeling better for having talked to her, and thinking he needed a will. And he needed that will to specifically state that he was not to be cremated and scattered in the cow pasture. He wasn't wild about spending eternity in a six-foot box either, but it beat his mother's idea of ashes to ashes and dust to dust.

He checked his watch. It was going on 2:30, and he'd put off talking to Deirdre for as long as he could. She'd seen him naked; and, what's more, she dressed him. This took their relationship to a whole new level. Deirdre was what his mother would call a nice girl. Nice girls got married. They had children. They went to church every Sunday. They didn't dress naked, intoxicated men and cover them with blankets and tend to their wounds and make sure they were all right before turning out the lights and leaving. Nice girls didn't do that sort of thing.

Naked. He'd been *naked,* for Chrissakes. Not that he was modest. Because he wasn't. And he wasn't ashamed of his appearance. Some pretty fair dames had called him handsome in his day. But some lines were not meant to be crossed. He and Deirdre needed to have a talk about that.

"Is your stomach ailing you?" Edwards asked as Baker pulled on his coat.

"No. Just thinking about Deirdre."

"Really? With such a sour look on your face? Thoughts of that particular young lady usually bring a smile to my face. You look as if you just ate a bad oyster."

"Mmm," was all Baker said as he pulled the door shut behind him.

He scowled at the delicate bell above the dress shop door that tinkled happily as he entered. Two old ladies searching the racks paused with their wrinkled hands poised in mid-air when Baker filled the doorway and nodded in their direction before scanning the store for Deirdre.

"Oh my," one whispered to the other. "A man."

The other nodded as if she couldn't quite believe it herself; and the two moved to a rack farther away, careful to keep him in their line of sight.

Baker moved deeper into the store and nearly stepped on Deirdre, who was kneeling on the floor beside the counter next to a mannequin, her mouth full of straight pins. Her brow was wrinkled in concentration as she pulled a pin from between her lips and placed it in the hem of a deep green dress. She looked up when he cleared his throat and held a hand out so Baker could help her off the floor.

She took the pins from her mouth and set them on the counter as she gestured to the dress. "Do you like it? It's a Christmas dress for Polly Olson. She gets a new one every year. Always dark green velvet and always too long by at least three inches." She shook her head. "I'm forever hemming her dresses." She smiled and waved as another woman entered through the front door, setting the tiny bell to tinkling again. "Be right with you, Gloria." Deirdre turned back to Baker. "I just love Polly Olson. She's my best customer next to Letty Babcock and Nancy O'Brien." She stepped to the counter and began poking the pins into a pincushion next to the cash register. "How's the case going?" she asked.

"It's going well." He stepped to the counter and watched her put the pins away.

She leaned over and whispered to him, "I'm sorry about last night. Edwards told me you were upset."

Baker's jaw clenched. "I wasn't upset," he lied. "Just surprised." When Deirdre raised her eyebrows, he continued, "I like to be awake when a woman sees me naked."

138

The woman called Gloria was staring at them, with her mouth hanging slightly open. Baker wondered if she'd overheard him, and he glared at her. She looked away, blushing.

Deirdre shrugged and began straightening the loose fabrics on the countertop. "You'd been injured. What was I supposed to do, leave you there naked and cold in the middle of the floor?"

"But you did leave me there," he said, wishing she'd look at him. "And for all I know, you had your way with me first."

She did look at him then; and a pink flush colored her face, neck and collarbones. Baker took a step closer, smiling when he realized he was making her uncomfortable. "I might have died," he whispered in her ear, watching the wisps of hair on her neck move with his breath. Her hair was loosely pulled back with combs, and Baker suppressed the nearly overwhelming urge to pull them out and watch her hair tumble over her shoulders.

She pursed her lips and pushed him away, trying to regain her composure. "I promise you I did not take advantage of your situation. I assessed that the bump on your head was just a flesh wound. Nothing seemed to be missing from your office, so I called Edwards and told him what had happened; and he assured me he'd be in as early as possible." She stared at him for a long moment. "And you were drunk."

Baker ignored that and picked up a red hat perched atop a head-shaped figure. "Is this your latest design?"

The women in the front of the store had given up all pretense of shopping and were staring at them openly now. Deirdre didn't seem to care. "Yes. It's my latest." She stepped closer. "Say, I wasn't wrong, was I?" she asked. "About them taking anything? You weren't robbed, were you?"

"No. I wasn't robbed. You weren't wrong about that."

She looked at the front of the store and licked her lips as she leaned close enough to whisper to him. Baker noticed she smelled like flowers. Something tightened in his chest, and he wondered about it for a moment before tossing it aside "Do you know what they were after?" she asked.

Baker studied her collarbone. It peeked out from her blouse, making her look pale and fragile; and he surprised himself by wondering what it would be like to rest his head there. "I have an idea," he said, his voice strained as he pulled his eyes away from that spot.

She sighed and took the hat from his hands, arranging it carefully on the figure again. "I'd hate to think of someone breaking in here at night." She looked at him pointedly. "I'm sorry about dressing you. But you really shouldn't go around without any clothes on. It's bad for business. Not just yours. Mine too."

Baker stepped back, his heart heavy and his head puzzling over why that was exactly. "I need to know if you saw anything last night. Saw anyone leave," he said.

Her brow creased, and she reached up and scratched her head where one of the combs held her hair in place. Baker held his breath, waiting for the hair to cascade over her shoulders; but the comb held it tightly. "I heard tires squeal," she said after a while. "You know, like someone was trying to drive away really fast. I was afraid the bank had been robbed. But then I knew that couldn't be the case because Phil showed me the vault." She rolled her eyes like it was a bad memory. "The walls of that thing are very thick. If the people in the car wanted to rob the bank, they would have had to use explosives." Her gaze shifted to the front of the store. "That particular dress costs sixteen fifty, Mrs. Hansen; but it comes with a matching handbag."

Mrs. Hansen, an eighty-year-old spinster who played the organ at the Lutheran church, was so intent on listening to Deirdre and Baker's conversation that she had pulled a backless evening gown covered in pink sequins from the rack. Deirdre hadn't batted an eye.

She turned her attention to Baker again. "So then I thought of you," she said, lowering her voice to a whisper. "I was concerned you might have gotten yourself in trouble with these letters you're looking for."

Baker smiled, the expression unfamiliar to him, but oddly pleasant. He wondered why that angered him.

She paid no attention. "So I peeked in your window and saw you on the floor. You looked very cold and miserable."

"How did you manage to…"

"Get you dressed?"

He nodded.

"My sister's a nurse. I used to help her take care of a paralyzed patient. You're much bigger, but I remembered what to do."

Baker cleared his throat. "Thank you."

She smiled. "Try not to drink so much. It lowers your IQ."

He nodded and left, not sure what else there was to say, and not liking the way he was beginning to feel whenever he was around Deirdre. The three customers giggled as he walked by.

Edwards' brow was creased with frustration when Baker blew through the front door. "It's about time, sir," he said. "Diana Kramer has called twice in your absence."

"Did you call Miss Marsh?"

Edwards nodded, taking Baker's coat and hanging it on the rack. "Of course. I rang Miss Marsh immediately after Miss Kramer phoned the first time to listen in. And I tried very hard to keep Miss Kramer on the phone during the second call, but she refused to speak to me. She insisted on speaking only with you."

Baker ran to his office. "Will Diana call again?"

Edwards checked his watch. "In three minutes, sir. Miss Marsh is standing by."

Baker lit a cigarette and paced while he waited, wondering what he would do if they were successful in locating the source of the call. Would he confront Miss Kramer? Would he turn her over to the police? Had she done anything wrong? Did she kill Chet Ferrebee? Did she look as good as she sounded? When the telephone bell rang again, he jumped.

"This is Detective Baker," he said, meeting Edwards' eyes as the enormous Brit stood in the doorway tapping his foot.

"Have you found my letters yet, Detective?"

"It's a little hard to find anything with you harassing Chet's widow every time my back is turned."

Diana gave a throaty laugh. "Ah, yes," she said, "poor Marian. She says she doesn't know a thing about the letters."

"So why do you keep hounding her?"

"Because she is lying." There was an edge of danger to her voice.

Baker sank into his chair. "What makes you say that? Woman's intuition?"

"I know she has those letters, Detective." Diana's voice was tight as she spoke. "I warn you not to be fooled by her. She knew about me from the beginning. All her sobbing and crying and begging forced Chet to stay with her. But it was pity that kept him from leaving. It was me he loved. And I want my letters." She was a spoiled child stamping her foot.

Baker played with his lighter as he debated lighting a cigarette. "What's in the letters, Miss Kramer?"

She blew a soft breath into the phone; and when she spoke, her voice was soft with memories. "My love for him was in those letters. Everything we shared is in them."

Baker frowned. "If it's as cut-and-dried as that, why is everyone so determined I drop the case?"

He could feel as well as hear her hesitation at the other end of the line, almost seeing the shrug she undoubtedly gave as she replied, "I would imagine they don't want their golden boy's reputation tarnished by a rumor of infidelity." She laughed softly. "But Chet was naughty. If they only knew him like I did."

Baker was running out of questions. He felt a burning need to keep her on the line, to discover what she had planned with regard to Marian Drake. But he didn't want to anger her. "What kinds of things did you know about Chet?"

"I knew everything about Chet," she snapped. "I know things Marian never could. She's a coward and she's weak."

Baker's flesh crawled. "She saw her husband murdered. She was nearly killed herself."

Diana was silent for a moment. When she spoke again, her voice was thin and brittle. "You tell Marian I want those letters, Detective. And if you can't get them for me, I'll get them myself."

"Careful, Miss Kramer. That sounds like a threat. The Drakes won't take kindly to that. Neither will the sheriff." But Diana was gone. She'd hung up, and Baker sat staring at the dead phone in his hand until Edwards spoke.

"Well?"

"Well what?"

"What did she say?"

Baker shook his head. "She sounded very anxious." He stood and grabbed his coat. "I'm going to check on Marian. Call me at the sanitarium if Rosemary gets back to you with any information about that call." He checked the clock on the filing cabinet. It was 2:45. "I've got dinner at the sheriff's at 6:00 and a meeting at Lenny's at 9:00."

"Lenny's, sir? That is a most disreputable place. Perhaps the gray suit is too nice."

There was a short, sharp knock on the door before it was flung open, coming to rest against the filing cabinet. Baker looked up to see Leadfoot Barone and an unknown thug standing in the doorway.

"See. I told you they'd be here," Barone said.

Baker sighed as he put his hat on. "No news on your sister, Barone. We told you we'd be in touch." He closed his eyes and shook his head, still having difficulty digesting the fact that Leadfoot employed him.

"Well, you'll forgive me if I want to make sure you're putting in as much time on this as it warrants." He gestured to the man standing beside him. "This is Joey. He's Frankie's brother. Frankie says 'hi,' by the way. The doctors don't think the limp will be permanent."

Baker opened his mouth to tell Joey to take a hike; but Edwards, ever the diplomat, stepped up. "The detective is just leaving," he said, draping an arm around Barone and Joey. The Brit towered above them, but neither seemed to mind as Edwards pushed them through the connecting door into his own office.

Barone smiled and looked over his shoulder at Baker. "Good," he said. "Joey will go with you."

"No way," Baker said.

Edwards hesitated a moment, then shrugged, as if he didn't have any opinion on the matter one way or another.

Barone just smiled. "Consider him invisible."

Baker looked at Joey. He was about 145 pounds of lean muscle on a five-foot five-inch frame. It was easy to imagine him being a pain in the ass, but invisibility didn't seem to be an option. Barone rocked on the balls of his feet. "He's going to be with you until my sister is found."

"Like hell," Baker said, pushing past them, through Edwards' office and out onto the sidewalk. Deirdre's shop was three steps away, just next door. And he knew she was still around. He hesitated for an instant, afraid of the little old ladies inside, but regained his courage and pushed his way in.

"I need to use the phone," he said, and Deirdre only smiled and nodded to the set behind the counter.

No questions asked. That was Deirdre.

Edwards answered on the third ring. "They still there?" Baker asked.

"I am unable to see directly next door, but I believe Joey is standing outside of Deirdre's Dress Shop watching you through the windows."

Baker looked up. Joey regarded him through the glass with cold eyes. Deirdre looked from Joey to Baker and back again. She waved at the thug and he turned away.

"Mmm. Okay, listen," Baker said. "If I'm not in the office tomorrow morning, check the alley behind Lenny's. And bring a stretcher."

Edwards said, "Very good, sir." And hung up.

Chapter 15

Heavy clouds swallowed the sunlight, and the air smelled of snow. As the Chevy spun its way through three miles of mud on the way to the sanitarium, Baker wondered how many pairs of shoes he would have to ruin before he remembered to wear galoshes. He hated galoshes. They were for old men.

His stomach burned as he headed out of town, and he realized he'd axed lunch again. Maybe he could talk this Joey character into driving back into Crane Haven and picking up something from The Diner. The thought of having Joey run errands made Baker smile, and the smile made him think of Deirdre. And that made him uncomfortable.

His Chevy splashed through the half-frozen mud of the sanitarium's parking lot, and he found himself staring at the back end of an enormous service truck. A second truck was parked ten feet away. Thick black hoses snaked from valves on the trucks' sides and over the ground, where they'd been carelessly dropped in the mud.

As he climbed from the car, he could hear the grind of the motors in the cylindrical housing on the backs of the vehicles. It appeared they were finally flushing the pipes. *About damn time*, Baker thought. He stopped a man in mud-caked coveralls to ask about the progress they were making, but the engine noise made communication impossible. In the end the man smiled and shrugged, and Baker went on his way.

Joey the thug had managed to get his small coupe into the lot and was tiptoeing through the mud a few paces behind Baker, doing his best to look tough. The two made their way up the wide steps to the verandah, careful to avoid stepping on hoses. Both the inner and outer doors to the vestibule had been propped open; and cold air whistled through, rustling papers and files on the nurse's desk.

Enid was on duty again today, busily anchoring documents with anything heavy: a stapler, a roll of tape, a potted plant.Baker stepped into the foyer and assessed the floor. No leakage, but the smell was no better. Beside him Joey coughed and held his nose, making a pathetic attempt to wipe his muddy shoes on the muddier floor.

Enid looked at Baker with something like weariness, a cloth tied tightly over her mouth and nose.

Baker gave her a half-hearted smile. "What's going on?" he asked, stepping out of the way of a sheriff's deputy, who hurried past, taking the stairs two at a time on his way to the second floor and disappearing into one of the rooms.

Enid's eyes narrowed, and the cloth over her mouth moved in a way that let Baker know she was frowning. "Not that it's any of your business," she said, slapping a stack of papers that threatened to blow onto the floor with her hand, "but Dr. Rogers ordered all the sewage lines flushed."

Baker watched the grim faces of the men in filthy white suits as they moved in and out of the building. "No luck in finding the problem, I take it."

"No luck. They're going to try the cistern out back next." She caught a file in mid-air as the wind blew it from the desk.

"So why is the sheriff's office here?"

Enid rolled her eyes and jerked her head in the direction of the parlor. "Marian took a tumble on the stairs. Says Diana Kramer pushed her. Ferrebee and his boys are here to check it out."

The hair on the back of Baker's neck stood up. "Did you see Miss Kramer? What does she look like?" He scanned the guest register again. She hadn't bothered to sign in today. There was no scratched-out signature on the page.

Enid's eyes shifted from Baker to Joey and back again. "Who's that?" she asked. "Friend of the family?"

Baker gave Joey a cursory glance. "He's nobody," he said. "Did you see Miss Kramer?"

"No. I didn't see her."

"Dammit," Baker said. The frustration he felt was obvious in his tone. "I told Judith to stay here with Marian."

"Judith was here," Enid said. "Jeffrey too. Marian just went upstairs to her room to get a sweater. She says Diana pushed her as she was coming down the stairs on her way back to the parlor."

Baker looked around. "Did Diana come in the front door?"

Enid shrugged. "I don't know how else she'd get in."

Baker gestured to the plumbers. "But these men have been here since early this morning."

"Yes."

"And surely *someone* would have seen her."

Enid sighed, becoming impatient. "Not necessarily."

Baker thought a minute. "I'd like to see Marian's room."

Enid frowned. "The sheriff's office has been in and out of there all morning. I don't know if Penny can take any more stress today. Dr. Rogers won't allow it."

"Who's Penny?"

"Marian's roommate."

"Did she see Diana Kramer?"

"She says 'no.'"

Baker's neck tingled. "I need to see her room."

"Already been searched," she said, securing more papers billowing in the wind.

"What would you say if I told you that Diana Kramer is dangerous?"

She studied Baker for a moment. "I think I'd believe you. She's got Marian terrified."

"Please, Enid," Baker said. "I need to see that room. I need to talk to Penny. She may be the only other person who's gotten a good look at Diana."

The deputy who ran up the stairs a few minutes earlier descended now, shaking his head and muttering to himself. Baker wondered if he'd just spoken to Penny.

"Follow me," Enid said when the deputy had passed. "And be quick."

Baker stayed close behind Enid. And Joey stayed close behind Baker as the three hurried up the winding staircase to the second floor. "Penny never leaves her room," Enid explained as they reached the top of the stairs. "Never. She eats in her room. She even bathes in her room."

"How does she…?"

"Chamber pot."

"Ah."

"She spends her time writing in journals, so if you see her writing something, don't ask to see it. She'll have a fit. And I mean a fit." She stopped moving and turned to face Baker. "And she's simple. She may not understand anything you ask, so don't get angry with her. If you mistreat her, I'll have your head."

147

Baker nodded.

Penny *was* simple. Baker recognized that when he walked in the door. For an instant, as he stared at the sad creature trapped in this room out of fear, pity filled his heart. Just as quickly, he chased it out again.

She wrote in a yellow notebook today, her lower lip caught between her teeth as the chewed nub of a pencil she used flew across the page. Baker couldn't read the words she'd written but recognized them to be the childish scrawl of a kindergartner. Over a dozen similar notebooks were stacked neatly on the table beside her bed, each well-worn.

He studied Marian's belongings, which were few. Her side of the room was tidy and impersonal. Other than a picture of Judith and Jeffrey sitting on her bedside table, there were no personal effects. Even the closet held only hospital issued garments.

Penny, resenting the intrusion, cringed as Baker surveyed the room.

Enid stood in the doorway and said, "I can't wait here all day, Detective. You have three minutes."

"Can't you leave us alone?"

Enid raised her eyebrows. Clearly she could not.

Baker shrugged and slowly made his way around the room. He checked the windows and found them secure. Peering through the glass, he noted it was a steep drop from the window to the ground. He didn't figure Diana Kramer as the type to risk a fall, even if coming through the window was the only way to get the letters. And there were no footprints in the snow outside. From this vantage point, he had a view of the entire rear of the property; and he could see two men in white coveralls standing beside a wide cylindrical cistern, deeply engrossed in a debate over something. After a moment, they started to push on the cement cap covering the hole. They appeared to change their mind about moving it when it proved to be too heavy. As they walked away, Baker closed the blinds.

There was nothing else in the room worth inspecting. It was a sterile, sad, stuffy room; and he couldn't imagine spending any length of time in here.

Slowly and with great care, he knelt on the floor in front of Penny and watched as she poured her childlike thoughts into the journal. When she spoke, she didn't look up from her writing. "Are you here to yell at me too?" she asked.

"Who yelled at you?"

"The sheriff." She made a big circle on the page and put an "X" through it. "He said I should have told someone about Diana Kramer."

"Then you've seen her?"

"No."

In the doorway Enid frowned and wrung her hands.

Baker kept his eyes on Penny. "Have you met her?"

"No."

"How do you know about Diana Kramer?"

"Because I'm here when she comes to visit Marian."

"I thought you said you've never seen her."

Penny looked up from her writing and met Baker's stare with the brown eyes of a little girl. "I'm here when she comes, but I can't see her because Marian is always in the way."

"I don't understand. How does Diana get in?"

Penny shrugged. "I don't know." She went back to writing on her paper.

Baker stared at Penny for a moment longer, wondering if she too was in danger from Diana Kramer. At length, Enid cleared her throat and Baker followed her from the room.

"I take it Marian wasn't hurt when she fell this morning," Baker said as he and Enid descended the stairs with Joey trailing behind.

"She didn't fall. She was pushed. And no, she wasn't hurt. Just scared."

Baker tested the banister as he moved along the stairs. It was sturdy—sturdy enough to hold his weight and certainly sturdy enough to support Marian. Next, he examined the stairs themselves. They were coated in mud that the sanitation crew tracked in, but the mud was dry and the stairs were not slick. He turned to tell Enid what he thought; but she was gone, already back at the desk sifting through charts. Baker strode to the parlor, wanting to see Marian for himself. Needing to see her for himself.

At one of the far tables, Ferrebee, Judith and Marian spoke in low tones with a heavily mustached man Baker suspected was Dr. Rogers. Jeffrey sat at another table speaking with a deputy Baker didn't recognize.

Marian's face was drawn and vacant. Her hair hung in greasy strands, partially concealing a fresh bandage on her forehead. Judith stopped speaking as Baker approached. "You," she hissed, getting to her feet. She looked at Dr. Rogers. "Doctor, I want you to keep this man out of here. He has done nothing but torment Marian."

Dr. Rogers turned and assessed Baker with intelligent eyes. "Is this true, young man?" The doctor was not a large man, but the directness of his stare made Baker feel like a schoolboy who'd just been caught tying a girl's braids together.

"*Torment* is a strong word," he said.

Judith scoffed. "He's a private detective, Doctor. He says he's been hired to find some letters. We've told him over and over again that we don't have any. And he refuses to listen." She noticed Joey lurking behind Baker. "And who is this?" she asked. "Have you brought along a tough to beat the letters out of us?"

The doctor stood and blocked Baker's view of the widow. "I'm afraid you'll have to leave," he said.

Baker's mouth tightened. "Fine," he said, looking around Dr. Rogers to the widow. "Marian," he said, "I'd like to apologize on behalf of my client. I was told she is the one who pushed you. If I ever find her, I'll let her know what I think of her." He turned to leave with Joey on his heels.

"Wait a moment, please," Dr. Rogers called after him.

Baker turned to see the doctor moving toward him with the easy grace of a European. Behind him, Judith squeezed her eyes shut and appeared to be whispering a prayer...or cursing Baker's existence. "Diana Kramer is your client, you say," the doctor said, rubbing his chin.

Baker nodded. "Mmm."

"Remarkable," Dr. Rogers said, removing his spectacles and gesturing to the table. "Please join us."

Baker turned to Joey. "Wait outside."

Joey glanced at Sheriff Ferrebee and nodded once.

Judith touched the doctor's sleeve. "Are you really going to let him stay?" she asked.

Dr. Rogers ignored her as he cleared his throat and gestured for Baker to sit down. "Tell us what you know about Diana Kramer," he said.

Baker shrugged. "Not much. She hired me to find some letters."

"You've met her?"

Baker shook his head and gave a bitter laugh. "No. She won't meet with me. We conduct our business over the phone."

"Where does she call from?"

"I don't know. I've got some people working on trying to find out." He looked around for a clock. "To be honest, I expected them to call me here."

Dr. Rogers smiled. "Oh, they won't get through."

"What? Why?"

Dr. Rogers and the sheriff exchanged glances. "There was an incident involving the phones, and I had to order them unplugged."

"What sort of incident?"

"I'm not at liberty to say."

Judith laughed and looked at Baker, amused. "It's not so coy when someone else says it, is it?"

"I'm done with Mr. Drake, Sheriff," the unknown deputy said, pulling out the chair beside Baker and shoving Jeffrey into it.

"Hey," Jeffrey said, nearly toppling over.

Dr. Rogers ignored them. "Tell me, Detective, do you know anything of hypnosis?"

Baker shook his head, watching as the deputy took a step back and stood behind them, arms crossed, eyes focused on what was unfolding at the shiny white table in the middle of this too-bright room. "What's this all about?" he asked.

Dr. Rogers looked at Marian and smiled the way a doting father would smile at his grown daughter. "We've been discussing the possibility of hypnotizing Marian in order to discover the truth about the night her husband was murdered."

"What's this got to do with Diana Kramer and the letters?"

Ferrebee rubbed his head. "I'm tired of hearing about these damned letters."

Dr. Rogers held up a hand to quiet the sheriff, but his eyes narrowed as he studied Baker. "What do these letters mean to you?"

"A paycheck."

"That's all?"

"Of course that's all. What is this?"

Dr. Rogers smiled, and it contained a pinch of condescension. "I am only making inquiries, Detective. As this is your line of work, one would expect you to understand."

Baker patted his pockets, searching for his cigarettes. "I need a smoke," he said, realizing he'd left his pack at the office.

Jeffrey pulled a crumpled pack from his pocket. "Here. Have one of mine." He passed one to Baker, who lit it, blowing the smoke out in a big cloud. "Thanks," he said. He took another deep pull on the cigarette and watched Dr. Rogers. "So what do you want from me?" he said after a while.

Dr. Rogers smiled. "I want to know everything about Diana Kramer. I want to know if she intends to harm Marian further." He looked around the table. "We all want to know."

The familiar loneliness engulfed Baker. Everyone stood to lose something in this case. Everyone but him. Finding the letters would help no one but Baker and Diana Kramer, who had just become a loose cannon. And once again Baker had the feeling there was more than just letters at stake here.

"I see you are troubled," Dr. Rogers said to him. "That is good. It means you are human." He stood and nodded to the women. "Mrs. Ferrebee, Mrs. Drake. I must go. I trust you will be fine now, Marian. No harm done. Sheriff Ferrebee, we will pursue the discussion of hypnosis again tomorrow." And he left the room.

Baker crushed out his cigarette and asked Jeffrey for another.

"May I have one?" Marian asked.

Jeffrey shrugged and passed one to her, holding the lighter to the tip with a trembling hand. Marian inhaled and coughed violently.

"What is wrong with you?" Judith said to Jeffrey, taking the cigarette from Marian and crushing it in the ashtray. "She doesn't smoke."

Jeffrey shrugged again, stood and staggered back to the windows. There he pulled his flask from his pocket and drank.

Marian folded her hands in her lap and looked at Baker. "I want to go home," she said. "It smells so bad in here."

Judith patted her shoulder. "After the hypnosis, if it's safe."

Ferrebee shook his head as he pushed away from the table. He pulled the unknown deputy aside where they talked in hushed tones. Baker returned his attention to the women before him. "Marian, how does Diana Kramer get in here?"

"She's not answering any more of your questions, Detective."
Judith's eyes were slits. "You've bothered my family long enough."
Marian lifted her head and looked at Judith. "Please," she whispered.
"I really do want a cigarette."

Judith shrugged and pulled a flat cigarette case from her pocket.
Marian held the cigarette between her bandaged fingers and leaned
forward as Judith lit it.

"How does she get in?" Baker repeated.

Marian's eyes watered from the smoke, but she didn't blink as
she looked at Baker. "Through the window. I open it for her."

Judith drew a deep breath. "But why, Marian?"

Marian shrank from her like a chastised child. "Because I have
to. She says Chet never loved me. She says he only loved her. And
she wants the letters back."

Baker thought about the window in Marian's room and wondered
how Diana Kramer managed to scale the building without falling. As
he was thinking, Ferrebee and the deputy passed the table. "We'll be
leaving now," Ferrebee said. "Detective Baker, this is Deputy
Reynolds. He's new."

Baker stood and shook Reynolds' hand.

Reynolds said, "A private dick, eh. I'm from Jersey. We hate
dicks over there."

Baker studied Reynolds with flat eyes, placing a finger in the
center of Reynolds' chest. "You have sauce on your tie."

Reynolds looked down to examine the tie. At the same time,
Baker brought his finger up, bumping Reynolds in the nose. It was a
schoolboy prank, and Edwards would highly disapprove; but it
humiliated Reynolds, and that made the whole thing worth it.

"See you tonight," Ferrebee said, giving Baker a smile that didn't
quite reach his eyes.

Jeffrey stumbled back to the table and stood behind Judith. "We
about done here? I need a drink." He shook his flask to indicate it
was empty.

Judith rolled her eyes. "In a minute."

Marian finished her cigarette and stood. She looked Baker in the
eye. "I can't tell you anything else right now."

"Can't or won't?"

"Isn't it all the same thing?" She looked at Judith. "I'm going to my room now. Alone."

Judith grasped Marian's hands and kissed them both. "I'll be back tomorrow."

Once Marian was gone, Jeffrey slid into her seat, sliding it as far away from Judith as possible. "She'll be all right," he said, nodding his head.

Judith looked at her husband, hatred in her eyes. "Are you reassuring me or yourself?" And the thing about married couples who no longer love one another is that the hate they begin to feel is as intimate as the love they used to share. It penetrates deep and pares out part of the soul. It's worse than what one feels for an enemy because when resentment follows dead love, there's the memory of what used to be good. And that just makes the hate bigger...more personal.

Judith and Jeffrey stared at one another with that hatred now, and Baker thought about Ginger. He cleared his throat. "If you'll excuse me, I've got a date with the sheriff for dinner."

Jeffrey turned from his wife, the smell of his rotting body competing now with the sewage stench from the front of the building. "Interesting," he said, his breath blowing fumes of smoke and gin into the room. "We've been summoned there as well."

Judith sighed. "To discuss the funeral, I'm sure." She looked at Baker. "This has been very hard on Effie. She hasn't left the house since all this happened. The sheriff says she hasn't even been to the church to talk with the minister. It's so sad."

As she spoke, the hatred fell from her eyes; and Baker felt that familiar pull in her direction. Resisting it, he cleared his throat and turned to Jeffrey. "Well, then," he said, "I'll see you both there."

Chapter 16

Baker was dressed to kill. With the Ferrebees and Drakes wanting to strangle him, he needed to look good. As he steered the old Chevy in the direction of Sheriff Ferrebee's house, he thought about the case. Ferrebee had tried to bribe him to stop looking for the letters. Baker wondered about that. Two thousand six hundred bucks went a long way. That was the sheriff's salary. Baker had checked. Whatever money Ferrebee made needed to stretch far enough for house and food. Most likely, he had a little left over for savings, depending on how frugal Effie was with the household budget.

And judging from the looks of the house as Baker pulled into the driveway and stood on the porch waiting for someone to answer the bell, Effie was frugal indeed. She said nothing as she opened the door and stared down her nose at Baker. Instead, she pointed to a threadbare rug and waited while he wiped his feet. Then she led the way through a small parlor and a kitchen whose only source of light was a weak bulb over the sink. The faint glow offered enough light for Baker to recognize the spotless nature of the kitchen countertops. Whatever dishes Effie used to prepare the delicious-smelling dinner had already been washed and put away. Even the stovetop sparkled in the dim light.

Baker followed her down a hallway, noticing she didn't turn on any lights to guide their way. He stepped carefully, afraid of tripping over a seam in the carpet...or a strategically placed board with a nail in it. She led him into a tidy living room where Sheriff Ferrebee and the Drakes were enjoying drinks.

Judith sat in a stiff chair, sipping a glass of wine as Baker entered. She regarded him with the cold indifference Baker had become accustomed to over the last couple of days. Jeffrey sat on the sofa with a gin and tonic and nodded dumbly in Baker's direction as Effie showed him in. "The detective is here," Effie said, her voice devoid of any emotion. As she held out her hand for Baker's coat, he realized he hadn't offered condolences on her son. He opened his mouth to speak, but Ferrebee was already off the couch and slapping him on the back. "Baker," he said. "Glad you could make it." He looked at his wife. "Effie, why don't you hang his coat in the front closet?"

155

She nodded with her blank face and disappeared down the dark hallway.

"Care for a drink, son?" Ferrebee asked.

Baker thought about the meeting coming up at Lenny's. "No thanks," he said.

Jeffrey tossed his drink back and said in a fairly sober-sounding voice, "Well, the gang's all here, Sheriff. Are you going to tell us who did it?"

Judith was appalled. "Jeffrey," she breathed.

Ferrebee's jaw tightened at the remark, but he managed to keep a tight rein on his temper. "Sadly, Mr. Drake," he said through clenched teeth, "my son's murder has not been solved yet."

Jeffrey had the grace to blush.

Ferrebee walked to the bar in the corner and poured out two scotches, handing one to Baker and keeping the other. "Have a drink, son. It'll help." He looked at the Drakes. "I thought that since we're practically family, you two should be present to hear what I have to say to the detective tonight."

Baker tasted the scotch and arched his eyebrows. "Am I to be crucified then, Sheriff?"

Ferrebee laughed. "No. Nothing of the sort. And I don't plan to discuss anything until I've have a good bit of my dinner." He gestured to a door off the living room. "Shall we?"

Baker allowed himself to be led to the slaughter, which was to be performed in a tiny dining room. He frowned as he realized that for the second time in a week he was seated at a meal with people who regarded him as the enemy.

Effie filled plates one at a time, passing them around the table with care. After she filled Baker's plate, she let it drop on the table directly in front of him. Gravy and meat juice splashed on the tablecloth and on the six-dollar tie Edwards hijacked from Pockets O'Hurley last month. He ground his teeth together. "Thank you," he mumbled. "Looks delicious."

She offered a stiff "Thank you" and leaned back in her chair to light a cigarette, not bothering to touch her food. "Naturally," she said, her voice cold, "I haven't felt up to entertaining." She glared at the sheriff. "But Doug insisted we have you over. It seems we need to impress upon you that our son was a good boy." Her eyes shifted to Baker. She took a drag on her cigarette and blew the smoke in his direction. "I must apologize for the way I look, Detective. You must think me a fright."

"Effie," Ferrebee said, with a warning in his voice.

Baker said, "You look fine, ma'am." But she didn't. She looked terrible. She looked like a woman who'd been forced by a man she couldn't stand to prepare a meal for people she didn't like. And now it was payback time. Baker set his fork down and waited for the fireworks.

"I don't look fine," she said, her voice shrill. "I don't feel fine. My son is dead." Her voice broke on the last sentence, and she buried her face in a napkin.

"For Chrissakes, Effie," Ferrebee said.

Judith said, "I'm so sorry for your loss, Mrs. Ferrebee. If there is anything I can do." She gestured to the table. "And dinner is delicious. I know you weren't prepared for all this. No one ever is."

Jeffrey excused himself to fix another drink.

When Effie had composed herself, she fixed her red-rimmed eyes on Baker. "What are you trying to do to this family?" she demanded.

"Effie," the sheriff warned again. "We talked about this."

Effie ignored him, keeping her hateful eyes on Baker. "I get to watch my son be put into the ground in two days. Did you know that?"

Baker nodded. His head was beginning to ache.

"He was our only child. I wanted more, but Doug was satisfied with Chet." She looked at the sheriff. "Chet was his pride and joy." She covered her mouth with a napkin and stifled a sob.

Sheriff Ferrebee rested his head on his hand. Judith rose and knelt beside Effie, drawing the woman into her arms. "There, there," she cooed. "There, there."

Jeffrey returned with his drink. "Oh Christ," he muttered, seeing his wife holding Effie. "This is all I need." He slumped into his seat at the table. "None of this is even my problem."

"What do you know about any of it?" Effie said, pulling away from Judith and glaring at Jeffrey.

"I know my sister wouldn't be the way she is if it weren't for your son."

157

Ferrebee dropped a huge fist on the table. "You played just as much a part as everyone else did."

Jeffrey tilted his head to the side and sipped his drink. "If I recall correctly, Sheriff, you paid me off."

The sheriff's voice was dangerous when he said, "You let me."

Baker sat back. Something sick was spreading through his stomach. He patted his jacket for his pack of cigarettes and realized he'd forgotten to stop at the office to pick it up. Jeffrey absently passed him his own pack as he and the sheriff retreated into themselves.

After a minute, Judith stood. "Perhaps we should leave," she said, wringing her hands.

Effie laughed but it was a hard, brittle sound. "Don't be silly, Mrs. Drake." She blew her nose loudly. "Don't you want to hear what my *husband*," she spat the word, "has to say?"

Jeffrey stood and disappeared for a moment. When he returned, he had disposed of his glass and was drinking gin straight from the bottle.

"Jeffrey, for God's sakes," Judith said, standing and prying the bottle from his hands.

"Oh dear," Effie said, suddenly a concerned hostess. "I'm afraid that's the last of the gin. "Doug can go get more if we need it." She thought for a minute. "I have a lovely Bordeaux in the kitchen pantry. I'll just be a minute." She bustled into the kitchen; and Baker could hear her rummaging through kitchen drawers, most likely in search of a corkscrew.

"She's off her rocker with all of this," the sheriff said by way of explanation.

Baker sat straight in his chair, smoking one of Jeffrey's cigarettes. "Mmm."

Ferrebee met his stare. "It's killing her," he said. "She thinks I'm going to offer you money to give up the case tonight."

"Did you tell her you already tried that?"

"What?" Judith asked, her mouth open.

Ferrebee shook his head. "We haven't been talking much lately." His face was haggard and sad. "I wanted you to see her. To see what this is doing to her."

"So," Baker said, studying the cigarette in his hand. "You bought

Jeffrey off in the past. You tried to bribe me yesterday." He let his eyes slide to Ferrebee. "Sounds like this might be a habit for you, Sheriff."

Ferrebee's eyes flashed. "Be careful, Detective. Be very, very careful."

Baker refused to be intimidated. "If Diana Kramer hadn't hired me, she'd have hired someone else."

"I don't think so, Baker. You're the only game in town with a private license. I think she knew that."

Judith looked at Baker, her eyes pleading. "Please, Detective. I've known Effie for a long time. The sheriff is right. This is tearing her apart."

Baker said, "Have you considered what Diana Kramer will do if she doesn't get the letters?"

Ferrebee banged his hand on the table. "She's only still looking because you're still on the case."

Baker banged his own hand on the table. "If I drop the case, she'll still look." He leaned back again, his face hard. "Look, Sheriff. All these people, all the ones you're trying to hide this from, they're wise about Diana Kramer. There is nothing these letters can expose that will hurt you. So Chet messed around. Big deal. Doesn't make him a bad kid." But the hairs on the back of his neck were standing up; and he knew that, as deep as things were, they were about to get deeper.

The sheriff shook his head sadly. "I can't make you understand."

Effie returned, her face sad again. "I forgot what I was doing."

"Wine," Ferrebee muttered.

"Ah." She snapped her fingers and returned to the kitchen.

Baker stood, shaking his head. "I'm sorry, Sheriff. I can't drop this. I think Marian's in danger now. I have to find the letters." He slid his chair in. "I've got to go. I have another appointment."

Effie returned with the bottle of wine and four glasses on a tray. "Are you leaving so soon, Detective?" she said with a hollow smile.

"Yes, ma'am. Thank you for dinner."

Outside Baker fumbled with his keys, resisting the urge to rub snow on the back of his neck.

"Detective," Judith called from the front steps.

He turned and regarded her with cold eyes.

Her own eyes were full of fear and shame. "Detective," she breathed, trotting down to where he stood. "I hate to ask you this, but Jeffrey…he's had too much to drink; and I can't get him up. I don't want to ask the sheriff to help me get him home." She waited, her breath making soft clouds in the night air.

Baker sighed as the damp cold sank into his bones. He wished it would snow already. The air held the expectant charge that comes just before a storm. It was what made animals restless and school children wild. And that's how he felt now. Wild. He looked at the sky and regarded the blackness there. Then he returned to the house and slung Jeffrey over his shoulder. Effie stood in the doorway and watched as Baker and Judith maneuvered Jeffrey into the back of Baker's Chevy.

"Will he be safe back here?" Judith asked.

"He'll be fine," Baker said, climbing into his car. It started on the first try.

"Right," she said. "I'll follow you."

Joey the thug sat at the curb in his coupe and moved out of the way as Judith and Baker backed out of the drive. He pulled in behind Judith as Baker led the way out of the dark neighborhood.

Baker cut through town and drove past his office. Deirdre's lights were still on, as well as his own lights, which meant Edwards was still on the job. He remembered the call from Diana earlier in the day and wondered if Miss Marsh had had any luck with the trace. If he had time after getting rid of Jeffrey, he'd drop by the office before going to Lenny's. And he'd hope that Edwards wouldn't notice the gravy on his tie.

He led Judith down the dirt lane to Marian's driveway, his neck burning as he watched the weak porch light punch a hole in the dark. Something burned in his gut, and he wondered if he were getting sick.

He didn't have time to be sick.

Judith climbed from her car and unlocked the back door to the house. Baker slung Jeffrey over his shoulder, holding his breath as the stench of booze enveloped him. Joey switched his coupe off and gave a wave to Baker but didn't offer to help get Jeffrey into the house.

Baker's movements were strained under Jeffrey's weight as he followed Judith up the narrow stairs to the second floor and into the bedroom with the twin beds. "Which one?" he grunted.

Judith pointed to the one nearest the door.

Baker tossed Jeffrey onto the mattress and stood, arching against the kink in his back. Judith busied herself removing her husband's shoes and loosening his tie. "He doesn't drink this heavily at home," she explained. "It's this place. It does something to him."

"Mmm."

She followed Baker down the steps. "You don't believe me," she said, turning on a light over the sink.

"It doesn't matter what I believe." He stood near the back door, leaning against the wall.

Judith stepped closer to him, her eyes darkening. "What if I say different? What if I say it matters a great deal?"

Baker's eyes were flat. "It doesn't matter what you say, what I believe, what either of us believes." He looked down at the mud on his shoes and realized he actually meant what he was saying. "It doesn't matter."

She stood in front of him now, so near he could feel her warmth. With a gentle hand, she reached out and tilted his face until his eyes met hers. "You've been hurt," she said.

Baker pulled his chin away from her. "I got hit on the head."

She gave him a tolerant smile that made him feel like a teenager. "I'm not talking about that." She reached for him again and traced a long finger along his jaw, beneath the bandage on his cheek.

Baker tried to swallow, but his tongue was thick. "I got cut with a knife."

She looked up at him, her eyes dark in the dim kitchen. "I'm not talking about that either." She drew back and studied him, her head tilted to the side. "Yeah," she said. "You've been hurt. And you want revenge on the world for it."

He pushed her hand away. "So what if I do? What's it to you?" He looked at the clock hanging on the wall. It was 8:30. He needed to get going if he were going to make it to Lenny's on time.

But Judith didn't know that. And even if she did, he doubted she'd care. She moved closer, the soft kitchen light making her hair glow golden. She smelled like honeysuckle. He was trapped against

161

the wall, and she was so close. He could see into the collar of her blouse, mesmerized by the way the skin stretched over her collarbone. What was it about collarbones? He swallowed and searched for his voice. "I have to go," he whispered.

She encircled his neck with her hands and pulled his head down to rest on her shoulder. Baker closed his eyes and breathed her in. She was everything womanly. She was soft and beautiful, and at that moment he wanted to stay just like this forever.

She lifted her head and moved it against his jaw, velvet against sandpaper. One instant he wanted to pull away for fear of hurting her cheek. In the next instant he wanted to crush her to him and kiss her like he knew Jeffrey never could. He was paralyzed. So he stood, suspended in indecision, until she pulled away and laid her hand on his cheek.

"Poor Detective Baker," she said, her eyes dark blue pools. There was no mockery in her voice, only understanding and kindness. "Not all women are bad."

He looked down at his trembling hands. He'd crushed the fedora he'd forgotten he was holding, and now he'd have to explain the tie *and* the hat to Edwards. He dropped the fedora on the floor and grabbed Judith by the arms, spinning her around and pinning her against the wall.

Ignoring the fear that filled her eyes, he said, "Not bad? Is that what you said?" He was a fraction of an inch from her face, his eyes filled with all the rage he'd kept a lid on for the last year. "If you're not bad, then explain to me how it is that you can turn me into a man who wants to bed a married woman? How is it you can turn me into what I hate the most? How is it that your husband can be asleep upstairs, and all I can think about is you and your touch?" There was a knife in his gut. A twisting, burning knife. Something was wrong.

He staggered away from Judith and retched painfully in the sink. Pain tore through his belly and dryness assaulted his mouth, making speech almost impossible. He retched again. When he was done, he turned on the tap and drank greedily with cupped hands.

When he stood again, Judith was still leaning against the wall by the door, her eyes full of fear. She took a step toward him. Then another. "Are you all right?" she asked.

Baker watched her, his breathing labored, the air heavy with the accusations he'd just made.

"Baker. Are you all right?" She was filled with golden light. It radiated from her, burning his eyes and stealing his breath.

"Don't come any closer," he begged. But he didn't mean it and she knew that.

He doubled over in pain, crying aloud as it peaked. She rushed to him, closing the distance in two dainty steps. "Something is wrong," she said. "You're ill." She reached down and helped him to stand.

He rose on weak legs, able to hold himself upright for a moment before he collapsed into her. She caught him, struggling under his weight. And suddenly her mouth was on his. He tried feebly to push her away, but his arms were made of lead and she was warm and soft.

He let her push him to the floor, moaning as she settled over him. But whether the sound he made was from the feel of her on him or from the intensity of the pain in his belly, he couldn't say.

She fumbled for his tie, working it from its knot with skilled fingers that left trails of smoldering flesh in their wake. Her hands were hot against his chest as she worked his shirt buttons loose. Baker lay on the floor and waited to die. Every breath was agony.

Summoning all his strength, he pushed Judith aside and rolled to his hands and knees. He used a kitchen chair to pull himself up and stood, breathing heavily, fighting to stay upright.

Judith got to her feet, her face flushed, her hair tumbling in a golden tangle over her shoulders. "I'm sorry," she said, lowering her eyes. "I just..."

Baker staggered to the sink and retched again. "See to your husband," he said, wiping his mouth on his sleeve. "He's had too much to drink."

He moved to the door. Judith reached out and touched him, the sleeve of her jacket sliding up her arm as she did. A clean bandage was fastened there securely...as if she'd been recently cut.

She watched Baker notice the bandage and hastened to pull the sleeve down. Baker shook his head. "I see," he said. "And did you find what you were looking for in my office, Mrs. Drake?"

She backed away. "No," she said. As Baker pulled the door open and stepped out into the night, she called after him, "Will you be all right?"

"I have no idea," he said, staggering into the blinding snow that had finally started to fall.

Chapter 17

Baker's heart pounded as he tumbled into the front seat of the Chevy. Joey watched with flat eyes, the window of his shiny coupe wide open. He blew smoke into the night air where it mixed with the snow in an angry fog before disappearing. Baker ignored him and concentrated on fighting the pain in his gut. The Chevy wasn't keen on starting, so Baker punched it in the dash a few times. He backed down the lane and careened out onto the road, moaning aloud as he was gripped by another pain. And the thirst that began in the widow's kitchen ignited his throat like a sparkler.

He was desperate for a cigarette and drove by the office again, thinking about stopping; but the windows were dark, and he was close to being late. He moved on. Joey stayed close on his tail, and Baker was disgusted that the man's presence made him feel somehow safer. Maybe the goon would give him a smoke. Christ, how he needed a smoke.

His gut clenched again, and he swerved to the side of the road. He climbed out, stood in the headlights and threw up in the dirty snow. Joey pulled the coupe up close to the Chevy but didn't get out. Baker wiped his mouth with his sleeve and made his way into the ditch. There he scooped up a handful of clean snow and packed it into his mouth to ease the thirst.

He'd been poisoned. He was sure of it.

At that moment he considered skipping the meeting at the bar. He was reasonably sure he was going to be jumped and left in the alley for the cats to eat anyway. But there was always the chance he'd get something useful from Bertie Sims or Jeremy Watts. And after the meeting, if he survived, he'd get to a doctor…and try to sort out where he'd gotten a belly full of poison.

As Baker made his way across town, clutching his gut, the already heavy snowfall got even heavier. The clouds ripped open, spilling the snow they carried in a fury that covered the ground in minutes and showed no sign of letting up for a long time to come.

Even in the blizzard, Lenny's Pub was easy to find. There were enough neon signs in the front window to light up a New York City block. Lenny had chosen an out-of-the-way place to sell his booze.

The narrow bar was wedged between a bail bondsman on one side and a pawnshop on the other. Dames in low-cut numbers lingered out front, a couple with feathered hats on. The feathers drooped in the snow, and Baker imagined Deirdre would be insulted on behalf of the hats if she were here.

He parked a block away and stepped into the night air, wiping the sweat from his face with his dirty tie. His gut was turning him inside out. He bent down and scooped up another handful of snow, praying it would cool the fire in his belly and take the edge off his thirst. Joey stopped his coupe a block down from Baker and made no sign of getting out of his car.

Blues music drifted out of the bar into the street, growing louder as Baker reached the door. "Hey, fella," a woman said as he passed. When Baker ignored her, she called after him, "Up yours."

A tough in a dark coat stood to the right of the door. He scrutinized Baker with a frown. "I'm expected," Baker said and flashed his ID.

The tough nodded, satisfied, and allowed Baker to pass. The bar was dim and smoke-filled; and, despite the pain he was in, Baker's mouth watered with the thought of cold bourbon and a long smoke. A long saloon-style bar lined the back wall; and Baker approached with guarded steps, careful not to jar his gut too much as he walked. Barstools had been bolted to the floor in front of the bar, and Baker climbed onto one near the back hall he figured led to the alley. A squinty man in a dirty apron stood behind the bar drying glasses with a dirty towel, his fleshy lips clamped tight over a soggy cigar.

"What'll it be?" he said as Baker sat down.

As much as Baker wanted a bourbon, he wasn't sure his belly could take it, so he shook his head.

"Drink or leave," the man said around his cigar.

"Bourbon."

The bartender poured out a drink and slid it to Baker with a nod. "There you are."

"Pack of smokes."

"Brand?"

"Lucky Strikes."

If the bartender noticed the sweat dripping from Baker's face onto his collar, he didn't let on. He slid the cigarettes and a pack of matches to Baker, who nodded his thanks and scanned the room. There were four other customers in the bar, none of them familiar. The bartender gave him a pointed look, so he tossed his drink back and signaled for another.

A waitress in a tight blouse took the stool next to his. "You're a tall one, aren't you?" She let a long, red fingernail trace the back of his hand.

"Taller than some," Baker said, cringing at her touch and pulling his hand away.

"You the detective?" she asked as the bartender set a fresh glass of bourbon on the counter.

Baker froze with the drink halfway to his lips. "I am," he said with his husky voice. He tossed the drink back, feeling a little dizzy, the fire in his gut dying a little.

The waitress slid from the stool. She and the bartender nodded at one another. "Follow me," she said. "They're out back."

Baker rolled his eyes. *Here we go*, he thought, loosening his tie. He said nothing but followed the waitress, feeling tired and cold and dizzy. He wasn't in the mood for this. He wondered if they'd answer questions first or skip to the part where they beat him up and left him for dead.

Halfway to the door, his steps faltered. He paused and stared at his feet, trying to get his bearings, then looked up. The waitress liquefied, smearing before him and shifting in and out of focus. Baker leaned against the wall to keep from falling.

"They're just through here," she said, her voice smearing like the rest of her. She tugged on his arm. "Almost there."

But Baker knew this was wrong. His legs wouldn't work the way they were supposed to. He wanted to stay against the wall. But she was pulling him, moving farther down the dim hallway. And his legs, his faithful legs, were obeying her. He pulled his arm away and said, "Wait a minute," but it didn't come out right. Actually it sounded like a lot of grunting. He knew he'd been drugged.

A Goddamned Mickey Finn.

Determined to make his legs obey him and not the waitress, he pulled his arm as hard as he could. He was free. The waitress toppled back against the wall; and he fell sideways, striking his head as he hit the floor. This was all wrong. He was on the floor and that was not the place to be. The fire inside him flared up again. He curled up into a fetal position and moaned, certain he was being ripped apart. But the waitress was there again, pulling him to his feet. Her face smeared and melted, only to reform, then smear and melt again. He tried to lift a hand to touch her, but his arms were too heavy. She was searching him, sliding her hands into his pockets. He felt her take his keys.

"Hey," he said. But it didn't sound right, and she wasn't listening.

"Here you go," she mumbled, opening the back door and shoving him into the alley. "Right out here."

There was the slight pressure of her palm as she pushed him out the door, followed by the metallic click as she closed it and threw the lock. And then he was alone.

A spasm of pain seared through him; and he doubled over, feeling heavier than he'd ever felt in his life. His body was made of lead; and he knew that if he stood still long enough, he would sink through the earth. But that wasn't possible, was it?

He laughed as it occurred to him that he'd been poisoned and drugged in the same night and wondered if he would live through it. Then he wondered if he cared whether or not he lived. His mother still needed him. And he hadn't made that will. He didn't want to end up scattered in the cow pasture like Stewie. He didn't want animals stepping on him and shitting on him and licking up bits of him with their grass. It was settled. He did not want to die. Not until he made a new will.

He tried to lift his arms. He would put up a fight if he could just lift them. But they were made from cast iron, and he couldn't get them above his waist. A set of headlights as the end of the alley switched on, blinding him. "Hey," he said, unable to shield his eyes.

Baker watched snow dance in the headlights and knew he was about to be run over. When the car began to move, slowly at first and then faster, he tilted his head to the side, fascinated by the way the shadows of the garbage shifted on the alley's wall as the lights floated closer. He should probably make a list about the poison and the drugs and the being run over come morning. If he survived.

He could show the list to Edwards.

Something struck him on the back of the head. Baker fell to the ground, dazed.

"Christ," a voice said. "He looks like hell."

Baker opened his eyes. There were feet here on the ground. Feet stuffed inside men's shoes. He reached out with a heavy arm and grabbed an ankle. As the foot stuffed inside the shoe attached to the ankle tried to pull away, Baker gave it a good tug. Bertie Sims collapsed on the ground beside him.

Another foot kicked him in the right side, but Baker didn't feel it. He couldn't feel much of anything right then, except a dark burn in his stomach like he'd swallowed a lit match. He grabbed the ankle attached to the kicking foot and pulled. Another man fell on top of him.

In the darkness Baker couldn't make out the face, but he managed to lift his weighted arms and punched at it with his heavy fists, satisfied when the flesh grew slick with blood.

A third man climbed from the car, a black shadow in front of the headlights. "That's enough," he said. "We can't talk here. Put him in the trunk."

Bertie Sims pulled Baker to his feet, and the second man punched him in the stomach a few times. Baker was allowed to fall to the ground again, where he lay in a heap, trying to breathe, praying for death.

"'That's enough,' I said," the third man warned.

Bertie and the second man, most likely Jeremy Watts, picked Baker up and tossed him in the trunk. Baker looked out into the cold night, felt the snow as it fell onto his face. "Once for luck," Bertie Sims said as he punched Baker in the face and closed the lid.

Darkness pressed in on Baker from all sides, and he struggled under the weight of it. His face ached. His head swam. He felt himself drifting into unconsciousness and fought to think...to pay attention to where he was going. But his gut was on fire...and there was such a thirst now. He knew he was dying. His last conscious thought was of Edwards. He hoped the Brit would look for him.

Someone dropped a safe on his head. Baker was sure of it. And maybe they'd put a knife in his gut. He was on fire. And his mouth had turned to sand. He felt like ashes...like the husk of someone burned at the stake.

"He's awake," Bertie said; but his voice was miles away.

169

Baker tried to sit up; but the world spilled, tipping him out the side. Bertie Sims grasped his shoulders and pulled him to a sitting position. Baker registered gray carpet, dirty walls, soiled bed. And he groaned as he realized they were in the Road King Motel.

"Drink this," another man said, shoving a glass of water into Baker's hands.

Baker gulped it greedily. "More," he said when he'd finished it.

The glass was refilled and he sipped it, doubling over in pain after he'd taken a swallow.

"Well, Detective Baker, you've given my boys quite an overhaul."

Baker looked up and blinked through the sweat dripping in his eyes. "Deputy Wally Sims," he said, his voice like dry leaves. "I wondered when I'd run into you."

Wally stared at him with blank eyes. He nodded to the glass in Baker's hands. "Need more?"

Baker shook his head. "You've aged since high school."

Wally was grim. "The sheriff mentioned you've been reading the yearbook."

Baker handed the glass to Bertie and rubbed his neck. "Why the rough stuff, Wally? Why not just arrest me? Afraid to get your uniform dirty?"

"I'm not afraid of anything."

"Then why the rough stuff?"

"Want me to kill him?" An ugly thick-necked fellow sat across the room with a bag of ice to his broken nose.

Baker grinned. "You must be Watts."

Watts looked at the deputy. "Let me kill him."

"Take it easy," Wally said. "He's just here to talk. Aren't you, Detective?"

"Seems like you're the one with all the answers, Wally."

Wally frowned. "It's like this, Baker. We want you to leave the Drake case alone. We'll even pay you to drop it."

Unbelievable. "How much?"

Wally looked at his brother. "Bert, get Artie in here. Tell him Baker's awake."

Bertie left and returned a moment later with Artie Pfeiffer. Artie carried a briefcase, which he set on the foot of the bed. He mopped his face with a greasy handkerchief as his eyes darted from Baker to the deputy and back again. "I don't like this, Wally. He looks pretty beat up. You said there wouldn't be any more of that. That's what you said."

Wally didn't move. "Shut the fuck up, Artie," he said. "Open the case."

Artie flinched but did as he was told.

The case was filled with cash. Artie mopped his face and stepped back. "Five thousand," he said. "You can count it if you want."

Wally stood and shoved him out of the way. "Enough, Artie." He turned and looked at Baker. "The detective trusts us, don't you?" He nodded toward the case. "Go ahead. It's all yours if you'll stop poking around for those letters."

Baker's jaw clenched. The burn in his gut was changing to nausea, and he looked around for a trash can. He pointed to it, and Bertie managed to get it under him just in time. Baker was noisily sick. When he was done, he lay back on the dirty pillow. Sweat poured from him; and the other men in the room looked at each other nervously, no doubt wondering if the Mickey Finn had been too strong. After a minute, Baker managed, "Suppose I don't want to drop the case?"

Wally smiled. "Should that be your decision, I will leave; and my friends here will rough you up so bad your own mother wouldn't recognize you. Plus, me and my boys get to keep our money."

"Let me at him," Jeremy Watts cracked his knuckles.

"It's like this," Baker began, interrupted by a pounding at the door.

"Oh my God," Artie croaked, a cold sweat breaking out on his forehead.

"Quiet," Wally hissed. "Bert, see who it is."

Bertie opened the door a crack, peered outside and said, "What do you want?"

Bertie was tossed backward as the door flew open, and Baker nearly laughed out loud as Edwards and Deirdre stumbled in. "So sorry to trouble you," Edwards slurred as he swayed drunkenly. "My date and I...."

Deirdre smiled stupidly, her small frame drowning inside an enormous fur coat. "Hello," she said with Jersey in her voice.

Edwards held her up. "My date and I were just over at the pub across the way." He gestured to a bar across the road. "No ale but a fine beer."

Deirdre giggled, leaning into him. "Very fine, I'm sure."

Baker kept his eyes flat. The pain in his belly surged, and he doubled over in pain. Deirdre jerked and made a move toward him, catching herself at the last minute and pretending to list to the side. Edwards swept her back and held her close to him. "Easy, love," he said.

She giggled, but it was forced. Baker lay down on the bed and waited to die. The poison was eating him alive, and he wondered if he would make it out of here.

Wally and Bert exchanged looks.

Edwards cleared his throat. "We were just readying ourselves to go home and discovered my tire is flattened."

"Flat as a pancake," Deirdre said, gesturing wildly with her arms, disappearing inside the fur for a minute.

Edwards bolstered her up a bit more in his arms. "As you can see," he said, "the lady is in no condition to walk; and it is so very far to Crane Haven."

"Call a cab," Jeremy said.

Deirdre's laugh was shrill.

Edwards smiled tolerantly. "When I first came to this country, I was told whenever I got into trouble to look for an officer of the law." He nodded at Wally and listed to the side. "I thought the deputy here would be good enough to give us a ride."

Deirdre let her eyes wander around the room. She let her gaze land on Baker and pretended to see him for the first time. Artificial recognition lit her features. "Detective," she exclaimed, pulling on Edwards' arm. "Eddie, look who it is. It's your boss. Ain't that a coincidence?"

Edwards managed to look shocked. "Sir. What a surprise. Have you been invited to the party too?" He assessed Baker's pale face, the state of the suit, the gravy on the tie. His silent rage was obvious only to those who knew him. Baker recognized it, and Deirdre edged away just the tiniest bit. The rest in the room were oblivious to their danger. "What happened to you, sir? You look terrible." His voice was dangerously calm.

Baker shrugged. "Car accident."

"My, but you do get in a lot of those," Edwards said. He looked menacingly at the men in the room, forgetting to be drunk. "Is that why these nice men are helping you?"

Deirdre said, "They look like they was in an accident too, don't they, Eddie?"

Edwards' eyes narrowed. "They do at that, dear." He let his eyes shift to Wally. "My good man," he said, all drunken charm again, "how about that ride? Always trust an officer of the law. That's what they say."

Wally stood, his body rigid. "Of course I'll take you to town," he said. He looked at the men in the room. "I'll be back."

Deirdre said, "Detective, there's a party in town at the Palms. I insist you come have a drink with me and Eddie." She crossed to him, pretending to examine his injuries. When he looked at her, she gave him a wink. "I won't take 'no' for an answer," she announced.

To seal the deal, Edwards crossed the room and lifted Baker to his feet. "You heard the lady, my good man. She insists."

"Come on," Wally said as he walked out.

Deirdre and Edwards followed, dragging Baker along.

Baker ignored the dizziness from the drug. He ignored the burning in his gut. He pulled away from Edwards; and, with eyes like steel, he crossed to the table holding the briefcase of money. He closed the lid and picked it up. Watts took a menacing step toward him but backed off when he saw Edwards looming in the doorway.

Edwards took the case from Baker; and, together with Deirdre, the two supported the detective on the way out to Wally's car. There they helped him into the back seat. As the car pulled away from The Road King Motel, Baker closed his eyes and prayed for the pain to end.

Chapter 18

A darkened room, a pressed tin ceiling, a red-hot poker in his gut. Baker was still alive, and he climbed into consciousness with reluctance.

He didn't recognize the ceiling above him, which led him to realize he was not in his office.

As if reading his mind, a voice answered him, "You're at my place." It was Deirdre.

Baker pushed himself up with brittle arms. His voice was weak. "Was it arsenic?"

She stood in front of the window, wrapped in a silk robe. Her dark hair was pinned loosely at her neck, and she held a cup of steaming coffee in her hands. "Yes. Dr. Phillips was here. He gave you thio...something or other."

"Thiomercapitrol," Baker supplied.

"That's it," she said. "You have a lot of experience with arsenic poisoning?"

He shrugged. "Some." He pushed back the covers and noticed he was wearing only his boxers.

Deirdre held up a hand when he cast a look in her direction. "Edwards undressed you this time. I had nothing to do with it."

He tried to stand but was too weak. "What time is it?"

"Four in the morning." She set her coffee down and moved to his side. "Dr. Phillips said you should rest as much as possible for the next day or two."

Baker spied his pants lying over a chair beside the bed. He reached for them. "I've got five thousand dollars in bribe money I need to unload. And I've got letters to find."

Deirdre blew out a breath. "Edwards said you'd be like this. He left you a fresh shirt and jacket. I'll go get them."

Baker remained seated on the bed, his head cradled in his hands. This night was far from over. She brought the jacket and a cup of hot tea. "I wasn't sure you could stomach coffee yet," she explained.

He took a sip and retched, handing the cup back to her. "Guess I'm not ready for anything just yet," he said.

Worry creased her brow as she took the cup. The robe parted a little as she moved, and he caught a glimpse of the side of her breast. She saw him look and closed her robe. "You really should rest," she said, moving away from him.

"Where's Edwards?"

"With Rosemary Marsh at the telephone office. They're going over long-distance calls."

"Why?"

"All the calls from Diana Kramer have been coming from the sanitarium. Edwards wanted to see if any long-distance calls were going out of the asylum to the same number on a regular basis. He was thinking maybe she had an accomplice or something."

"Mmm."

"He said he'd be back soon."

"I don't have time to wait." Baker stood and, with sluggish movements, put on the jacket. "Are you sure he said the calls came from the asylum?"

She nodded.

Baker moved to her. "Thank you for your help tonight. For everything." He put his hands on her shoulders. "You make a hell of a drunk."

"That's a compliment coming from you," she said, and there was no malice in her eyes. Just a smile.

Baker smiled back. And this time it didn't make him angry.

There was a knock on the apartment door, and Deirdre smiled at him once more before moving into the living room to answer it. Baker followed.

"Edwards," he said, relieved to see the big Brit filling the doorway.

"Barone's man is downstairs in your office asleep."

"You mean Joey?"

Edwards nodded. "I found him sleeping in his car outside Lenny's bar when I went to retrieve your Chevy. Said he'd dozed off waiting for you to come out again."

"Some tail he's turned out to be."

Edwards reached into the hallway and tugged a tiny blonde woman with enormous brown eyes into the room. "May I present Miss Rosemary Marsh."

Rosemary Marsh was around five-feet two-inches tall, which put her at the level of Edwards' chest. Baker guessed she weighed around a hundred pounds and smiled at Edwards' description of her as robust and vigorous.

"Pleased to meet you," Baker said.

Deirdre cleared her throat. "I'm pleased to meet you too, Miss Marsh. I'm Deirdre."

"I bought a dress from your store once," Rosemary said, shaking Deirdre's hand.

"I hope it served you well."

"It did."

Deirdre smiled. "Why don't we all sit down for some tea?"

Baker was impatient to get rid of the bribe money, but he also needed to talk to Edwards. And he felt weak. Plus, he couldn't stop thinking of Deirdre in her robe...or how soft her bed was.

Miss Marsh smiled her thanks when Deirdre poured her a cup of tea. Baker declined, but Deirdre poured a cup for him anyway.

Baker said, "Glad you found me last night, Edwards," knowing that was the only thanks the Brit would accept. Edwards nodded, and Baker noticed his knuckles were bruised and scraped.

"I convinced Miss Deirdre to help me follow you to Lenny's, sir. Just in case."

Rosemary sat stone still with the teacup halfway to her lips. Edwards continued his explanation, his own cup like a child's toy in his enormous hand. "When you didn't emerge after a considerable length of time, I decided to have a look inside."

"He made me wait in the car," Deirdre said, oblivious to the look of ice Rosemary tossed in her direction.

Edwards cleared his throat. "I asked the barkeep what had become of you, and he claimed he couldn't recall you ever having been there." He paused and sipped his tea. When he spoke again, a frown darkened his face. "And then I noticed your car keys on the bar."

"So he talked," Baker said, wanting to hurry this up so he could get going.

"No, sir. His jaw was very tight. I had to extract a couple of teeth in order to loosen his tongue."

Rosemary gasped. "Walter Edwards," she said, "you are so brave."

Edwards' cheeks turned a pale pink color, and he cleared his throat. "Yes, well, we found you, sir. All's well that ends well. Now, if you don't mind, I'd like you to explain this business about the briefcase."

Baker dared to take a sip of tea. His gut lurched, but only slightly. "They wanted me to stop looking for the letters, same as everyone else."

Deirdre frowned. "They don't think you killed Chet or anything crazy like that, do they?"

"No. Nothing like that. They say they don't want his reputation ruined."

Rosemary snorted. "You don't buy that, do you?"

Baker regarded her for a moment. "No, actually I don't." He scratched his chin. "But I find it interesting that Bertie, Wally and Jeremy all want me to stop looking; but David Holden said he'd talk to me."

"But he hasn't talked to you," Edwards said. "You're right. Maybe I'll go see him tomorrow and remind him that we need to meet."

"I wonder why he's been so helpful," Deirdre said. "He's in the photo too. I thought Marian hated all of them."

"What photo?" Rosemary asked.

"Maybe David was involved in tonight's little escapade too," Edwards said. "And you just didn't see him."

Deirdre snorted. "David Holden would never be involved in the drugging and kidnapping of a detective."

"What photo?" Rosemary asked again.

But Baker and Edwards weren't listening. They were staring at Deirdre with their mouths open.

"What?" she said. "We had a date once. Not that it's any of your business." She folded her hands on top of the table. "He makes a very fine chocolate milkshake. He would never abduct a man and hold him hostage in a dirty motel room."

"Someone tell me what photo," Rosemary pounded the table with her tiny fist.

Edwards smiled tolerantly. "I'll explain it all later," he said.

She pouted for a moment, then smiled back. "Yes, you will," she said.

Baker said, "I think you're wrong, Deirdre."

"About what?"

"About David Holden. He is involved. They're all involved." When she started to protest, he held up a hand. "Maybe not in the kidnapping or the bribery, but he's definitely part of the big picture."

"Picture of what?" Rosemary asked.

Deirdre's eyes were wide with fright. "A picture of something that happened a long time ago."

"During a winter they all want to forget," Baker said, frowning. He turned to Rosemary. "And these calls, Miss Marsh? You're sure they're coming from the sanitarium?"

She nodded, her eyes wide.

"Right," Baker said, standing. "I'm going to the city to get rid of this cash. I'll be back later this morning."

By 5:30 a.m. Baker reached the city limits. He'd lit two cigarettes during the drive but tossed each out the window when his gut rebelled. He stopped at the first diner he came to and went in to use the pay phone. The phone was old, one with a speaking tube and an earpiece. It was covered in greasy fingerprints. He dialed information, got the number he wanted and braced himself for the sound of her voice.

"Hello?" Ginger's voice was sleepy and warm. He wondered if she still wore the blue nightgown.

"Ginger," he said.

Silence settled on the line. He knew she was sitting up in bed, reaching over to turn on the bedside lamp. He knew the lamp would be the one that once sat in the bedroom they shared. She'd never get new lamps on a cop's salary.

"Ham?" she breathed. "Ham, is that you?"

"I need to talk to Lewis. Put him on."

"Ham, I'm so sorry about Stewie. I've written to your mother. I…"

"Put Lewis on, Ginger."

There was a muffled exchange of words, both confused and surprised, between the couple. Why had he called? What did he want at this hour?

"Baker," Lewis' voice was guarded.

"I need to meet you. Now."

There was silence for a moment. "Forgive my lack of enthusiasm, Baker. It's 5:30 in the morning."

Baker's jaw tightened. "I've got a case full of money a few locals tried to bribe me with. I want to turn it over to you."

There was another long pause and the sound of Lewis' nifty Zippo lighter snapping open. Baker heard him take a drag and blow the smoke out before speaking again. "Why not the sheriff?"

"Because one of his guys was the ring leader."

"Christ. Where are you?"

"I'm just inside the city limits. I'm at a diner called The Locomotive. You know it?"

"All night diner on Ponderosa and L."

"Yeah. That's it. Get here as soon as you can. I'll be waiting at a table in the back."

Lewis' uncombed hair stood like a blonde Brill-o pad, and the hair in his usually impeccable mustache lay at angry angles.

"You look like hell," Baker said.

Lewis looked Baker over. "I'm guessing I look better than you. Why am I out of bed?"

Baker set the case of money on the table.

Lewis inspected the contents and gave a low whistle. "Wow. You said one of Ferrebee's guys was in on it?"

Baker nodded. "Wally Sims."

Lewis sat back in his chair. "Who else?"

"Bertie Sims, Artie Pfeiffer and Jeremy Watts."

"This about those love letters?"

Baker nodded.

"You going to drop it now?"

Baker stood. "No. Not now. Something's not right about all this."

Lewis nodded at the money. "Why you turning this over to me and not some other guy on the force?"

"You're a cop, aren't you?"

Lewis was suspicious. "There's lots of cops around."

Baker smiled. It didn't reach his eyes. "Yeah. But not all of them are working this case. Besides, Wally and his friends are going to

179

come looking for it. They'll likely rip whoever's got it to shreds." He looked Lewis in the eye. "No one deserves that more than you."

"Right," Lewis said, his eyes flat.

"Detective Lewis," a waitress said, approaching the table. "Your wife is on the phone. She says it's an emergency."

Lewis smiled. "She can't stand to be without me."

Baker frowned. He was done here. No reason to hang around and watch Lewis' face as he listened to her low voice over the wire. Baker watched anyway. And in the end, he was glad of it because whatever Ginger said was bad. Lewis blew out a breath and raked a hand through his wild hair. He slammed the receiver down and returned to the table. "I'll take care of this," he said as he picked up the case. And then he was gone.

Baker followed from the parking lot, careful to keep his distance. Lewis was heading to Crane Haven, sirens off, lights flashing. A knife of fear stabbed through Baker's heart as he thought of Diana Kramer. And Marian Drake. Suspicion had sprouted inside him, and he could feel it taking root as he drove through the dawn.

Sunlight pierced the horizon, spilling its light over the snow, reflecting orange light into flat fields. Baker shielded his eyes from the glare, thankful the roads had been cleared. Lewis pulled into a slot in front of The Diner. Baker pulled in right behind him.

A bad feeling hung in the air. Ferrebee leaned against the hood of his car but moved forward to shake hands with Lewis as he approached. Baker stepped from the Chevy and made his way through the early morning crowd of onlookers, hoping to peek in the windows. Wally Sims stepped from the shadows and put a restraining hand on Baker's chest. "What are you doing here?" he asked.

Baker slid his eyes to the sheriff and Lewis, who were deep in conversation several feet away. "I have an appointment with David Holden. He around?"

Wally's eyes narrowed, his hand resting on the butt of his gun. "He's dead. Somebody shot him."

Baker's gut tightened, and he hid his surprise by scratching his chin. "Mmm. You do it yourself this time, or did you get one of your goons to do it for you?"

Wally lunged forward, but Lewis was there to hold him back.

"Take it easy, Deputy," he said to Wally. But his eyes were on Baker. "So you followed me. I might have guessed."

"You might have."

Lewis lit a cigarette. "Maybe you can shed some light on this for us, Baker."

"Sorry. I don't even know what 'this' is." He thought about David Holden, the one man who had helped him. And the second man from the photo to die.

"Suppose you and I have a talk tomorrow," Lewis said.

Baker turned on his heel and walked back to his car, ignoring the heated stare Wally gave him. "Can't, Lewis," he called over his shoulder. "I have things to do."

Baker climbed into his car. Nausea bubbled up inside him, and he knew it was no longer due to the poison. This time it had everything to do with guilt and rage and the knowledge that there was a lot more going on here than what was in a handful of love letters.

Chapter 19

At 7 a.m. Baker sat at his desk and sipped the weak coffee he'd made, careful to hold it in his mouth for a moment as a silent warning to his gut that something was coming down. He retched anyway, but at least the coffee didn't come back up. It was arsenic he'd been given. And he knew where he'd gotten it. He also knew he wasn't the intended victim, just an accidental casualty. But he didn't know who had done it. Or why.

Baker fingered Wally as the ringleader for what went down last night at the motel, but Wally wasn't the murdering kind. His blood ran hot, not cold.

It was hot blood that drove a man's passion. And it took passion to kill a man on impulse. Baker could accept one murder as passion-driven. Maybe Chet was going to go public with whatever was in the letters, and Wally felt he couldn't let that happen.

Maybe. Baker remembered the report about Chet's body. It was passion that tied the noose around his neck…passion that choked the life from him.

But passion couldn't have driven Wally to commit a second murder. A second murder would require planning…the decision to kill. Baker didn't figure Wally to be a calculating man, capable of planning a murder. He was probably capable of offing someone impulsively. Probably.

No. Two bodies indicated a killer with cold blood.

Unless there was more than one killer.

Baker chewed on that thought for a minute. Two crimes. Could there be two killers?

Suddenly he felt very tired. Edwards would be in soon, provided he hadn't overslept. They had, after all, had a very long night.

He leaned back in his chair and let his mind wander. A pounding at the outer door interrupted his thoughts. "Come in."

The sound of the door leading into Edwards' office as it flew open and struck the wall was loud enough to shake the coffee mug on Baker's desk. Then there was silence.

Baker wondered if Barone had become impatient about the case of his missing sister and had finally decided to send some muscle to get Baker to work faster. Baker drew his gun and sat, waiting.

He saw the silhouette on the other side of the glass before his door creaked opened. Wally Sims leaned against the doorjamb. "Baker," he said, his voice weak. Then he fell forward onto the floor, blood leaking from a hole in his middle.

Baker made it to him in two strides and knelt to press a hand to the wound.

"Call the doctor," Wally whispered. "And lock the door."

"Let me try to stop the bleeding," Baker said.

But Wally grabbed his arm. "Call the doctor. They can't kill me if the doctor is here."

Baker's neck tingled. He made the call. "There's an ambulance on the way."

Wally seemed to relax. A little. Baker pressed a towel to the hole and listened to Wally's raspy breathing. What the hell happened?

"You're going about this all wrong," Wally said, gritting his teeth against the pain Baker knew he must feel.

"Who shot you?" Baker asked. But Wally just shook his head.

There was a ruckus from Edwards' office, and Wally looked at Baker with wide eyes. "You didn't lock the door, did you?" And the way he said it was not a question.

Ferrebee and Lewis charged in, looking from Wally on the floor to Baker with the towel pressed to the deputy's belly. "Which way did he go, Wally?" Ferrebee asked, his gun drawn. He and Lewis were moving toward the door again. "We followed your blood here. Did you see which way he ran?"

Wally's smile was weak as he shook his head a second time. He and Ferrebee regarded one another for a long moment. Then Wally said, "Didn't see a thing. He got away clean."

Baker thought he saw a look of relief cross the sheriff's face.

A siren cut through the quiet morning; and, as paramedics poured into the office, Baker stood back and watched. Wally reached for him as he was wheeled past on a stretcher. "Baker," he said and Baker leaned forward to hear. "Stop asking *who* she is. Ask yourself *why* she is."

Baker stepped back and rubbed his chin. Three more deputies pushed their way into the office and stood staring at the pool of blood Wally Sims had left on the floor. Lewis looked too, his jacket parted by hands that rested on his hips. His gun was visible, and Baker supposed that was the point.

Ferrebee hitched up his pants and murmured something to Lewis, who nodded. Then Sheriff Ferrebee shifted his red-rimmed eyes to Baker. And Baker took a step back.

Gone was the broken man with a dead son. Gone was the jolly sheriff with a ready laugh. Ferrebee was full-fledged one hundred percent pissed-off lawman now. And he wanted answers. "What did Wally say to you?" he asked now.

Baker knew he needed to be careful. Something in the back of his mind was whispering to him, but he couldn't yet hear what it was.

He thought of dinner at Ferrebee's house with Jeffrey sitting beside him at the table.

"You paid me off."

"You let me."

Ferrebee's eyes were boring into Baker. "Answer me, Detective. Did Wally add anything to his statement?"

Baker scratched the bandage on his cheek. "I wasn't aware he'd made a formal statement while he was here, Sheriff."

Lewis snorted. "Cut the bullshit, Baker. Who shot him?"

"You tell me."

"We'll be glad to take you into custody," Ferrebee said.

Baker sighed. "He didn't say anything. Look, I need to get to the asylum to check on Marian. I'm concerned about this Diana Kramer woman bothering her. I'll stop by your office later, Sheriff. I promise."

Ferrebee was grim, but he nodded and waved Baker on his way.

Baker pushed through the assembly of brown uniforms huddled in Edwards' office, amused at the thought of Edwards' annoyance when he found his office stuffed with deputies.

Leadfoot Barone rested against the bumper of his white Packard as Baker stepped out onto the sidewalk. Baker ignored him and climbed into the Chevy, pointing it in the direction of the sanitarium once he got it started. Barone was driving himself this morning and pulled in behind Baker.

Deep tire tracks cut through the mud and snow-packed road to the sanitarium. Baker noted with some satisfaction that Barone's

Packard had difficulty maneuvering up the steep hill. The big car slid dangerously close to the edge of the road twice. And Baker found himself wondering if he'd get out to help the gangster if his car turned over on the road.

Clouds were darkening the sky again, and Baker felt the fatigue of the last day catching up with him. He also felt a pang of hunger and figured that was a good sign.

He pulled into the lot and Barone pulled in next to him.

"I want to talk to you, Baker," the man said.

"I'll find your sister, Barone. Really, I will. But this case…"

Barone held a jar filled with amber liquid out to Baker. "I got this in my mailbox yesterday."

Baker took the jar and swirled the contents around. A preserved frog floated in the murky liquid. "It's a frog."

"No shit, it's a frog," Barone said. "Look closer. It's got four fucking eyes."

Baker looked closer. "Mmm."

"It's from my sister."

Baker handed the jar back. "Good. So you found her."

Barone handed him an envelope. "Hell no, I didn't find her. I don't know where the hell she is. The jar was shoved in my mailbox. It wasn't actually mailed to me."

"Mmm."

"Mmm," Barone mimicked. "Don't give me that. What the fuck are you going to do about it?"

"Where's Joey?" Baker asked. "He was a much quieter tail than you are."

"He's at his mother's. You wore him out."

Baker took the jar again and swirled it around. "Any letter or note with this? How do you know it was from your sister?"

Barone handed him an envelope. Baker pulled out the slip of paper inside.

"Larry, Keep this in case anything happens to me. I'll explain when I can."

"You're sure it's from her?"

"Hell yes, I'm sure. I want you to find her."

"Fine. I'll get right on it. Let me finish what I came here to do."

Baker handed the jar back to Barone, who said, "Fine. But I'm

185

coming with you."

"Suit yourself."

Barone's gasp as he caught the first whiff of the smell of the sanitarium carried through the foyer, causing Enid to look up from her papers as the men entered the building. "Dear God," Barone said.

"Who is that?" Enid asked, pointing at the gangster with her eyebrows raised.

Barone smiled. "Someone who wishes he could take you away from all this."

Enid ignored him and glared at Baker. "Well?"

Baker shrugged and signed the guest register. Barone was content to lean against the desk and gaze at Enid's masked face. Baker let them talk and made his way to the parlor. Marian was not inside. Baker returned to the foyer. "Where's Marian?" he asked.

Enid was in the process of prying her hand from Barone's grip. "Her brother has gone missing," she said. "She and Judith are with Dr. Rogers."

Baker moved to his left toward a hallway leading under the stairs and toward the back of the house. "I don't think they'll want to be interrupted," Enid said. But Barone was talking to her again, and Baker didn't wait around to hear what the gangster had to say.

He found himself standing outside the kitchen beside a door opposite a large bathroom. He didn't bother to knock.

Judith's face was pinched and pale as she sat across the desk from Dr. Rogers. Marian sat farther away, in a well-cushioned chair in the far corner. Dr. Rogers puffed on a pipe as he sat behind his desk and surveyed Baker through his spectacles.

"Jeffrey's missing," Judith said, meeting Baker's eyes for an instant and then looking away. Baker figured she was still sore about him rejecting her last night.

He looked at Dr. Rogers. "I thought you should know that David Holden is dead and that Wally Sims has been shot."

Dr. Rogers continued to watch him with curious eyes. He pulled the pipe from his mouth and tapped it in an ashtray perched precariously atop a leaning stack of papers.

Baker said, "I'm afraid it's my client. I'm afraid Diana Kramer is doing these things. We need police here. A guard. Something."

"Detective," Judith began, but Dr. Rogers held up his hand.

"Ladies," he said, "I would like a few moments alone with the detective. Would you be so kind as to wait in the parlor?" He turned to Judith. "And the sheriff's office will be here as soon as they can, my dear, to take a statement regarding your husband."

Judith's face showed no emotion as she helped Marian to her feet.

When they were gone, Dr. Rogers leaned forward, rested his arms on the desk and closed his eyes for a long moment. When he opened them again, he said, "I find myself in a difficult position, Detective."

Baker was silent.

Dr. Rogers regarded him for a long moment, as if debating what, or how much, to say. "I'm not sure how much information regarding Mrs. Marian Ferrebee I should disclose." He stood and paced, picking up his pipe as he passed the leaning stack of papers. "Are you working on the Ferrebee murder?"

"No. I'm only after the letters Diana says she wrote to Chet."

"Ah, the mysterious love letters."

"That's what everyone calls them. Mysterious. I'm beginning to wonder if they really exist."

"Oh, they exist, I assure you. I've heard all about them." He sat at the desk and began to fill his pipe with sweet-smelling tobacco from a leather pouch. "In the short time Mrs. Ferrebee has been here, she has had difficulty following a routine. Initially I attributed this difficulty to a potential brain injury sustained during the attack at the motel or the psychological trauma of seeing her new husband strangled." He pressed the tobacco tightly in the pipe bowl and struck a match, puffing frantically for a few moments, until smoke began to come from his mouth. "After all," he continued at length, "she has been unable to recall anything about the attacks on herself or her husband. Naturally amnesia seemed the correct diagnosis. At first."

"I don't understand."

Dr. Rogers gestured with his pipe. "Amnesia affects old memories as well as new. In Marian's case, I initially believed that amnesia was what made it difficult for her to learn a new routine: meals, activities, washing and so forth. Do you understand me so far?"

Baker nodded.

Dr. Rogers began to pace again, clutching his pipe between his teeth and clasping his hands behind his back. "After our first few sessions together, it became apparent that she was missing chunks of her life, not just the events leading up to and following the wedding as I would expect with a true case of amnesia. And yesterday the most curious thing happened."

"What was that?"

Dr. Rogers stopped pacing and resumed his seat. He leaned forward, resting his arms on the desk again. "I mentioned a discussion she and I had just the day before. I asked her about an event she described to me. She had told me about a weekend she and Chet spent at his parents' lake house. I wanted to clarify something, so I asked her to repeat part of the story." He removed his spectacles and stared at Baker. "Marian became very defensive. She insisted she would never spend the weekend with a man who was not her husband, even if they were engaged." Dr. Rogers shook his head. "She left my office in tears."

"Sounds like amnesia to me."

"Not if she remembered the event clearly the day before. And there is more than that. Sometimes she smokes, sometimes she doesn't. Most of the time, Marian is very modest and shy. And somewhat clumsy. But there are times when she possesses grace and confidence as well."

"Like she's two different people?"

The doctor snapped his fingers. "Exactly." He pulled a piece of paper from his top drawer. "Look at this," he said. "I have written Marian Drake's name on this piece of paper. Underneath I have written Diana Kramer's. You will notice that with the letters from Marian Drake's name, the name Diana Kramer can also be spelled."

"But Marian's last name is Ferrebee now."

"Now, yes. But Diana Kramer came into existence before Marian and Chet got married."

"I don't understand."

"Marian Drake and Diana Kramer are the same person."

Now Baker stood to pace. "So I'm searching for letters from the very woman who has hidden them." He pinched the bridge of his nose. "This is giving me a headache."

"I know just how you feel," Dr. Rogers said. "Believe me. However, it will make a nice case study for the *Journal of Psychiatric Medicine.*"

Baker wasn't listening. He sat down again. "Diana Kramer has been calling my office from this building. She's made threats against Marian."

Dr. Rogers frowned. "It is my belief that Diana knows all about Marian. And vice versa."

"Your belief?"

"Keep in mind, Detective, that I have only just put these pieces together myself. I have not yet had time to speak at length with Diana Kramer."

"But she's Marian Drake."

"Diana Kramer is an entirely different person. She just happens to share the same body. I hope to hypnotize Marian to see if I can bring about some convergence of the two personalities."

"I still plan to look for the letters."

Dr. Rogers arched his eyebrows. "I suspected as much. Obviously there's more in them than just love, or there wouldn't be so much violence happening because of them."

"Exactly," Baker said.

"Something quite traumatic happened to Marian long ago. In the few sessions we've had together, it has become apparent that the chunks of her life she is missing occurred after she started high school."

"How much younger is Marian than her brother?"

"Three years, I believe. Why?"

Baker chewed on his cheek. "No reason."

A knock on the door sounded, and Enid poked her head in. "There's a Detective Lewis here for Detective Baker."

Baker stood. "Looks like I've got to go." He shook the doctor's hand. "You'll let me know about the hypnosis?"

"I'm afraid I've disclosed far too much already, my good man. Any information about the hypnosis will have to come from the family."

Chapter 20

Judith stood at the nurse's desk, speaking earnestly to Detective Lewis. She looked thin and frail and very worried.

"Mr. Baker," Lewis said, patting Judith on the shoulder as he stepped away. "The sheriff wants to see you in his office. He sent me to pick you up."

"I'm busy."

"And I'm tired of waiting. Come on, let's go."

Baker looked around for Barone, who had conveniently disappeared. Where were good muscle and a heavy boot when you needed them? "I'll be along in a minute. I'll follow you."

Lewis smiled and shook his head. "Sorry. I'm here to provide a personal escort."

"Why?"

Lewis shrugged. "In case you decide it's in your best interest to avoid the sheriff."

"Why would I do that?"

"You tell me."

Judith watched the exchange with wide eyes. "I told him Jeffrey's missing," she said to Baker. Under normal circumstances, Baker would smile and tell her not to worry…that Jeffrey was drunk in a ditch somewhere. But during the night he'd pieced together where he'd gotten the arsenic. It had been in Jeffrey's cigarettes. Someone wanted Jeffrey dead. Baker wondered if it were the same someone who had killed Chet and David and shot Wally Sims. So when Baker looked into Judith's eyes, wanting to shrug and say, "I'm sure he's fine," he found he couldn't. Because it would be a lie.

He said, "How long has Jeffrey been missing?"

"Since early this morning," Judith said. "He was gone when I woke up."

"Let's go, Baker," Lewis said.

"Since when do you do the sheriff's job, Lewis? And isn't this completely out of your jurisdiction?"

"I'm a consultant on this case, Baker. They don't get many homicides up here. Funny thing is, since you started poking around, they've had three."

"Three?"

"Wally Sims died a couple of hours ago. So now you're wanted for questioning in a homicide."

"I had nothing to do with Wally's murder, and you know it."

Lewis shrugged. "Let's talk about it at the station."

"I'm not leaving my car here," Baker said as he followed Lewis outside.

"Reynolds will take it for you."

Baker tossed the keys to the waiting deputy and climbed into Lewis' car.

The sun disappeared, and snow began to fall in a steady rhythm as the men made their way down the hill into Crane Haven. At the station Lewis put Baker in a small interrogation room and said he'd be back with the sheriff.

Baker was left alone with his thoughts and felt the weight of the day settle in around him. He needed sleep. He needed food. It was past noon, although how far past he couldn't say. He tried to think about the four-eyed frog Barone had showed him, but he couldn't get his mind off of Marian Drake and Diana Kramer.

He'd been banking on Diana being the killer. But if she never left the sanitarium, then she couldn't have committed the murders. Unless she was sneaking out, which was very unlikely.

A short man with thick glasses slipped into the room, carrying a cup of coffee. "Thanks," Baker said. "Is there a phone around here I can use?"

"Sorry. No phone calls."

"I'm entitled to one, aren't I?"

The man shook his head and chuckled. "You ain't been arrested yet, so you don't get a phone call."

"Isn't that a violation of my constitutional rights?"

"Anybody read you your rights?"

"No."

"Then they haven't been violated. Now sit there like a good bird and start singing when the big city cop starts asking questions, and you'll be out of here in no time."

Baker frowned. "Thanks for nothing," he said.

"My pleasure," the man said as he left.

Baker nursed the coffee, wishing he had a sandwich to go with it.

And he thought about the case some more. He reached for his notebook and the small stub of a pencil he kept in his pocket as Lewis walked in with the sheriff. "Got a nail file in there, Baker? Planning to make a break for it?"

"Up yours. What do you want?"

Ferrebee sank wearily into the chair opposite Baker. His eyes were red again, but he was calmer than he'd been at the office earlier. "We need some answers about last night."

Baker nodded, wondering what he could tell them that they didn't already know. He was exhausted. And he was hungry. "I need a cigarette," he said. "Mind if I smoke?"

Ferrebee waved a hand. "Not at all."

Lewis strolled around the room. "You followed me to David's place after I left The Locomotive."

"Is that a question?"

"Yes."

"Then phrase it as a question." Baker blew a cloud of smoke into the room.

"Did you follow me from The Locomotive to The Diner?"

"Yes."

"Why?"

"I figured something else happened, and I wanted to see what it was."

"Ah."

"I also figured you'd never solve the case on your own."

Lewis dove for Baker, but Ferrebee jumped up and held him off. Lewis regained his composure and stood, smoothing his jacket. "I'm fine," he said to Ferrebee, who sat down again. Lewis resumed his strolling. "So you want to be a wise guy," he said. "What happened when you got to The Diner?"

"I pulled up, figuring I'd pump one of the deputies for information." He glanced at the sheriff. "Sometimes we exchange notes on cases."

"Go on," Lewis said.

"Deputy Sims was there."

"And you spoke to him."

"Is that a question?"

Lewis slammed his fist on the table. "Did you speak to him?"

Baker smiled. "He spoke to me. Told me Holden was dead." He looked Lewis in the eye. "And then you spoke to me, Detective. Or don't you remember?"

Lewis gave a tight smile. "Go on. Where'd you go next?"

"To my office."

"You in the habit of going to work so early in the morning?"

"Yeah. I am. What's it to you?" Baker crushed out his cigarette and lit another. His gut gave an unfriendly rumble.

"You okay, son?" Ferrebee asked.

"Haven't eaten today," Baker said. "Plus I was sick last night."

Ferrebee stood and walked to the door. "I need sandwiches in here," he yelled into the hallway.

Baker gave him a weak smile of thanks.

"Moving on," Lewis said, impatiently. "What were you doing in your office when Deputy Sims showed up?"

"Polishing my Tommy gun."

Lewis lunged forward across the table and backhanded Baker across the mouth. "A cop is dead, Baker. Show some respect."

Baker sprang from his chair, grabbed Lewis by the neck and shoved him against the wall. "I didn't kill him. We all know that. And while you stand here blustering about a cop being dead, let's not forget that same cop tried to bribe me earlier in the evening."

Ferrebee blanched. "What?"

Baker let go and wandered back to the table. He sat down and wiped his face on his sleeve. Then he gestured to Lewis. "Ask him. He knows all about it. I gave him the money."

"Nice try, Baker." He handed the sheriff a receipt. "This is from my department. The money is locked up, and the matter is being investigated."

The sheriff studied the receipt and handed it back to Lewis. "I see."

Lewis put the receipt back in his pocket. "What happened after Deputy Sims got to your office?"

"I stood to help him. He fell onto the floor. I called the ambulance."

There was a knock on the door, and the short man entered with a tray of sandwiches. He looked at Baker. "You started to sing yet? I told you that it'll go faster if you sing."

"That's enough," Lewis said, shoving him out the door again. He sat down and shoved the tray toward Baker. "Eat," he said. "But you're not leaving until we get to the bottom of this."

Ferrebee called for some milk to be brought, and the short man brought it right away. "You want cookies with this?" he asked.

"Beat it," Lewis said.

The food helped. Baker felt his strength returning.

Lewis was growing impatient. "What happened after Sims fell to the floor?"

"I told you. I called the ambulance. I tried to stop the bleeding."

"Before he fell, then. Did he say anything?"

"Yeah. He said, 'Please don't shoot me.'"

Lewis smiled and leaned back in his chair. "I got all night, Baker. I got all night."

"Then arrest me and read me my rights, because this conversation is over. You've got no reason to hold me, and you know it." He gestured to Ferrebee. "He knows it too." Baker stood and shoved a sandwich into each of his coat pockets. "Thanks for supper," he said to the sheriff.

Baker picked up his car keys at the staff sergeant's desk and was told his car was in the back lot. He pushed his way out the front doors into the snow that was still falling. He was bone tired. And his car was nowhere to be seen. Confused, he circled the lot on foot. His car was not there. He circled a second time; and then he saw it, or part of it, sticking out from a drift. It had been deliberately driven into a snow bank and now sat buried under six feet of snow. He figured it had taken at least five men the better part of an hour to pile that much snow on top of it.

Baker leaned against the nearest patrol car and ate a sandwich. When he was done, he tightened the sash on his coat and pushed his hat low on his head. Then he began the long trek back to his office.

Chapter 21

Baker trudged the twelve blocks to his office through lightly falling snow. By the time he got there, exhaustion was all he knew. Standing on the deserted sidewalk, he fumbled in his pocket for a key. He found only the remaining sandwich from the sheriff's office. He dropped it in the snow and continued searching.

"Detective, is that you?"

"I think so," he said. It hurt to speak. "I've lost my key."

"Here, let me help you."

He looked up and saw a red hat. Deirdre. "You're soaked," she said. "Come with me." She reached out and took his hand. Her touch was soft and gentle, and Baker allowed her to lead him into her shop. There it was warm and dry. And dark.

"What time is it?" he rasped, too exhausted to put any effort into making small talk.

"Six o'clock. You're all wet. What have you been doing?" She led him to the back of the store, past racks of dresses and frilly undergarments he wasn't comfortable looking at in her presence. She stopped in front of a narrow white door in the back of the shop. She opened it and led him through.

"I've been walking," he mumbled as he followed her through the door and up the narrow flight of stairs to her apartment. "I need to call Edwards," he said.

"Fine. But you can't wait for him with those clothes on."

She turned on a lamp in the living room and the light above the sink in the kitchen. Baker stood on the mat just inside the door, afraid of dripping on her rug. He tried to pull his coat off, but it was damp and clung to his suit. "Here, let me do that," she said, helping him to remove his coat and then taking him to the kitchen where she pushed him into a chair.

His eyes were half-closed when she put the kettle on, and he was dozing by the time she set a cup of steaming tea in front of him. "Drink this," she said.

"I'm dying," he said.

She laughed a little at that, and Baker realized he liked the sound of it. "You're not dying," she said. "You're cold and tired, and people keep using you as a punching bag."

"Mmm." He sipped the tea.

"Plus, you were poisoned yesterday too, if you recall."

"Mmm."

"And, by my estimation, you had about two hours of sleep last night."

Baker sipped some more of the tea, and Deirdre set a sandwich in front of him. "I have one of those in my pocket," Baker said.

"Not anymore," she said. "You dropped it on the ground in front of your office."

Baker shrugged and took another sip of tea. Deirdre let him eat the sandwich before she pointed down the hallway to the door across from her bedroom. "Bathroom is there. I'm going downstairs to rummage through abandoned dry cleaning. I'm sure I can find something dry for you to put on. Take a shower. Get warm. I'll be back in a few minutes."

Baker pushed back from the table, entered the bathroom, closed the door and rested his head against it. He needed sleep. But he was cold and wet, and he needed to take care of that now before real sickness set in. He forced himself away from the door and turned the shower on, letting it warm up while he got undressed.

The bathroom floor was pink and white tile. And he was surrounded by wallpaper covered in pink roses. He climbed in the shower and let the hot spray wash over him, pulling the bandage from his cheek when it became soggy. The case was beginning to unwind. It was a yo-yo spinning at the end of a string, and he didn't have the slightest idea how to pull it back into his grasp.

He was growing more and more certain that Chet's murder was what sparked the killing of David Holden and Wally Sims. But why? Yesterday he considered the possibility of two murderers and dismissed it as unlikely. But was it really so improbable?

There was a knock on the bathroom door. "Just me," Deirdre called. "I'm setting some pajamas inside the door. Put them on and come out when you're done. I'm warming some brandy."

The door closed softly, and Baker counted to twenty before turning off the water and stepping out onto the plush pink bath mat. The pajamas she left were gray flannel and well- worn. He put them on and felt comfortable for the first time in days.

"Those fit perfectly," Deirdre said as he shuffled into the kitchen. She pointed to a chair. "Sit, please."

"Thanks."

She wrinkled her brow as she studied the stitches in his cheek. "Looks better. How's it feel?"

"Fine. I think the stitches can come out soon."

She handed him a brandy. "This will fix you."

He sipped the brandy while she phoned Edwards. She was still on the phone when Baker stumbled to the living room and collapsed onto her sofa.

He knew nothing more until much later, when he opened his eyes and noticed the slant of a streetlight's glow arcing across the room. He sat up on the sofa in Deirdre's apartment and rested his arms on his legs. Edwards must have decided to leave him here, the bastard. Baker wondered if the Brit had at least left a key for him to get back into the office.

A soft green quilt was draped over his legs and he shoved it aside, irritated. It seemed Deirdre was everywhere lately: finding him drunk in the office, putting him in pajamas when he was naked, rescuing him from the snow, fixing him sandwiches.

He needed a cigarette. He pushed off the couch and made his way into the dark kitchen where he fumbled through the cupboards for a pack of cigarettes. He didn't know why. Deirdre didn't smoke. He came across the bottle of brandy from last night and thought about pouring a snifter full. Then he thought better of it.

It was cold in the apartment, so he wrapped the quilt around his shoulders and peered out the windows to the street below. Somewhere in the night, the snow flurry had changed to a storm. Main Street was already buried under a new carpet. Phil Farmer's car was parked across the street in front of the bank, drifted in on all sides. Baker swore softly when he found himself absently patting at his pajama pockets for a pack of cigarettes.

He trudged to the bathroom, thinking he'd get dressed and phone Edwards for the damned key; but his clothes were still wet, and there was no way he was leaving Deirdre's in a pair of borrowed pajamas. Not with the possibility of Phil Farmer being at the bank this early.

He stomped into the kitchen then and made as much noise as possible as he filled the teakettle with water and rummaged through the icebox for something to eat. Deirdre slept on.

He was halfway through his third pot of tea when the first rays of sun peeked through the windows. Deirdre floated into the room and smiled at him as if he sat in her kitchen every morning drinking tea.

"Edwards dropped off a key last night," she said, laying it on the table. "You were asleep and he didn't want to wake you."

"I'm sure."

"I hung your clothes over the shower rod last night, but they're still damp. I'm sure Edwards will bring a new suit for you. In the meantime, I'll make breakfast."

Baker's irritation faded as he realized he liked the way she looked in the morning. Her hair was tangled around her face, her eyes were sleepy and her skin looked soft and warm. "It's cold in here," Baker said. "You need a decent furnace."

She laughed as she pulled eggs from the icebox. "Don't fret about the cold. It'll put hair on your chest."

Baker grumbled but said nothing.

"I forgot to tell you something last night," she said.

Baker wasn't particularly interested in what she had to say. He was watching the way her bottom moved beneath the robe as she whisked the eggs.

"Detective?" she said, turning around.

Baker met her eyes, hoping she hadn't guessed where he'd been looking. "What?" he said.

"I saw Jeffrey Drake outside your office last night."

Baker gave her a sharp look. "Judith says he's missing."

"Well, he wasn't missing last night. I saw him plain as day."

"When was this?"

"Shortly before you got there. I was on my way to the druggist, and he was fumbling around in the snow like he'd lost something. I stopped and he said he'd lost a key. I helped him look, but we didn't find anything." She poured the eggs into a pan. Baker watched her bottom again.

Thoughts crowded in on him. He raced to the bathroom and began searching his clothes. First the trench coat, then the pants. Finally he found what he was looking for in his jacket pocket. Stupid Judith. Baker never put anything in his jacket pocket. No wonder he hadn't found the key last night.

Suddenly Judith's amorous intentions made sense. He replayed them in his mind. He thought about Judith in the foyer, kissing him, her lips warm and full. Most likely, she had taken the key at that time. And in Marian's kitchen, when she kissed him and he was on the floor. Had she been trying to put the key back in his pocket? He'd been in too much pain at the time to pay much attention.

When he discovered the bandage on her arm, he knew she and Jeffrey were the ones who had broken into the office. But why would they have needed to break the glass if she had the key? And why would Jeffrey be looking for the key outside the office door if Judith had returned it the night before?

Had she killed Chet, or David Holden, or Wally Sims? And if she and Jeffrey were after the letters together, why was she so concerned over his whereabouts?

"You know what you should do?" Deirdre interrupted his thoughts.

"What?"

"You should have a dinner party to flush out the killer."

Baker arched an eyebrow. "Like Nick Charles in *The Thin Man*?"

She snapped her fingers. "Exactly." She spooned eggs on two plates and slid two pieces of bread into the toaster. "If you had everyone come in and sit down...wearing fancy dresses and tuxedoes, of course..."

"Of course."

The toast popped up, and she hastily spread butter on the warm slices. "And you just proceeded to question them...I'm sure the killer would confess eventually."

Baker smiled at her as she set a plate in front of him and sat down across the table with her own plate. Her cheeks were flushed from the heat of the stove, and he noticed there were freckles on her cheeks. He realized he was sitting across from a beautiful woman in a bathrobe...himself dressed in pajamas...enjoying breakfast. And he was shocked to realize he was as comfortable as if he did this every day of his life.

That's when he choked on a piece of egg.

"Oh dear," she said. "Are you all right?"

He nodded and swallowed some coffee. "Your plan would never work."

She set her fork down, straightening in her chair. "And why not?"

"Because…"

A hammering on the door interrupted his train of thought. Deirdre excused herself to answer it and returned a moment later with Edwards strolling behind carrying two suits, two hats and five neckties.

"Oh my," Deirdre said as Edwards draped the suits over a kitchen chair. "Those are lovely."

Edwards bowed. "Coming from you, my dear, that is a compliment."

"Would you like some tea? I have eggs and toast too."

"That would be lovely." Edwards pulled out a chair and sat, grimacing when he saw Baker. "Deirdre tells me you've ruined another suit. And you're in someone else's pajamas again, I see. The entire town is beginning to think I don't know how to clothe you."

"If the town is worried about another man dressing me, then we've got big problems," Baker said dryly.

"Where do you find such magnificent suits?" Deirdre asked, fingering the sleeves on one of the jackets.

Edwards cleared his throat. "Secret of the trade, I'm afraid, Miss Deirdre. My father was a manservant, and he informed me it is in very bad taste to disclose the source of an employer's clothing."

Baker studied his hands, suppressing a smile. Deirdre nodded, her brow creased. "I see," she said.

Edwards looked at the suits he brought. "The dark green today, sir," he said, handing Baker a suit and shirt. "Please go and change immediately."

Baker carried the suit to the bathroom and dressed. When he returned, Edwards was sifting through neckties. He looked at Baker, then back to the ties. "This one," he said after a moment. "It will counteract the shadows under your eyes." The tie was pale green with yellow flecks.

"Fine," Baker said, taking the tie to a mirror in the living room to knot it. When he returned to the kitchen, Edwards was seated in the chair Baker had vacated just moments ago. And Baker was surprised to find he'd come to consider the chair his own. He worked fast to stamp out the jealousy that bubbled in him.

"Edwards," Deirdre said, "don't you think we should have a dinner party to flush out the killer?"

Edwards cocked an eyebrow. "Madam?" he said.

"Like *The Thin Man*. That's how Nick Charles does it."

Baker took the chair Edwards had originally sat in and leaned back, crossing his arms and hoping Edwards realized he was a big, fat chair stealer. And an intruder.

Edwards didn't notice. He was studying Deirdre. "*The Thin Man* is fiction, Miss Deirdre. Real life is much more complicated than the movies, I'm afraid."

She chewed her lip. "Yes, I suppose you're right." She looked at Baker. "But I'm telling you Jeffrey Drake is no more a missing person than you or I. I saw him last night. I think he's hiding, plain and simple."

Baker said nothing. But he believed Deirdre was right.

Chapter 22

Baker's head was spinning when he exited Deirdre's shop on the way to his own office. Edwards kept tactfully quiet about Baker sleeping on her couch last night, and Baker appreciated it. However, he couldn't help blushing when he nearly bumped into Judith, who was leaning against the locked office door when they returned.

"Good morning," she said. "Getting a late start this morning?"

Baker ignored that and reminded himself that she'd stolen a key, broken into his office and seduced him as a ruse to put the key back in his pocket. And he still didn't know why the hell she broke Edwards' window. The blush turned into a flush of anger.

He mumbled, "Good morning" to her as Edwards unlocked the door. Edwards stood aside and allowed Baker to usher Judith inside. "Good morning, Madam," Edwards said as she passed. "Please come in. I'll put some coffee on."

Baker moved silently through Edwards' office and into his own, feeling, rather than hearing, Judith behind him. "Have a seat," he said as he hung up his hat. When he was seated, he lit two cigarettes and passed one to her. "Did Jeffrey come home yet?"

She shook her head, not looking any the worse for wear. She looked, well, perfect. As always. "Not yet," she said, handing Baker a dark envelope. "But he sent me this. I wanted you to see it before I took it to the sheriff."

Baker examined the dark brown paper. "Special messenger," he said aloud.

She nodded. "I had to sign for it. I thought maybe we could trace it to his location." She paused. "Or to whoever sent it."

Baker took a deep drag on his cigarette and read the note.

"Judith,

I killed Chet and David. I can't tell you everything, Jude. I wish like hell I could. I lost the bet and can't pay. Things are a mess and it's best if I go.

Yours,

Jeffrey"

Baker stared at the note for a long time. When he looked up, his eyes were cold. "Well, I guess that solves the case."

Judith stood, a cloud of smoke billowing from her perfect mouth. "You can't possibly believe Jeffrey had anything to do with this."

Baker rubbed the back of his neck, suddenly tired of the plastic woman before him. Had he really found her charming in the beginning? "Sit down," Baker said, "Of course I don't believe he had anything to do with it. Jeffrey's a coward. He'd never have the guts to pull the trigger."

If Judith was insulted by what he said, she hid it well. Baker saw nothing but her plastic perfection sitting in the chair across from him. Her expression was the model of composure.

She sat for a moment and tapped her foot impatiently. When Baker did nothing but stare, she stood again, smoothing her skirt and straightening her jacket. "Should I take that note to the sheriff?"

Baker shrugged. "Not unless you want them to hunt down and arrest your husband. And remember, the real killer is still running around. Could be Jeffrey's a target, and he only confessed to keep the killer from coming after him."

She sat down and tapped her foot again. "What do we do?" She was pouting now, her lips full and red. But Baker couldn't see the beauty in it today. Today he was tired of this woman and her problems.

"We don't do anything. We wait until he comes back."

She dabbed her eyes with a handkerchief, somehow managing to look forlorn. "I'm so worried. Won't you please try to find him? I don't have the money for your fee, but I can get it when Jeffrey returns."

Baker studied her for a moment, wondering if her concern was genuine. He'd smoked his cigarette down to the filter and crushed it out in the ashtray. The smoke that hovered between them, above the desk, began to clear. "I can shake a few trees and see what falls," he said.

Judith's face shifted into a small smile. "Thank you, Detective. For me and for Marian."

"I'd like to thank you for returning my key," Baker said, taking a sick delight in the discomfort the statement seemed to cause for her.

Her hands fluttered around her throat; and she blinked rapidly, as if trying to think of something to say. "I...I'm sorry, Detective."

"Why did you take it?"

"To find the letters." Her voice was a whisper.

"You didn't find them."

She shook her head.

"Why did you break Edwards' window?"

Her hands were at her collar, fiddling with the button there. "That was an accident. Jeffrey was behind me and he tripped, and my arm went through the glass." She regarded him for a moment, and he couldn't tell if the expression in her eyes was one of anger or amusement. "I'm sorry."

"My neighbor saw Jeffrey fumbling in the snow outside my door for the key last night."

"Jeffrey? Where did he go from here?" She ran to the window and looked up and down the street, as if he would be there somewhere, poking his drunken head out of a storefront.

Baker rose and turned her to face him. "Why didn't you tell him you'd returned the key?"

She stared at Baker, her eyes wide. "He was gone when I woke up, before I had the chance to tell him...Oh, God." She covered her mouth with her hand and moved back to her chair.

"Why was he after the letters?"

Judith shook her head and tried to look away, but Baker moved to her and grasped her chin, holding her face so she had no choice but to look in his eyes. "Why did he want the letters, Judith?"

She blew out a breath. "I don't know exactly," she said. "He said if the wrong person found the letters, he might end up in jail for a long time."

"Why?"

"I don't know, Detective. But he's the only family Marian has. I couldn't just let the letters be found and turned in...not if there were something I could do to help."

Baker stood and showed her to the door. "You owe me five dollars for the window," he said as she left.

He relaxed when the door closed behind her. "Edwards," he said softly, fearing Judith might still be listening in the hallway. "I'm going out."

"Very good, sir. Would you like some coffee before you go?"

"No. But keep it warm. It's going to be a long day."

Outside the air was warming rapidly. The sky was still overcast, but the snow was tapering off to a steady rain. Rivers of dirty water ran through the gutters. Baker did his best to avoid the mess as he walked the four and a half blocks to Artie's Used Car Emporium, reminding himself to have Edwards retrieve the Chevy as soon as possible.

Chances were good that Jeffrey was still lurking about somewhere. If that were the case, the man was certainly sick from the poisoned cigarettes. If that were the case, Jeffrey was in need of medical attention. There were only a few people in town Jeffrey would be comfortable calling on for help, and Artie was on the list. If Judith were going to pay Baker to shake trees, then he'd shake trees.

Unfortunately "Artie's Used Car Emporium, Where America Buys Cars," was closed. Artie, no doubt acting out of fear, had locked the door and pulled the shades. Baker circled the building and peered through a back window, where the shade hadn't been pulled completely closed.

He could make out the cluttered office on the other side of the glass. A small lamp burned on the edge of a desk covered in stacks of files and loose papers. Baker pounded on the window. "Pfeiffer, I know you're in there." He waited. When Artie didn't answer a second time, Baker moved to the front and kicked the door in.

"Pfeiffer," he said, stepping over splintered wood. "I know you're in here."

There was a small shuffling sound from the back office; and then Artie, perspiring heavily and looking nauseated, slunk into the reception area, his hands raised. "I'm here, Baker. I w-was just on the ph-phone back there is all. No need to get upset. Haven't opened for business yet today." He gave a nervous laugh. "Snowed so much last night I didn't think anyone would come in for a test drive, if you get my drift." He mopped his moist face with a handkerchief. "Sorry about the other night. That was all Wally's idea."

"Wally's dead."

Fear lit Artie's eyes. "I heard," he said.

Baker slunk forward like a cat, keeping his face impassive as he grasped Artie's lapels and backed him into a wall.

"Come on," Artie whimpered. "You can't still be mad. Bert and Jeremy, they wouldn't have hurt you. Not very bad anyway."

"Why the bribe, Artie?"

Artie trembled. "We warned you, Baker. I warned you myself, remember. I told you some people would get angry if you kept looking for those letters."

Baker leaned close enough to touch Artie's nose. "I know Diana Kramer and Marian Drake are the same woman." He let Artie go.

Artie sank into a chair and mopped at the sweat running from his face. "I'm as good as dead," he muttered. "As good as dead. There's no way out now. We're all dead men."

Baker supposed he was right. "Where's Drake?"

But Artie wouldn't answer. He shook his head and muttered to himself. Baker slapped him. "Where's Drake?"

Artie shook his head. "He's going to kill me, don't you understand?"

"Jeffrey's going to kill you?"

Artie's eyes were wild. "We're all dead men."

Baker said, "I need a car. Mine's buried in snow."

The thought of potential business brought Artie back to life. "I have just the car for you," he said.

Baker pulled Artie from the chair and shoved him against the wall again. "I'm not going to buy it, Artie. I'm going to borrow it. Give me a set of keys. And the car better be reliable or I'll kill you myself."

Artie smoothed his jacket as best he could and, with trembling hands, handed Baker a set of keys from the key rack on the wall. "The '38 Buick in the third row. She's just been detailed. She'll plow through anything."

Baker jangled the keys and tipped his hat. "Be seeing you, Artie."

The bay doors at the Ford garage were shut tight against the cold, the interior lights illuminating the windows in the gloom of the day. Baker entered the garage through the grimy office, glaring at Shep, silently daring the man to stop him. Shep made a move to lift his bulk from the chair…then waved his arm. "Ah, go ahead," he said. "They're useless to me today anyway."

Baker nodded once at Shep, then silently stepped into the garage, careful not to draw attention to himself. Bertie Sims slumped on a stool in a dim corner. His coveralls were covered in grease, and even from across the room, Baker could tell the man hadn't bathed; and, judging from the rum bottle clutched in his hand, Bertie's blood was 80 proof.

Bertie looked up, and Baker saw recognition dawn in the man's eyes. "Detective Baker," he slurred. "Didja hear? My brother's dead." He shook his head and cried softly. "My only brother. He was a deputy. And he's dead."

Baker looked down the length of the garage to where Jeremy Watts was stooped over an old Hudson. "I heard about your brother, Bertie," Baker said, keeping his eyes on Jeremy while bending down to pick up a wrench from a toolbox on the floor. "I'm sorry." Jeremy backed out from under the hood of the Hudson, returning Baker's stare.

Baker was once again surprised by the enormity of the man. More than that, he was surprised at the ease with which Jeremy Watts moved. Even now, as Watts walked forward, wiping his hands on a greasy rag, he was graceful. Baker moved toward him, the wrench hanging loosely at his side. Watts stopped moving and watched Baker approach.

"What the hell do you want here, Detective?" he asked, his mouth tilted in what Baker supposed was a smile of some sort. "Come for another beating?"

Baker stopped moving, the wrench held limply at his side. And for some inexplicable reason, he thought of Stewie, of his face the last time they spoke. When Stewie gave him the car. Baker crushed the memory.

"I'm going out to the Ferrebees' lake house," he said. "And you're going with me."

"Is that so?"

"I figure Diana Kramer's got a friend or two still lurking around. I figure I'll use you as a human shield in case someone's out there holed up."

Jeremy snorted and drew his arm back to throw a punch. He was fast. But Baker, who was faster, sidestepped at the last second and lifted the wrench, delivering a bone-crushing blow to Watts' jaw.

Jeremy crumpled to the ground, moaning.

Baker smiled at the wrench, then looked down at Watts. "So," he said, "let's take that ride." He looked over his shoulder. "Bertie, you come too."

"I think you broke my jaw," Jeremy mumbled from the floor.

Baker helped him to his feet and pushed him out through the office, across the dirty drive and shoved him into the Buick. "Feel free to bleed on the seats," he said as he shoved Watts into the back.

Bertie had followed them out and stood, swaying, the rum bottle dangling at his side. "Climb in," Baker told him.

"I feel sick," Bertie said as he climbed into the front seat.

"That's okay. It's Artie's car."

"You broke my jaw," Watts said, his words spewing blood between the fingers that cradled his mouth.

"I promise your jaw isn't broken. How do we get to the lake house?" Edwards had been to the lake during his search for Barone's sister, but Baker hadn't accompanied him and was not in the mood to get lost this morning. He pulled out of the garage lot and headed north through town.

Bluebird Lake was long and thin; and, depending on which end the cabin was on, one needed to head either north or south out of town. "This the right way, Watts?"

"I'm not talkin'."

Baker slammed on the brakes and Jeremy flew forward, slamming his face against the back of the front seat. He moaned.

"I'm sorry," Baker said. "What was that? I should turn where?"

Bertie was noisily sick on the floor in the front.

"Aw, come on, Bertie, that stinks," Watts moaned. His words were nearly unintelligible. Blood oozed from his mouth, and Baker noted with satisfaction that it was landing on the upholstery in the back.

Baker hit the brakes again, propelling Jeremy into the seat once more. Bertie answered with a retch.

"All right, all right," Jeremy slurred. "Take the highway south out of town. Drive to Bluebird Lane. It'll be about four miles out on your left. Turn there. Take the third right. Drive to the end of the lane and turn left. Take that until it dead ends. The cabin is the last one on the left. Now let me out of this goddamn car."

Baker had to concentrate to understand Watts' words through the swelling that was rapidly spreading through his jaw, widening the cut from the wrench into a jagged black chasm. "Come on, Watts. Don't you want to see where the famous Diana Kramer and Chet Ferrebee had their love nest?"

"I don't feel good," Bert said.

"You get sick again and I'll pop you one," Watts said. "It reeks in here." Blood dribbled from his mouth as he spoke, making his words sound wet.

Baker followed the directions Watts gave, forcing Artie's car through the snow and mud-packed roads and making the ride as miserable for his unwilling passengers as possible. He smoked, he played the radio and he talked about his Aunt Laura's prawn soup. "Feels like the temperature is dropping. I'd better turn the heat up, boys."

"I'm going to be sick again," Bertie protested.

"I'll kill you, Baker," Jeremy promised.

But Baker wasn't listening. He was thinking about the lake house and the mystery of Diana Kramer's letters, which were now linked to three murders and one disappearance.

The lake house was quiet and dark, and the rain did nothing to make it inviting.

Baker turned the car off and pocketed the keys. "So this is the place," he said, looking at his passengers. "You coming in?"

"No," they answered together.

"Want me to leave the heat on?"

"NO."

Baker shrugged and climbed from the car.

Chapter 23

Baker circled the small cabin before trying the doors. In the rear a small dock led from a large, screened-in porch to the water. He checked under the mat. No key. He circled to the front again and checked under the mat there. Again, no key.

Bertie and Watts were still in the car, Watts cradling his bleeding jaw, Bertie cradling his entire head. Baker smiled and waved at them, and Watts made a gesture with his left middle finger.

Baker made his way around back again, this time checking the screen door. It was unlocked, and he entered the porch quietly. Cloth-covered furniture lined the walls, and the smell of dust hung thickly in the air. He peered through the back door's small window and knocked once. From where he stood, he had a view of the kitchen and a small dining nook. A vase of dead flowers sat in the middle of the small table. Clean dishes sat abandoned in the rack where they had been placed after being washed. There was two of everything. Two plates, two cups, two bowls. He shook his head, thinking about the bizarre relationship between Chet and Diana Kramer and Chet and Marian Drake. Clearly the man recognized they were both the same woman. Baker didn't know whether to be disgusted...or impressed.

He backed away. The cabin was dark and quiet, and he felt slightly better about breaking in knowing that no one was around.

He pulled a set of lock picks from his coat pocket and was inside in seconds. Now he could see the full kitchen. A set of canisters resting on a small Hoosier cabinet held flour, sugar, coffee and tea...all fairly fresh. Off the kitchen was a small living area with modest furniture surrounding a large stone fireplace. The front door was located in the middle of the far wall. Baker looked through the front window to the Buick. His passengers were still inside and still miserable.

Off the living area was a door leading to a bedroom and bathroom combination. Baker was grim as he entered. Here was the personal touch missing from Marian's home. The long pine dresser was covered with photos lovingly arranged on its dusty surface. Here was the woman Chet loved, hidden away in the woods like a fairy tale princess.

Baker spent a long time at the dresser, studying the photos. Here was the abundant evidence of the couple's mutual affection. A photo of them on the dock, waving to the camera. A photo of them with Sheriff and Mrs. Ferrebee, smiling broadly. A photo of the couple at Christmas. One of them on a picnic.

But was it Diana in the photos? Or Marian?

Something sick settled in his gut, and he looked away from the photos to begin a careful search through the bureau drawers. Here the clothes were brighter and more modern. Diana Kramer's wardrobe, he realized. Marian's clothes, drab and frumpy, were hanging in the dingy house at the end of a muddy lane.

He found no letters in the bureau. A small night table sat next to the bed; and Baker opened the drawer carefully, expecting to find the letters, expecting not to. Inside a withered rose sat atop a small envelope. The drawer was otherwise empty, except for a discarded pink ribbon lying near the back. Baker pulled the rose from the drawer and laid it atop the night table. He opened the envelope as carefully as he could. Inside was a small card from the local florist.

"Diana,

For all your forgiveness and all your love, I give you my heart. With all my love, now and forever, Chet"

"Oh brother," Baker mumbled, stuffing the card in his pocket and dumping the rose back into the drawer.

He found a phone in the kitchen and dialed the office. "Edwards," he said when the Brit answered. "I need you to come and get me. I'm at the Ferrebee cabin."

Baker stood on the dock smoking a cigarette when he heard Edwards' car pull up in front. He dropped the cigarette on the wood planks, crushed it with his shoe and felt in his pocket for Artie's keys.

Next, he rolled his shoulders a few times to loosen up and hurled the keys as far out over the ice-covered lake as he could. If Artie wanted the car back, he could get the keys himself.

The day was turning out to be quite pleasant, he thought as he made his way around the cabin. The rain had stopped, he'd found another clue and two of the bums that beat him up were stuck in a car, soon to be trapped out here with no one around to give them a lift back to town.

Edwards was peering into the windows of the Buick as Baker came around the front. "Sir," he said. "These men look as if they need medical attention."

Baker strode to Edwards' car and climbed into the front seat. "Let's go, Edwards," he said, not looking at the Buick. "Time's a-wastin'."

Edwards stood, undecided, for a moment, then followed Baker's lead and climbed into the driver's seat. "Should we telephone someone?" he asked.

"Yes, we should, Edwards," Baker said, lighting a cigarette. "Drive to the nearest gas station. We'll order a ride for them."

Edwards' brow creased. "We're just going to leave them there?"

"We are indeed."

At the pay phone Baker had the operator connect him to Artie Pfeiffer's Used Car Emporium. "Artie," he said when the man answered. "Jeremy and Bertie need you to come on out to the lake house and pick them up. I left the Buick with them." He hung up before Artie could say anything.

As he climbed back into the car, he was smiling. "Drive on, Edwards," he said.

"Where to, sir?"

"To the sanitarium. It's time to retrieve the letters."

The sanitarium stood white and forbidding against the gray sky, but Baker felt less revulsion at having to enter its rancid halls than he had previously. Edwards, however, had never been to visit the widow and had difficulty stifling his reaction to the smell.

"Egads, sir."

"You'll get used to it."

"I rather doubt it. How can something that looks so clean smell so bad?"

Enid looked up and smiled at Edwards as the men entered the foyer. "Hello, Detective. Who is your handsome friend?"

"This is Edwards. Edwards, Enid."

Enid batted her lashes. Edwards was not charmed. "Madam, how do you stand the stench?"

She shrugged. "I usually don't notice it."

"I'm here to ask you about that," Baker said.

Enid's eyes widened. "The smell?"

Baker nodded. "Have they found the problem yet?"

"No. They plan to check the cistern tomorrow morning."

"I'd like to look at it now, if I may."

Edwards groaned and covered his mouth and nose with a handkerchief. "Perhaps I should wait in the car."

"Fine, Edwards. I won't be long."

Enid said, "The cistern is out back. I'll have to get someone to help you with the lid."

Baker nodded. "Take your time. I need to speak to the widow first."

Marian sat alone in the parlor today with her back to the windows. Winter light cast a black halo around her head; and Baker swallowed a lump in his throat as he looked at her, stunned by her dark beauty.

She met his gaze with curiosity. "Detective," she said, her eyebrows raised. The bruises on her face had healed to a dull yellow, giving her a pallor that was unusual, but not unappealing. "Isn't it a beautiful day?" she asked.

Baker sat down across from her, wondering where Judith was, but somehow afraid of what the answer might be were he to ask.

Marian leaned forward. "Judith says you've spoken with my doctor."

"Yes."

"Then you know."

"Know what?"

"That I'm crazy."

"You don't look crazy."

She leaned back in her chair, her mouth curved in a crooked smile. "You've told me that before," she said.

"Yes."

"May I have a cigarette?"

He lit two and passed one to her.

Baker watched as she inhaled and held the smoke in her lungs a good, long time. "I know where the letters are, Marian," he said.

She blew the smoke out on a laugh. "Really?" she said, her eyes narrowing. "How do you propose to get them?"

"I'm going in after them."

She shrugged and looked away. "Take them. I don't care anymore. Dr. Rogers is going to help me get rid of Diana Kramer once and for all." She looked at him, and her eyes were black slits in her pale face. "So the letters don't really matter much at all anymore, do they?"

"If people are going to keep dying because of what's in them, then I think they must matter a great deal."

She waved her hand carelessly. "There's nothing in them, really. This and that. Love talk. Read them yourself. You'll see."

"Why did you take the letters?"

"Because Diana doesn't exist, and Chet fancied himself in love with her. With a woman who wasn't real."

"She was real for him."

Pain flickered across her face, followed by a cold indifference that startled Baker and made his neck tingle. Marian began to laugh. "Don't worry, Detective. You can keep the fee. I won't ask for it back."

"I'm not concerned about that."

She crushed out her cigarette and leaned back. "What are you concerned about?"

"Did Diana Kramer kill Chet?"

Her face fell for an instant. Her shoulders slumped, and an inner pain caused her eyes to drift shut. "No," she said after a moment. "She loved him. And he loved her." Marian opened her eyes and looked at Baker, a smile playing around her mouth now. "And I loved him and he loved me. We were all very happy together." She laughed silently, but a tear leaked out of her eye and ran down her cheek.

"Did you see who killed Chet? Did Diana see who killed him?"

She shook her head and looked at the table. "I don't know."

He studied her for a moment. "Marian, how did Diana come to be?"

Marian was silent for so long that Baker was sure she would not answer. At last, she spoke. And when she did, her voice was husky with emotion. "Something bad happened a long time ago. I don't remember what it was. Dr. Rogers thinks Diana remembers. I think my brother remembers too."

"Can I talk to Diana?"

Her laugh was a mixture of amusement and grief. "No, Detective, you can't. I told you I don't need her anymore. Chet's gone and Diana will be gone soon too." She looked at her hands as they rested on the table. "And then I'll be alone."

"You have Judith."

She rubbed her eyes. "Judith thinks Jeffrey and I have money. That's the only reason she married him and the only reason she's nice to me."

"I don't think..."

Marian's look cut him off. "Jeffrey told her we had wealthy relatives. She believed him. She hates him but won't divorce him. If you ask me, that says it all."

"Says what?"

She sighed and rubbed her temples. "Says she stays with him because she thinks he'll be rich someday. Can I have another cigarette?"

Baker handed her one and leaned across the table to light it. There was nothing more to say. He had reached a dead end. He'd been hired by a woman who didn't exist to find letters that didn't say anything but were getting people killed. There was no need to finish the job. If the letters were just love notes, they could be left alone.

Baker stood. Whether Diana Kramer was real or not, the money she'd given him certainly came in handy; and he would finish this job. "Guess I'll go fetch those notes, Marian."

But Marian wasn't listening. She was smoking her cigarette and staring at the table.

Chapter 24

Enid told Baker that the janitor would meet him out at the cistern. In the end it took Baker and the janitor, whose name was Bill, as well as Edwards, to push the lid from the squat cylindrical tube that served as the top of the cistern.

Above ground, the tube stood three feet high. Inside, however, it dropped ten feet below ground level. As the stone lid was slid to the ground, Edwards stood back and covered his nose.

"This hasn't been used for drinking water in over fifteen years," Bill said. "They use it to route sewage now."

"Really," Edwards said dryly. "How fascinating." He brushed at the dirt clinging to his suit jacket.

"Oh, we've found all kinds of stuff in here," Bill said, scratching his head. "People drop it through this hole over here." He pointed to a large defect in the cement where a chunk had been knocked away. "Found a whole set of china in here three years ago." He scratched his head again. "Well, not the whole set, to tell the truth." He chuckled to himself. "Just the sugar bowl and cream pitcher. Some man dropped 'em in after he caught his wife cheating."

Baker and Edwards stared down into the hole. "Why on earth wasn't the cistern checked when the smell first started?" Edwards asked.

Bill shook his head. "Well, most things thrown in here sink to the bottom, see? And if they sink to the bottom, they don't obstruct the flow of sewage from the building. He pointed down into the hole. "This was a bad plumbing design from the get-go. And I told them that too."

Baker removed his jacket. "Hold this," he said, lowering the ladder Bill had provided into the hole.

"I forbid you to go in there, sir."

Baker ignored him and moved down the ladder into the murk of the cistern's sewage-ridden depths. He lowered himself until he was waist deep.

Edwards groaned. "I loved that suit," he said.

Bill was watching Baker closely. "Now listen to me," Bill said. "The sewage enters the cistern from the south end. If you feel on the north end over here," he stepped around to the other side, "there will be a hole around twelve inches down from the surface of the water. That's where the fresh water pours in to dilute things."

Baker moved his hands along the wall beneath the surface, trying not to think about what he was touching. After a moment, he felt a cool current of water passing his fingers. He followed it to a hole in the side of the blocks. "I found it," he called.

"Is it putting out water?"

"Yes, but the flow is weak."

"That's because of the backup. It's pressure sensitive to prevent overflow in the cistern."

"Yes," Edwards called down to Baker. "We wouldn't want the cistern to overflow, sir. Much better to have it back up inside the building."

Bill scowled. "Hey, like I said, the design was flawed from the start."

"I'm just pointing out..." Edwards started.

"If you nancies are done nagging one another up there, why don't you tell me what to do next?"

Bill peered over the side again. "Feel around the fresh water supply," he said. "The drain is twelve inches below that and is about a foot wide.

Baker felt around as low in the muck as he dared without immersing himself any deeper. His fingers brushed suction once and he moved his hand closer to the wall, probing the slimy cement blocks. Even with his fingers stretched as far as possible, he couldn't find the hole. Closing his eyes, he lowered himself to his chest and fumbled in the filth.

His nails scraped against something semi-solid and he felt it ooze into the creases of his fingernails. "God dammit," he muttered.

"Find the blockage?" Bill asked.

"Shut the hell up," Baker said. "I'll let you know when I find it." He dropped a little further and reached. His fingers struck something hard and metal and he closed his eyes as he felt around, imagining the shape of the object in his head. It was a flat, rectangular box of some sort and it was sucked up tight against the drainage tube.

Baker pried it loose, and immediately the level in the cistern began to drop. He examined what he held in his hands. It was a flat tin case, and he didn't need to open it to know it contained the letters. He held the case above the water level as he waded to the ladder. "Found it," he called, climbing to the surface.

Bill examined the case. "So that's the culprit," he said.

"Sure is. There a shower I can use?"

"Must we put that thing in the car?" Edwards groaned.

"It's not going in the car, Edwards. It's going in the trunk."

"Sir, please. I beg of you. You have no idea where that's been."

Baker's smile was crooked. "On the contrary, Edwards. We both know where it's been. We've both smelled where it's been. Now open the trunk, or I'll have to hold it on my lap in the front seat."

"I was rather hoping you'd ride in the trunk as well."

"I took a shower."

"Yes, well, some smells take a while to wash out."

Baker pinched the bridge of his nose. "Stop blubbering and open the trunk."

Edwards did. Then he stood back and allowed Baker to set the metal case inside. After Baker showered, Enid lent him a white hospital gown, slippers and a pair of loose-fitting white pants worn by the male patients. Edwards threw the ruined suit into the incinerator, declaring it beyond any hope of cleaning. Baker feared the Brit would cry; but, in the end, Edwards bore up rather well.

When they were settled in the front seat, Edwards said, "Please roll down your window, sir."

At the office Baker changed into a clean suit. Edwards cleaned the outside of the tin as best he could, and the two worked together to sort the contents. "I can't make any sense of these letters," Baker said after a time.

"Mmm, yes," Edwards agreed. "Happily, this mess is your job, not mine. Now," he said, moving to the pile of hospital clothing Baker had just changed out of, "may I discard this latest ensemble?"

Baker kept his eyes on the letters. "No," he said. "I told Enid I'd return them."

Edwards' face fell, but Baker wasn't paying attention. He continued to stare at the letters. "Edwards, how could a man love two women at once?"

"It's every man's dream."

"Not when the women share the same body, Edwards. In this case I think Chet got twice the headache, not twice the fun." He held up one of the letters. "These don't say anything useful."

Edwards picked up one of the notes and scanned it. "I don't know about that," he said. "This one is rather graphic in nature."

Baker snatched it away. "I'm talking about her past, Edwards. I was hoping for a clue about Chet's murder. All these letters refer to, other than making whoopee, is how much she loves him and how she forgives him for what he did to her."

"Hmmm. Yes, rather nauseating."

"And look here," Baker pulled the note he'd swiped from the lake house out of his top desk drawer. "I found this at the cabin." He handed it to Edwards.

"This is from Chet."

"Exactly. All these letters are from Diana. This card probably came with a bunch of flowers or something. He thanks her for forgiving him. What the hell did he do that needs forgiveness?"

Edwards scratched his chin. "He cheated on her?"

"We already know he was technically involved with two women sharing the same body. God help us all if there's a third one in there somewhere."

Edwards smoothed his jacket and straightened his tie. "Whatever mystery lies in these letters is no longer your concern, sir. You have solved your case. You should be celebrating, not brooding."

Baker cracked his knuckles. "Marian knows we have the letters. She'll spread the word. The killer will want to shut everyone else up."

"He's not done?"

Baker pointed to the yearbook lying on his desk. It was open to the all-too-familiar photo. "I'm guessing the killer won't stop until all these men are dead."

"Hello? Anyone home?" Deirdre called from the outer office.

"In here, Miss Deirdre." Edwards crossed to Baker's door and gestured for her to come in.

"Brought your suits," she said, carrying a full garment bag.

"Ah, very good. I'll take that." Edwards relieved her of the suits and carried the bag to the closet.

"Ooh," she said, spying the letters. "What are those?"

Baker leaned back and looked at her, liking the way she looked standing in his office. He smiled and lit a cigarette. "Those are love letters."

She raised an eyebrow. "Yours?"

"Chet's."

She clapped her hands and squealed with delight. "You found them. That's wonderful. May I?"

"Sure."

She picked one up and read it. First she blushed; then she began to fan herself. "My, my. She had it bad."

"Yeah."

"It would appear so," Edwards said, returning from the closet.

Deirdre adjusted her hat. "Well," she said, "A hearty congratulations to both of you." She moved to the door. "I'm off to watch the fire."

Edwards' eyes widened. "Fire?"

She rolled her eyes. "Didn't you hear the sirens? Artie Pfeiffer's office is burning. Everyone's gone to watch." She patted the pink hat she wore. "See? I've just made this, and someone is bound to ask me about it. I'll make a dozen sales at least."

Baker stood and crushed out his cigarette. "Shrewd," he said, earning him a smile. But he wasn't thinking about Deirdre and her hats. He was thinking about Artie's Used Car Emporium and wondering if Artie was the latest target for murder. He was also wondering where Jeffrey Drake was and if he were still alive...or if he'd been the one to set the fire. He set his hat atop his head, running a hand over the crease and flipping the brim down over his left eye. This earned him another smile from Deirdre.

"Are you coming with me?" she asked.

"Wouldn't miss it," he said, tucking her hand in the crook of his arm.

Deirdre chatted happily for the two and a half blocks to Artie's, waving at Mrs. Beirbaum, Mrs. Kendall and Madge Hobbs, who all *adored* her hat. "Told you," she said sideways to Baker. But he wasn't listening. He was smoking. And wondering.

Artie's Used Car Emporium was a charred ruin, still smoldering, and surrounded by sooty water. Firemen milled around in the lot, ignoring Artie as he barked orders to move the cars farther back. "For God's sake," he cried, "they're all unlocked. Just slip them in neutral and roll them back."

The firemen walked past him as if he were invisible. Artie threw his hands up in the air and paced anxiously back and forth along the sidewalk. His face and clothes were smeared with black, and his pants were soaked to the knees from trudging through the dirty water.

He spied Baker after a minute and froze. "You ruined my car," he shouted, jogging over, his face red, the veins in his neck bulging. "You owe me six hundred bucks."

Baker shrugged. "I just gave a couple of guys a ride. You shouldn't mind, seeing as how they're friends of yours."

Deirdre looked from one man to the other and cleared her throat. "Well," she said. "It looks as if you two have something to discuss, so if you'll excuse me, I'll just wander around." Baker gave her a half-smile before she turned and moved through the crowd to model her hat.

"You threw my keys in the lake," Artie said, thrusting a fat finger into Baker's chest. "It was the only set I had for that car."

"They're not under water yet, Artie. Just crawl out and get them. Stop being such a nancy."

Artie sighed and took a step away from Baker. He looked at his used car emporium and blew his nose loudly. "What a day," he said, forgetting the ruined car and the keys sitting on ice in the middle of Bluebird Lake.

Baker nodded to what left of Artie's office. "What happened?"

Artie shook his head and swiped a hand over his face, smearing the already sticky grime farther down on his cheeks. "Someone locked me in," he said, his eyes darting from the soot- covered firemen to the spectators and then to Baker. "I smelled the smoke and got curious. When I tried to open the door, it was stuck. Locked from the outside. So I tried to use the phone, but the lines had been cut. Then the whole place went up." His eyes were still touched by panic. "I couldn't get out."

One of the firemen smashed a Chrysler's front windows to pass a fire hose through. Artie jumped up and down, stamping his feet. "Put it in neutral and roll it back. You'll pay for that." He ran a filthy hand over his scalp and began to pace again. "Jesus Christ," he muttered.

Baker's eyes were narrowed. "Who called it in?"

Artie looked at him as if he'd forgotten Baker was there. "What?" he asked. "Oh. Right. The fire. Some lady saw it when she drove by. Thought it looked funny."

Baker didn't point out that a fire in the middle of town would indeed look funny. Instead, he scanned the crowd, looking for anything more abnormal than a burning used car office. He stifled a groan as he spied Lewis strolling toward him. Someone had given him a hard hat. "Baker," he said as he approached. "Figured you'd show up. You here to chase the ambulance?"

Baker ignored that. "What are you doing here? This a homicide?"

Lewis didn't answer. He looked at Artie. "Was anybody else in there with you, Pfeiffer?"

Artie stared at his feet.

"Answer me here or downtown, Artie. The choice is yours."

Baker said, "Technically he's out of his jurisdiction, Artie. But he's a consultant with the sheriff's office right now, and he can make one of them arrest you." Artie stared at him with wide eyes. Baker shrugged. "Personally, I'd answer him here. The coffee at the sheriff's office is terrible."

"Keep out of this, Baker," Lewis said. To Artie he said, "Answer the question."

Artie's voice was barely a whisper. "Jeffrey was in there. Jeffrey Drake. He's dead."

"How?" Lewis asked.

Artie shrugged. "I don't know. He was sick. Kept getting sicker. Said he needed a place to lie down where his wife wouldn't nag him to death. He fell asleep and when the fire started, he wouldn't wake up." Artie blew his nose again. "He was just dead."

A sick feeling spread through Baker, starting in his gut and creeping up until it touched the back of his throat. "Where are Bertie and Watts?" he asked.

Lewis' eyes narrowed. "Stay out of this, Baker."

But Baker wasn't listening. He stood and looked Artie in the eye. "Where are they?"

"I—I," Artie stammered.

Baker grasped him by the shoulders and shook him. Hard. "God damn you, Artie, where are they?"

"The garage," Artie said. "Doc stitched up Watt's jaw, and they went back to the garage."

Lewis grabbed Baker's arm. "Let me handle this. You're not a cop."

"Fuck you," Baker said. And he punched Lewis in the mouth. Then he took off at a dead run for the Ford Garage.

Chapter 25

The garage was silent as Baker approached. He entered through the office, and Shep pushed his bulk up from the greasy chair. "Hold up there, Baker. There's the matter of your car to discuss." He laid a fat hand on Baker's arm and left a smudge on the sleeve.

Baker looked at the smudge and then into Shep's face. "Thanksgiving is next week," he said. Then he punched Shep in the mouth and moved on into the garage.

He was out of breath from the run, and sweat dripped into his eyes. He ran a hand over his face to clear his vision as he stepped into the first garage bay. He spied the toolbox and the wrench he'd used earlier. He picked it up and noted Jeremy's blood had mixed with the grease in a congealed black glob. Baker held the wrench by his side as he moved into the garage.

He could make out Bertie's inert form on the stool in the corner again, propped against the wall, dozing. Jeremy stood, staring out one of the garage windows, silent. When he heard the sound of Baker's approach, he turned.

"What the hell do you want, Baker?" His eyes were tired and his jaw was swollen. Baker could see the stitches Doc had put in, and he smiled a little.

His grip on the wrench tightened. "I came to warn you," he said. "Drake is dead. And if my hunch is right, you're next on the list."

Bertie snorted and sat up. "What's going on?" he mumbled.

"Drake's dead," Baker informed him, not taking his eyes from Jeremy Watts.

Bertie straightened in his seat. "We didn't do it."

Baker, his eyes still on Jeremy, said, "My guess is you two are next on the list, Bertie."

Jeremy shrugged and traced a circle in the filthy glass with his finger. "My guess is you should shut up."

Bertie leaned forward. "Maybe he could help us, Watts."

Watts turned and took a menacing step toward his friend. "Shut up, Bertie."

"I don't want to end up like Wally. I don't want to be dead. Tell him, Jeremy."

Jeremy's shoulders slumped; and he stared out the window at the smoke—and into the past, Baker supposed.

Baker leaned against a car. "Tell me what you know about Diana Kramer."

He watched Jeremy, waiting for the tale to spill out, waiting for the story that would explain the last week and all the crazy things that had happened, waiting for Jeremy Watts to help him understand how Marian's mind had fractured enough to support two separate lives. But Watts was silent. It was Bertie who spoke. "She was the most beautiful girl," he said.

"Shut up, Bertie." But Watts' voice wasn't threatening, just tired. And sad.

Bertie's eyes were far away. "She was shy, you know. She wouldn't talk to anyone except her brother. She looked up to him."

"I said, 'Shut up.'" Watts' fists clenched at his sides, and he took a few steps toward Bertie; but Baker raised the wrench menacingly, and Watts backed off to resume his post at the window.

Baker looked at Bertie and nodded. "Go on."

Bertie trembled, but he continued. "Chet wanted to take her out." He looked Baker in the eye. "You know, date her. Chet was a good guy. Our leader. He wasn't bossy or mean or one of those tough guys. He was the best. And his dad was the sheriff." Bertie shook his head. "Everybody loved Chet. He asked Jeffrey if he could take Marian out some time."

Watts' back stiffened. Bertie watched, appearing nervous; but he cleared his throat and continued, "Jeffrey said no. Said his mother would never allow it. Marian had duties at home." His eyes slid to Baker. "Their father had left, you see. And their mother, Norma, worked two jobs to put food on the table. And Marian couldn't be spared for something silly like getting an ice cream soda." His eyes were serious when he regarded Baker. "It was the Depression, you know."

Baker nodded. He knew.

"Chet wasn't one to take 'no' for an answer, especially from the likes of Jeffrey Drake, who was a runt back then." He laughed. "Wasn't he a runt back then, Watts?"

Watts didn't answer.

Bertie said, "So Chet asked Jeffrey again. And Jeffrey said 'no' but that if maybe Chet could come up with thirty dollars, Jeffrey could arrange it so that Marian would be alone on the road after the bus dropped her off one afternoon; and Chet could do whatever he wanted with her for a while."

Watts raised his hands and pressed his palms flat against the window where they made dark smears against the cold glass.

Baker's jaw tightened.

Bertie twisted in his chair and looked at Baker with a half-smile on his face. "But it was the middle of the Depression, like I said, and no one had thirty dollars. Did they, Watts?"

Watts held his tongue.

"Anyway," Bertie continued, "Jeffrey must have needed the money sorely, or he would have never done anything like that. And Chet didn't even have thirty dollars. Besides, all he wanted to do was take her out or maybe walk her home from school." He thought for a moment. "Of course, she did live five miles from the school so that wouldn't have worked. Besides, no one had any money. And one day we were all at the diner talking about how none of us had any money, and isn't Jeffrey Drake a crumb for suggesting something like that?" He looked at Watts. "Remember how David's dad ran the place back then, Watts? He charged us only half- price for a soda. So we could all share one sometimes. Remember that, Watts?"

Baker studied Jeremy Watts. The man was silent, his hands pressed tightly against the greasy window. And even from where Baker stood, he could sense the tension, the agony in the man.

"Anyway," Bertie went on, his words sounding dry and tired now, "Chet told us he knew what Jeffrey offered was wrong; but he was so sweet on Marian that he would give just about anything, even thirty dollars, to spend just ten minutes with her." His voice broke, and he took a moment to regain control. "After a minute, Artie says he has five dollars he'd be willing to give to Chet but only if he could have a few minutes with Marian too. He said, 'Five bucks is worth five minutes.' Didn't he say that, Watts? And then I said that I could probably find five dollars too. And before you knew it, everyone says they have five dollars or could get their hands on that much. So we agreed on five minutes each with Marian to tell her all the things we couldn't on account of her brother being around all the time." He wiped his sweaty hands on his coveralls. "We all just wanted the chance to say we courted her. Marian wasn't ever supposed to know anything about the money." He looked at Baker for some sort of reassurance.

But Baker couldn't give any. He was sick. He wanted to break something.

After a minute, Bertie continued, "We gave the cash to Jeffrey the next day at school. He said he'd find some excuse to stay late so Marian would be alone when she got off the bus." He hung his head and was silent so long Baker tightened his grip on the wrench in case persuasion was needed. But again, Bertie continued his tale, "So anyway, the day comes and we all wait in the trees along the lane from the road to the Drakes' house. And Marian gets off the bus alone, just like Jeffrey promised." His eyes were far away. "She was the most beautiful girl I'd ever seen. And we all just stood there in the trees thinking the same thing. She was beautiful. And I wanted to be the first to tell her." He looked at his feet then, and Baker saw his lower lip tremble. "I guess we all had the same idea. We all wanted to tell her. We all stepped out of the woods at the same time."

Baker's breath came out in a sharp hiss. "You scared her."

Bertie nodded. "We didn't mean to, but, yeah, we scared her. She didn't scream or anything, but she started running. And Chet wanted to talk to her so bad he just started running after her, yelling at her to wait. And then before you knew it, we were all running after her; and she was so scared. But Chet was fast and he caught her. And she fell in the mud." He wiped a hand over his face. "And then we were all there, and she was so beautiful; and Watts shoved me out of the way...."

Watts punched the window and it shattered, the pieces falling at his feet where they reflected broken light.

Bertie flinched. "No one blames you, Watts; but you did shove me."

"What happened?" Baker asked. His stomach was in knots. He knew the answer to the question, even as he asked it; but he needed to hear it. He *needed* to hear it.

Bertie licked his lips. "Well, when she fell, her skirt caught on a stump or something; and it ripped way up her leg. We could see her underpants." He shrugged. "We were just young boys, and we hadn't ever seen anything like that before. And David leaned down and tried to kiss her, but she kicked him. And then me and Artie and Watts—" he choked and started to cry "—we held her down, and David climbed on top of her. And then she screamed, and Chet tried to shove David off of her. Said we were making her scared."

Baker swallowed.

But Bertie wasn't done. "Artie picked up a rock. And he hit Chet in the head with it. Chet fell over." Bertie shrugged. "He didn't get back up. And without Chet to rein us in, we lost our minds." He was crying freely now.

"Then what?" Baker asked, unable to hide the disgust in his voice.

Bertie cradled his head in his hands and began to sob. "Oh, God. We didn't mean it."

Baker crossed to Bertie in two strides and, with a steady hand, held the wrench covered in Watts' blood beneath Bertie's chin and tilted the crying man's face to his. "Then what?" he repeated.

Bertie swiped his nose with a dirty sleeve. "I was worried Chet was dead, but he was just knocked out. Marian struggled and fought, but we held her arms and legs; and David unbuttoned his pants and he—he—"

"You fucking bastards," Baker said.

Bertie choked. "There was blood—because she was a virgin, you see. And it didn't take David long. And then we all had a go."

"You all raped her."

Bertie nodded.

Watts spoke and Baker started at the sound. "I tripped on the way back through the woods," he said. "No one knew. Not even you, Bert. You all just kept running. I fell and hurt my leg. I rolled over on my back and looked up. There were no leaves on the trees. Their branches were like black fingers pointing at me and up at the sky." He squeezed his eyes shut. "I can still see those long black fingers pointing at me."

"Chet would never have let it happen," Bertie said. "He loved Marian."

"So you all raped Marian and left her lying in the cold with your best friend, who you knocked unconscious."

"I was sick about it," Bertie said. "We all were. She didn't move or anything. She just lay there, staring at the sky."

Baker squeezed his eyes shut, willing the nausea he felt to disappear. "What happened after you left her?" he asked.

Bertie cleared his throat and wiped his face. "The next day Jeffrey showed up at the Christmas tree lighting and tried to give the money back. He said he called Chet's dad after he got home and saw what we all did to his sister." He cleared his throat again. "The sheriff threatened us all if we told anyone. Well, he didn't need to do that. There's no way any of us wanted anyone to know about what we did."

Baker shook his head. "Ferrebee knew? And he did nothing? None of you faced charges?"

Bertie shook his head. "The sheriff said we'd all suffered enough and that Marian would keep it quiet and so would Jeffrey. He said he'd fixed it so the Drakes wouldn't tell their mother about it. As far as I know, they never did."

"Unbelievable."

Bertie's eyes flashed for the first time. Baker thought he actually looked angry. "We were kids. And Chet was everything to his father. You have to understand that. The sheriff would have done anything to protect his name."

"Like kill everyone involved when Diana Kramer starts asking for the letters she wrote."

Watts turned around. "No one said anything like that, Baker. No one said Ferrebee's responsible."

Baker set the wrench on the hood of the nearest car, leaned back and lit a cigarette. "No one had to. And if you boys know what's good for you, you'll find Detective Lewis and spill all this to him before Ferrebee gets a crack at you."

Bertie looked scared. Watts shrugged and looked through the broken window. "Looks like the fire's out," he said. "I suppose he'll be along soon."

"I'm already here," Ferrebee said, walking in from the office. "I heard everything you said, Bertie."

"Look, Sheriff," Bertie said, rising from his perch on the stool and backing farther into the corner. "I didn't mean any harm."

Ferrebee nodded, his face sad. "I know, son. I know." He looked down. "I came to advise you to get out of town. Run." He looked at Baker. "And I'm begging you, please stop looking for the letters.

This is out of control now."

Baker shook his head. "I've already got the letters, Sheriff."

Ferrebee's face fell. "Where are they?"

"They're safe."

Ferrebee wiped a hand over his face and slouched in defeat. "You don't know what you've done. You have no idea what you've done. Holding onto those letters was the only thing keeping Marian alive." He looked Baker in the eye. "You've killed her."

"What are you talking about?"

Ferrebee ran a hand through his thick hair. "After Chet died, Effie snapped."

"Effie?" the three other men in the room said in unison.

Ferrebee nodded. "She snapped. She wouldn't eat or sleep; and when she did sleep, she had nightmares. Then right on the heels of the murder came the search for the letters. She was sure Chet's reputation would be ruined. She said she couldn't let that happen."

"So she killed David Holden?" Baker asked.

"Only after he spoke with you," Ferrebee said. "I blame myself for that. I told her I'd visited with you both in The Diner. She knew you were after the letters, of course, and that they might implicate Chet in what happened to bring Diana Kramer into existence."

"But they don't. There's nothing in those letters. Nothing but the usual love letter mumbo jumbo."

"Oh God," Ferrebee said, shaking his head. "We had no way of knowing that, Detective. Effie panicked." He gestured with his hands. "She was determined to get rid of everyone. Dr. Rogers and I were working to get her committed before it was too late. But then Wally...I don't know how she got Wally alone. Maybe he was on his way to your office when she caught up with him."

"What about Jeffrey?"

"You borrowed a cigarette from him at our house, remember? Then you got sick. I found arsenic in the medicine cabinet. I believe she poisoned his cigarettes." He laughed. "Smart lady. She figured if Jeffrey was sick or dead that Marian would be more likely to hand over the letters."

"But Jeffrey was always sick."

Ferrebee's smile was grim. "No. He was always a lush. After he started smoking the bad cigarettes, he got sick. And Marian didn't really care what happened to him. So it didn't work the way Effie planned."

"At least Artie didn't die."

Ferrebee nodded. "I put him in the trunk of my car."

Watts gave a snort.

"What?" Ferrebee demanded. "He's safe enough there. If I hadn't locked him in, there was a chance that Effie would see him or that he'd run away screaming and then she'd kill him."

From the window, Watts said, "It's starting to snow."

Ferrebee walked to Baker and rested his hands on the detective's shoulders. "Look, we've got to get to the sanitarium. If my wife finds out Marian gave up the letters, it's all over. The only thing keeping Marian alive is the hope that she'll lead Effie to the letters. My wife is not in her right mind, Detective. We've got to stop her."

Baker nodded, feeling the storm coming, wondering if they were all strong enough to weather it.

Chapter 26

"Edwards," Baker said, blowing into the office, accompanied by a blast of snow and cold air. "Get my guns. Effie Ferrebee is going to kill Marian Drake."

Edwards sat in his desk chair, sipping from a cup of tea Deirdre had just poured for him. "What?" Deirdre said, standing.

"I don't have time to explain," Baker said. "But we have every reason to believe that if Effie finds out the letters have been recovered, she'll try to kill Marian."

Edwards stood stiffly at his desk. "And you plan to gun down an old woman in a heroic attempt to protect an insane one. Very good, sir. I shall retrieve your weapons at once."

Baker had no tolerance for British sarcasm at the moment. With exaggerated patience he said, "Effie killed Holden, Sims and Drake. The fire at Artie's was her work too."

"Jeffrey Drake is dead?" Edwards asked, helping Baker into a set of twin shoulder holsters.

"Yes. The poison I took was in the cigarette I borrowed from his pack at the sheriff's house during dinner. He smoked the whole pack and God only knows how many tainted packs prior to this latest one. Of course he died."

Edwards stood straight. "I'm shocked. I don't know what to say."

"Oh my God," Deirdre said. "I saw Effie downtown at the fire. She asked how I thought your case was coming along; and I told her you had found the letters, and she had nothing to worry about." She stared from Baker to Edwards. "What have I done?"

Baker turned to Edwards. "I'm going to the sanitarium to head Effie off. The sheriff and his deputies are already on their way." He held out his hand. "Give me your car keys."

Edwards didn't move. "I'm afraid I can't allow that, sir."

Baker stared at him, open-mouthed. "Why not?"

"I've seen you drive. I'll take you myself."

"It's snowing. There's a blizzard on the way."

"I am well aware of that, sir. My driving skills are impeccable." He donned a wool overcoat and red muffler. He took his time pulling on his gloves and working over the crease in his fedora. "Will I need galoshes, do you think, sir?"

"Good God, man, a woman's life is at stake. Move!"

Edwards gave a long-suffering sigh and said, "Oh, very well."

The sheriff's car was nowhere in sight as the pair made their way up the treacherous slope to the sanitarium. "Can't you go any faster?" Baker demanded of his friend.

"Only if we wish to die, sir."

Baker huffed and looked out the window. His trigger finger was starting to itch, and that was never a good sign. Effie Ferrebee, cold-blooded killer. Who would've thought?

The wind blew Edwards' car from one side of the road to the other, and the Brit struggled to keep it pointed straight ahead. As they neared the top of the big hill, the snow began to blow horizontally. "Dear God, sir, I fear we may need to turn back."

"Nothing doing, Edwards. Shut your yap and keep your foot to the floor."

In time, they crested the hill and plowed through a foot of snow into the drifted parking lot. Three sheriff's cars sat, already disappearing beneath the white, their lights quietly rotating as the storm raged around them. Baker wasted no time in jumping from Edwards' car. He took the steps two at a time, bursting through the vestibule's outer and inner doors without waiting for Edwards. Enid was not behind the desk. He paused to catch his breath, noticing as he did that the building was eerily quiet.

Edwards' entrance was silent. "I must say," he whispered, "it smells much better in here today."

"Shh," Baker said, drawing his left-sided gun. "Listen."

Edwards was silent for a moment. "I don't hear anything, sir."

"Exactly." Baker made his way toward the ladies' parlor, thumbing back the hammer on his Colt as he moved.

"Really, sir," Edwards said. "She's an old woman. Is that really necessary?"

"It's necessary, Edwards. Now shut up." The door to the parlor was closed; and Baker crouched low, peering through the keyhole.

"Do you see anything, sir?"

Baker took his time. Muffled voices exchanged angry words. Someone was crying. He listened harder. It was Marian. Marian was crying. He rotated his body to the left, trying to get a better view. She sat on a chair in the corner. Judith was beside her.

"I see Marian Drake," he whispered to Edwards.

"Has she been harmed?"

"I don't think so."

"Is Mrs. Ferrebee there?"

Baker twisted again, trying to view as much of the parlor as possible. "I don't see her," he said. Judith and Marian were close to the windows. Sheriff Ferrebee, Deputy Reynolds and two others stood behind them. Enid sat at a table on the opposite side of the room. Baker recognized Penny, Marian's roommate, sitting next to Enid. He had seen several of the other women in the room as well. At least a dozen male patients sat in various chairs and on the floor. Several nurses and orderlies moved slowly back and forth, making sure the patients were unharmed. No one else moved. "Looks like everyone from the whole place is in there."

A shadow passed in front of the keyhole, and Baker's head snapped back involuntarily. "Geez," he breathed.

"What is it?" Edwards whispered.

Baker crouched lower. "Effie's right inside the door."

Edwards pulled Baker out of the way. "I'll handle this, sir," he said, knocking on the door. "I have a way with old women."

Baker tensed as the voices inside quieted in response to Edwards' knock. A silence that was somehow louder penetrated the building. After a moment, they heard a loud, "Who is it?" Baker recognized the shrill voice as belonging to Effie.

Edwards cleared his throat. "If Madam is ready, I have prepared tea."

"Are you crazy?" Baker hissed.

"She is a lady. All ladies like tea."

"Not this one, Edwards. She's a loon."

There was silence on the other side of the door, followed by the unmistakable click made by the release of the safety belonging to a Thomas sub-machine gun. "Oh dear," Edwards muttered. "She's got a Tommy-gun." He and Baker dove for cover.

Effie opened fire, splintering the parlor's antique wooden door and spraying bullets down the long hallway. Debris rocketed past Baker and Edwards, spraying them with dust and plaster.

"Obviously she's armed," Baker said through clenched teeth.

"So it would seem, sir."

"Any other bright ideas?"

"Yes. We shoot her."

"What about the helpless old woman bit?"

"She's ruined my suit."

"On three then?"

"On three."

"One..."

"Two..."

"Three," they said together, racing for the door.

The wood frame had been blown apart. Edwards reached the door first, pulling what remained from its hinges and allowing Baker to dive through the opening headfirst. Effie lifted the gun again, but Baker reached out his arm and knocked her legs out from under her.

The heavy gun rattled across the floor, toward Edwards; and he stepped through the doorway, picking it up. Effie clawed at Baker's face with her hands. "Get away from me," she shrieked.

Sheriff Ferrebee stood and rushed to her side, pulling her off of Baker. "Calm down, Effie," he said, pulling her to her feet.

Baker hopped up and dusted his suit off as he quickly scanned the room to make sure everyone was all right. Enid walked toward them, a straight jacket in her hands. "Mrs. Ferrebee," she said softly to Effie. "You look cold. Try this on."

Enid nodded mutely and Enid slipped the jacket on her, hastening to buckle it tight in the back.

"Is that really necessary?" the sheriff asked.

Enid gestured to the destroyed doorway and the bullet holes riddling the wall in the corridor. "I believe so, Sheriff," she said. She helped the sheriff get Effie to a comfortable chair to sit down. "I'll go call Dr. Rogers," she said once Effie was settled. "And the city police, of course. I'm sure we'll need their help with this, seeing as how it directly involves the sheriff."

Ferrebee took a chair beside his wife.

On the other side of the room, Marian was in Judith's arms. "There, there," Judith murmured. "It's all over now. You're safe."

Baker nodded as he approached. "Ladies," he said. Then, looking at Marian, he said, "You okay?"

She nodded.

Sheriff Ferrebee supported his wife, who leaned heavily against him as a bewildered Deputy Reynolds led them away. As they made their way down the hallway, Detective Lewis appeared, leaning against the doorway, a smoldering cigarette between his index and middle finger.

He spotted Baker, and his mouth turned grim. He offered a curt nod and took another drag on the cigarette. Baker gave a mock salute and turned his attention back to the women at the table. "Mind if I sit down?" he asked.

Marian nodded, her mouth tight, and Baker sat. Edwards sat beside him, his face blank.

Judith leaned forward, her eyes wide and curious. "How did you find out about Effie?" she asked, keeping a reassuring hand on Marian's arm.

Baker leaned back in his chair and lit a cigarette. "Ferrebee told us. Seems she snapped after Chet was murdered." He watched Marian for any reaction.

There was none.

"Effie didn't kill Chet?" Judith asked.

Baker kept his eyes on Marian. "No," he said. "Effie didn't kill Chet."

Judith looked from Baker to Marian and back again. "I don't understand," she said, sounding nervous now.

"Perhaps Marian can help you out," Baker said, taking a deep drag from his cigarette and flicking the ash on the floor. The ashtray had been knocked from the table sometime during Effie's hostile takeover and shattered.

Marian kept her eyes on her fingers, which tapped on the table.

"Marian?" Judith asked.

"Tell her, Marian," Baker said. "Tell her how you killed Chet."

Marian looked up then, her eyes nearly black with fury. "You tell her, Detective. You seem to know so much about me."

Despite her crime, Baker felt a surge of pity for the widow now. He pitied her for the loss of a good husband and for what the future held for her. In that moment he wondered what it was like to be two people with different hearts, different minds. He wondered if they had different souls as well.

Diana Kramer loved Chet, wanted to build a future with him. Marian Drake thought he'd participated in her rape and could never forgive him for being there...for loving her in the first place.

Pity almost overwhelmed Baker at that moment, and he thought seriously of rising, walking to the door and making his way out into the blizzard and away from this crazy place and these crazy people. But the job was almost finished. And wasn't that what he said he'd do at all costs? Finish the job?

Judith was watching him with open curiosity. He knew she'd find out about Jeffrey soon. He also knew he wouldn't be the one to tell her.

He kept his eyes on Marian, willing himself to avoid watching Judith. He couldn't bear to think about her being a free woman now. She wasn't the right sort for him, he thought. She'd tricked him and used him. And he wouldn't forgive that.

"You never wanted to marry Chet," he said, his eyes boring into Marian. "Revenge was on your mind from the start." He took another drag on the cigarette, knowing Lewis was behind him, listening. "But Diana Kramer loved him. She loved him and forgave him."

"Shut up," Marian whispered. "I don't want to hear any more."

"Jeffrey tried to keep you safe. He tried for years. But money was tight for you all, so he let Chet have a chance with you. It was Chet's friends who let you down. Chet's friends and your brother. Chet wanted nothing but to keep you safe."

Marian leaned back in her chair now, a small smile playing at her mouth.

Judith sat beside her, bewildered. "I don't understand, Detective," she said.

"Marian killed him," Baker said, not looking away from Marian. "It's that simple. She hated him. She killed him." He watched Marian's eyes smolder, could see the hatred still bubbling beneath the surface. "You knew how to tie a knot like a fisherman. Your father taught you that. But I'm curious as to how you convinced Chet to let you put the sheet around his neck." He thought for a minute and then snapped his fingers. "I bet you pretended to be Diana, didn't you? 'Let's play a game, Chet.' Is that how it happened?"

"Shut up," Marian whispered.

"I imagine he was surprised when you kept tightening the knot."

237

Baker blew out a cloud of smoke. "I bet that's when he tried to fight back. Gave you that shiner. Broke your nails." He clucked his tongue. "He tried to protect you that day after school, Marian. If you had read the letters from Diana more closely, you would have known that. If you had asked him yourself, you would have known that."

"I don't believe you," she said. But her eyes were wide with fear.

"Artie Pfeiffer knocked him out. He was unconscious when his friends raped you. And afterwards, they left him there, cold and bleeding, just like you."

A tear rolled down her cheek. Then another.

Baker stood, filled with pity for the broken woman sobbing in front of him. He spared a look at Judith, who sat wide-eyed and hollowed. Her nightmare was just beginning. "Come on, Edwards. Let's get out of here. I'm sure the police will want a word with us."

Lewis waited in the foyer and followed as Baker pushed his way out through the vestibule and into the blizzard. "Hell of a case," Lewis said when they were outside, like they were old buddies.

Another sheriff's deputy approached Edwards, and the two stepped to the side so Edwards could answer questions.

"Yep," Baker answered. "Hell of a case."

"I imagine the sheriff will be retiring after this."

"You'd have to ask him that, I guess."

Lewis shuffled his feet a little. "You'll need to answer some questions for the sheriff's men. You know that, right?"

Baker nodded. "I'm heading to the station with Edwards right now."

"I'll be wanting those letters as evidence, Baker. You know that too, right?"

"Drop by and get them any time." He pushed past Lewis and made his way to Edwards' car.

"Maybe I want you to bring them to the station," Lewis called after him.

Baker turned around. "Maybe I want you to kiss my ass," he said, climbing in the car and waiting for Edwards.

The drive down the hill into town was slow. Snow pelted the windshield, and the wipers struggled to keep up with it.

"I should warn you, sir, that Mr. Barone plans to stop by this afternoon."

"Oh, great," Baker mumbled.

"Seems he received another jar of something or other in his mailbox yesterday."

"Not another four-eyed frog, I hope."

"No, sir. It appears to be a human finger. He says it belongs to his sister."

"Well, hell." Baker mumbled, looking out the window into the snow.

The End

J. Busskohl